W9-AVM-280

HEART OF WINTER

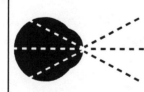

This Large Print Book carries the
Seal of Approval of N.A.V.H.

HEART OF WINTER

DIANA PALMER

THORNDIKE PRESS

An imprint of Thomson Gale, a part of The Thomson Corporation

THOMSON

GALE

Detroit • New York • San Francisco • New Haven, Conn. • Waterville, Maine • London

LIBRARY OF CONGRESS CATALOGING-IN-PUBLICATION DATA

Palmer, Diana.
  [Woman hater]
  Heart of winter / by Diana Palmer.
    p. cm. — (Thorndike Press large print basic)
  ISBN-13: 978-0-7862-9411-4 (alk. paper)
  ISBN-10: 0-7862-9411-6 (alk. paper)
  I. Palmer, Diana. If winter comes. II. Title.
  PS3566.A513W66 2007
  813'.54—dc22   2006100761

Published in 2007 by arrangement with Harlequin Books S.A.

Printed in the United States of America on permanent paper
10 9 8 7 6 5 4 3 2 1

CONTENTS

■ ■ ■ ■

WOMAN HATER

■ ■ ■ ■

CHAPTER ONE

When Gerald Christopher first suggested going to his family ranch in Montana to rest his recently diagnosed ulcer for a few weeks, Nicole had instant reservations. He was the boss, of course, and if he wanted to go to Montana, there was no reason he shouldn't. But Nicole liked the pleasant routine of life in Chicago, where she'd spent the last two years working for the Christopher Corporation. At twenty-two, Nicole White had found a nice, pleasant rut for herself and she didn't particularly like change.

The problem was that if Mr. Christopher went to Montana for a month, as he was threatening, and closed down his personal office while he was gone, Nicole would be out of a job until his return. Despite her adequate wages, trying to live for a month without any salary was a frightening thought. That was almost laughable considering her background, because Nicole's family had been one of the old moneyed ones of Kentucky. Her father, in fact, was still one of the jet set, a noted sportsman as well as a horse-racing magnate, and lived the part. Nicole had long since renounced her share of the family fortune and gone to work for a living.

Her mother's death had been the last straw. Her father had been with his latest mistress at the time, not that he'd ever been home a lot. That hadn't mattered at the time, because Nicole had been sure that her new fiancé, Chase James, would set up their marriage and that his job as a real estate agent would make it possible for him to support the two of them. She'd figured wrong. Once Chase found out that Nicole had been foolish enough to give up her family fortune — and when he realized that she couldn't possibly be talked out of it — he asked for his ring back. His immediate defection to one of Nicole's moneyed and eligible girl-friends had shattered her young life.

At the age of twenty, she'd left the elegant brick mansion of her childhood in Lexington, Kentucky, and a racehorse farm worth millions, to live the frugal life as a secretary in Chicago, where she had a friend with whom she could room. She smiled, remembering her lack of skills at the time, and how patient Mr. Christopher had been until she'd crammed in some courses at the local secretarial school. Lucky for her that he'd liked her personality and had decided to take a chance on her secretarial skills improving. They had. She'd graduated from the course at the top of her class.

It all seemed a long time ago now, a part of her life that was like some slowly fading photograph of a reality she no longer belonged to. . . .

"You'll like it there, Nicky," Gerald Christopher said dreamily, staring out the window. "The ranch is in the southern part of the state, nestled in the Rocky Mountains. It's rich with forests, lakes, rivers, peace and quiet. Just the thing to help me get over this ulcer they've diagnosed. We can work in peace and you can have plenty of free time to yourself."

"But your brother and his family — won't they mind having your secretary to house and feed?" she asked, her pale green eyes hesitant in a plain but interesting oval face, surrounded by naturally curling short dark hair. Despite the fact that she'd worked for him for two years, she knew very little about his private life. He'd never made a habit of talking casually about anything personal, as some employers did. She knew he had a brother, and he'd mentioned a woman named Mary, whom she'd assumed was his sister-in-law. But that was really all she knew about him in any personal way.

"Winthrop doesn't have a family," he said, smiling as he turned toward her. He was tall with brown hair and dark brown eyes. Not a bad-looking man and he seemed pleasant enough, but he wasn't a woman chaser or a ladies' man. He was very businesslike and a terrific boss, and Nicky adored him. In a purely businesslike way, of course. Her heart was pretty impregnable these days, hardened by Chase's cruel defection. That had ended her dreams of marriage. The hated wealth that had blinded her to men's greed was gone now, too. And without her designer clothing and her diamonds, men didn't seem to notice her at all. Of course, her manner was stiff and off-putting with most men, but she didn't even realize it.

"Your brother came to the office once, didn't he?" she ventured, recalling vaguely a tall, very cold sort of man she'd barely glimpsed on an unusually hectic day and had learned later that it was Mr. Christopher's mysterious older brother.

"Yes, he did," he said. "Winthrop owns a small share in the corporation, you see, but he's the silent partner. He doesn't care for desks and boardrooms. Dad left him the ranch, which is worth a mint, and I have an equally small share in that. He's primarily a cattleman, and I'm a businessman, so we each have what we like most. He's something of a loner. But as long as we keep out of his way, we won't have any trouble."

That sounded ominous. She looked at the green-lined white steno pad in her lap. "A month is a long time," she said slowly.

"Come on, Nicky, what have you got going that you can't walk away from?" he chided gently. "No boyfriends, no evening classes. A month in the country would do you good. If that wealth of potted plants you surround your desk with is any indication, you must be a country girl at heart. Or at the very least, a frustrated gardener."

She laughed. "I do love plants. And, yes, I'm a country girl. I was born and bred in Kentucky," she confessed, "and I guess I do miss it sometimes. My people were farmers," she added, tossing off the white lie as easily as she twirled the pen in her slender hand. That was the story she told people, anyway, and it prevented a lot of embarrassing questions about why she'd given up all that money.

"And farming isn't the best profession to

be in these days," he agreed with a fond smile. "I can see why you came to the big city. But since you do like the country, I presume, where's the problem?"

She sighed. "It's not quite orthodox."

"No, little puritan, it isn't," he agreed. "But for the next month, you're my private secretary and I'll even increase your salary to make it more acceptable."

"Oh, but that's not nec—" she began.

"Certainly it is," he countered, waving a lean hand at her. "I'm tired of the rat race, Nicky. I need rest or this ulcer is going to put me in the hospital. We'll both benefit from some mountain air."

"It's October," she reminded him. "Late October. Doesn't it snow in Montana in late October?"

"Oh, frequently," he agreed. "And the ranch is way up in the Rockies, near the Todd place —" he paused, glancing at her with an odd expression "— you remember Sadie, don't you?"

"Yes. She was very nice." A nurse, in fact, and Nicole's taciturn young boss had dated her and had been devastated when she left several months ago to take care of her invalid mother. Hmm, Nicole thought; that was about the time his health problems reared their ugly head.

14

"Anyway, the ranch is near the Todd place," he continued, "and we used to get snowed in a good bit. But we always get a chinook when we need one, and we can dig our way out. Stop worrying."

"What's a chinook?"

"A warm wind that comes unexpectedly to melt the snow," he said, smiling. "You'll love it there, Nicky. I promise."

I hope so, she thought. All at once she wondered if he had more than just health reasons for wanting to work at home. Sadie had managed to drag him out of his shell, and there had been a tangible something between them before her abrupt departure. It might turn out to be an interesting trip. "All right, I'll go," she agreed. "But you're sure your brother won't mind?"

He looked vaguely disturbed for a second. Then he smiled. "Of course I'm sure."

Nicky wondered later about that hesitation. Mr. Christopher had hardly ever mentioned his brother in all the time she'd worked for him. But through the office grapevine there had been some small bit of gossip about the Montana rancher, something someone had whispered just after his brief visit. If only she could remember it.

Becky, a blond and vivacious woman who worked for one of the vice presidents, breezed into the office after Mr. Christopher had left for the day.

"What's this I hear about some exotic vacation you're taking with the big boss?" she teased.

Nicky laughed. "If you call the backwoods of Montana exotic, then I guess it's true." She sighed as she covered the computer. "I do hope you'll come to my funeral. I have visions of being eaten by a puma or carried off by a moose."

"You might be carried off by Winthrop." Becky grinned. "Or haven't you heard the grizzly tales about him?"

Nicole turned, her eyes wide and curious. "Is he terrible?"

"A wild man, from what we hear. They said some society girl threw him over a few years back, and he actually went to her engagement party with a Hollywood movie star — a girl who turned out to have been a school friend of his and owed him a favor. He called up the friend and paid her expenses all the way from Hollywood, just for the occasion. Ruined the event, of course, since the movie star got all the attention. He used to be a ladies' man and he's always been well-to-do, and he traveled in those very ritzy circles. But since then, he's pretty much given up his playboy status and

16

turned to the great outdoors. They say his experience with the blond heiress has soured him against rich women in a big way. Can't blame him too much, can you?"

"He sounds . . . interesting." Nicky chose her words carefully; it wouldn't do to show her fear.

"Looks that way, too, except for the scars and the limp. Although the scars had faded nicely the day he was in here." She grinned at Nicky. "He sure gave you a look, but you were so busy you didn't even notice him."

"I remember him, but I didn't look long enough to see the limp." She frowned. "How did he get it?"

"From the wreck. Deanne Sharp — of the Aspen Sharps, you know, ski-resort wear and accessories, and Winthrop's fiancée at the time — was driving. They crashed. He almost lost his leg, and during his recovery, she walked out on him. I guess she only liked him for his athletic ability. He was an Olympic-quality skier and they met on the ski slopes. He missed the Olympic team by a few points when he was younger."

"That was what I was trying to remember. Someone said he'd been in a wreck, but I forgot what happened."

"The lovely Deanne happened. I hear she's on husband number three now, and has millions. But all that happened three years ago, the year before you came to work," Becky said. "We all heard about it. What he did at that woman's engagement party might have sounded cruel, if you didn't know it all. We were in Winthrop's corner, all of us. He got a bad break. As it is, he gets around pretty good, but he isn't the pinup he used to be. An experience like that could make a man bitter, you know."

Nicky drew in a slow breath. "A real woman hater."

"Now that's the truth," Becky laughed. "No, he doesn't like women. So if you go to the ranch with the big boss, make sure you take lots of warm clothing. That way you won't get frozen — by the weather or Winthrop."

"We may get snowed in," Nicky moaned.

"The snows come big in Montana," she was told. "Six feet deep and more, sometimes. My best friend worked at the hospital here until she had to go back to Montana to take care of her invalid mother a few months ago. You might remember her — Sadie Todd? The boss used to take her out."

"Yes, I remember," Nicky said with a smile, and kept her mouth shut about what Mr. Christopher had told her.

"They grew up together," Becky added. "I

visited her once. Montana is lovely country, but brutal. It's frozen a lot of people, but if you want to get away from the world, there's no better place."

"I don't think I want to go."

"Don't be silly," Becky chided. "The big boss is a doll. Winthrop can't be too horrible."

But Nicky still wasn't sure. She went home and got her small apartment in order, still with misgivings. It didn't take long to pack, because there wasn't a lot to pack. She had jeans and sweaters, some blouses and a single jersey dress, because she had the feeling that she would be roughing it. She took a thick winter coat as well, and some leather boots left over from the past. Her lips twisted in a thin smile when she surveyed the contents of her suitcase and she thought about the clothes and lifestyle she'd once taken for granted. She missed that easy luxury once in a great while, and when she had to pinch pennies to meet the rent, her principles didn't help much. But she was a different girl from the arrogant little miss her parents' financial indulgence and emotional indifference had created. And that meant a lot. She'd learned about reality in the past two years, and about real people, who didn't put a dollar sign on their friendship. Even though her friend Dana, with whom she'd roomed, had married a year ago, Nicole still had friends like Becky, and they often went to movies or the theater together.

She pulled on a pair of cotton pajamas, washed her face and went to bed. It wouldn't do any good to worry about the past or the future. It was enough to cope with the present.

A week later, Nicole and Mr. Christopher flew out to Montana in the corporation jet. She wore the gray jersey dress for the flight, along with a minimum of makeup. She looked sweet and young and totally unlike a glamorous socialite. She didn't want to start off on the wrong foot by deliberately antagonizing the elder Mr. Christopher, who had plenty of reason to dislike that type of woman.

"You don't mind if I work?" Gerald Christopher asked with a smile, looking up from the papers in front of him.

"Not at all," she assured him. "I'm not nervous of flying."

The flight seemed to take a long time, but perhaps that was because Nicole wasn't reading. She stared out at passing clouds, a little anxious about the welcome she was going to get when they got off the plane.

"Mr. Christopher, your brother does know I'm coming?" she asked him when they were over Butte and about to land.

His dark eyebrows arched. "Of course. Don't worry, Nicky, everything's going to be fine."

Sure it was. She knew that the instant they got off the plane and she got a good look at the expression on Winthrop Christopher's face.

She recognized him at once. He was a big man. Taller than his brother, broad shouldered and lean hipped. He was wearing work clothing — jeans and dusty boots, with a checked shirt under a massive sheepskin jacket. On his head was a battered black Stetson twisted into an arrogant slant over one dark eye. He looked like a desperado. He hadn't shaved, and the white line of a scar curved from one cheek into the stubble on his square chin with its faint dimple. His face was rather square, too, and his features severe. He had a straight, rather imposing nose, and his black eyes gleamed with a cold light. In one lean, dark-skinned hand he held a burning cigarette. And the look he was giving Nicky would have curdled fresh milk.

"Hello, Winthrop," Gerald said, shaking

his brother's hand. He glanced at Nicky with a smile. "In our childhood days, I used to call him Winnie, but I gave it up when he blacked one of my eyes. Despite all that, I know he'd die for me," he added with a grin, which the older brother didn't return. He was too busy glaring at Nicole, his dark eyes cutting into her oval face, looking for imperfections, making an unpleasant inventory of what he saw. "Winthrop," Gerald continued quickly, "this is my private secretary, Nicole White."

"How do you do, Mr. Christopher," Nicky said politely and she actually managed to smile, but her knees felt unsteady. This was no welcome at all. Dislike was too mild a word for what she read in those eyes. Wounded man, she thought, even while she wished she could run. She understood the meaning of betrayal, because she knew it intimately. For the first few months of her exile, Chase's handsome face had imposed itself over every letter she typed, every book she read, every television program she watched.

Winthrop's dark eyes narrowed. His thin, chiseled lips pursed thoughtfully, but there was no smile to ease the hardness of that rugged, unshaven face. "Yes, I remember you," he said curtly. His voice was deep and curt. "You're young."

"I'm twenty-two," she said.

"Young." He turned abruptly, with a care that no physically fit man would have had to take. "I've got the pickup. Does your pilot want to come out to the ranch and have something to eat?"

"No, he's due back to fly one of the other executives over to New York," Gerald replied, clapping an affectionate hand on Winthrop's shoulder. Brave man, to touch that walking inferno, Nicky thought as she fell into step behind them.

"I'll get the luggage." Winthrop started toward the plane, favoring one leg, and Nicky hesitated, her eyes speaking her thoughts. He gave her a look that stopped her from moving or speaking. He could have stopped a brawl with that glance. Her half-formed offer to help was frozen solid on her lips. With a violent flush, she turned away and followed Gerald.

"Don't ever offer to help him," her boss cautioned in a soft, quiet tone. "He's a little less sensitive about it these days, but soon after it happened, he threw a punch at one of the cowboys just for offering."

"I'll remember." She felt stung. The older brother was going to be hard going, and her first impulse was to ask if she could go back to Chicago.

Gerald Christopher seemed to sense her feelings, because he put an affectionately careless arm around her shoulder. "Don't panic," he teased. "He doesn't bite."

"Thank God I've had all my inoculations," she sighed, but she smiled back.

Behind them, the older man was watching that exchange of smiles and the arm around Nicky and putting his own connotation on what was going on between his younger brother and his secretary. The look in his eyes was both threatening and disapproving as he picked up the cases and followed them to the cream-colored pickup truck.

It was a long ride to the ranch, down a highway dwarfed by the towering, autumn-hued peaks of the Rockies. Soon Winthrop turned off onto some mountainous dirt roads that didn't actually seem like roads at all. To Nicky, squashed between the two men, it was a cold and unnerving experience. She could feel Winthrop Christopher's long, powerful leg come in contact with hers every time he pressed on the accelerator, and her body was reacting to the feel of his shoulder against hers in ways she hadn't expected. He made her tremble with awakening sensation, made her feel alive as she hadn't felt since her late teens. She didn't like that, or him, and her face took on the hardness of stone as the road wound on and on, through fir trees so tall and thick that Nicky stared in fascination at their girth. The forested areas were becoming thick now that they were off the rolling plain that had led to them, down country roads where houses were miles apart and traffic was practically nonexistent. Nicky, who'd read about Montana, hadn't been prepared for its vastness, or for the glory of orange-tipped aspens with their thin silvery trunks, and cottonwoods fluffy and yellow-hued, and those incredibly big pines. Or for the sheer splendor of the mountains and the crisp, clean coldness of mountain air. She watched, rapt, as the mountains shot up in front of them. Winthrop turned onto a tiny dirt road and they started to go up.

"Not what you expected, Miss White?" Winthrop chided as she stiffened on a sudden hair-raising curve as he gunned the truck up what seemed like a mountainside. "Montana isn't all pretty little photographs in coffee-table books."

"It's very mountainous," she began.

"That it is." He wheeled around another curve, and she got a sickening view of the valley below. It was just like the Great Smoky Mountains, only worse. The Smokies were high and rounded with age, but the Rockies were sharp and young and much higher. Nicky, who had no head at all for heights, began to feel sick.

"Are you all right, Nicky?" Gerald asked with concern. "You've gone white."

"I'm fine." She swallowed. Not for the world would she let Winthrop see what his careless wheeling was accomplishing. She held onto her purse for dear life and stared straight ahead, her jaw set, her green eyes unblinking.

Winthrop, who saw her stubborn resolve, smiled faintly to himself. Nicky might have been surprised to know how much it took to make him smile these days.

Another few miles, and they began to descend. The valley that opened before them took Nicky's breath away. She forgot her nausea in the sheer joy of appreciation. She leaned forward, with her slender hand on the dash, her eyes wide, her breath whispering out softly.

"Heaven," she breathed, smiling at maples gone scarlet and gold, at huge fir trees, delicate aspens and fluffy cottonwoods and the wide swath of a river cutting through it all, leading far into the distance like a silver ribbon. "Oh, it's heaven!"

Winthrop's eyebrows levered up another

fraction as he slowed the truck to give her a better view. At the end of the road was a house, a huge sprawling two-story house that seemed part of its environs. It was made of redwood, with decks on all sides and an enormous porch that seemed to go all the way around it. It had to have fireplaces, because smoke was coming from two chimneys. Maples were all around it, too ordered not to have been planted deliberately years before, and with the mountains all around, it had a majesty that a castle would have envied.

"Lovely, isn't it?" Gerald sighed. "Every time I leave it, I get homesick. Winthrop hasn't changed a single thing about it, either. It's been this way for forty years or more, since our mother planted those maples around the house when our father built it."

"I thought they looked as if someone had planted them." Nicky laughed. "They're in a perfect semicircle around the back of the house."

"Some city people might think that trees grow in perfect order," Winthrop mused, glancing coldly at Nicky. "Amazing, that you were able to pick it out so easily."

"Oh, Nicky grew up on a farm, didn't you, country girl?" Gerald grinned, tweaking her hair. "Way over in Kentucky."

"Good thing they plant trees in perfect order in Kentucky, and teach native sons and daughters to recognize the difference between a planted tree and a naturally seeded tree," Winthrop said without looking at her. "I guess there are people who assume God planted them in rows."

That was a dig, and Nicky wondered what the big man would do if she leaned over and bit him. That amused her and she had to fight to keep from grinning. He was watching her again, his eyes darkly piercing. He disturbed her so much that she dragged her gaze away and felt her cheeks go hot. It was incredible how easily this man got through her defenses. She was going to have to be careful to keep out of his way.

"Did I write you about the Eastern sportsmen I'm expecting week after next?" Winthrop asked Gerald unexpectedly. "I've organized a moose hunt for them, but I'll warn you in plenty of time to keep out of the section I'm planning to hunt."

"I remember," Gerald nodded. "I hope they have some savvy about weapons. Remember the solitary hunter who came one winter and shot your prize bull?"

Winthrop glared at him. "That wasn't funny," he said and glared at his two passengers, who were fighting smiles.

"Damned fool couldn't tell a stud bull from a deer. . . ." Winthrop wheeled the truck up the dirt drive. "These are my Herefords," he added, nodding toward the red-and white-coated herds grazing across the flat plain toward the river. "They're in winter pasture now. I rent some government land for grazing, but I own most of it. It's been a bumper crop of hay this year. There's enough to spare for a change."

Nicole, who knew about farming and winter feed, nodded. "The southern states aren't having such luck," she remarked. "Drought has very nearly ruined a lot of cattlemen and farmers." She didn't question the way he spoke with possession about the family ranch, since Gerald had already told her that Winthrop had complete control of it.

Winthrop frowned as he glanced at her, but he didn't say anything. Her name, her last name, rang a bell, but he couldn't remember why. No matter, he thought; he'd remember eventually where he'd heard it before.

He parked the truck at the door of the huge house and got out, leaving Gerald to help Nicky to the ground.

A big, elderly woman came ambling out

onto the front porch to meet them. She had high cheekbones and a straight nose, and she was very dark.

"That's Mary," Winthrop said, introducing her. "She's been here since I was a boy. She keeps house and cooks. Her husband, Mack, is my horse wrangler."

"Nice girl," Mary muttered, watching Nicole closely as the three newcomers came up onto the porch. "Long legs, good lines. Plain face but honest. Which one of you is going to marry her?" she demanded, looking from Gerald to Winthrop with a mischievous smile.

"I wouldn't have a woman, fried, with catsup," Winthrop replied without blinking, "but Gerald may have hopes."

Before Gerald could say anything, Nicky got herself together enough to reply. She did it without looking at Winthrop, because her cheeks were flushed with temper and embarrassment.

"I'm Mr. Christopher's secretary, Nicole White," Nicky said quickly, and forced a smile as she extended her hand. "Sorry to disappoint you, but I'm only here to work."

"And that is a disappointment," the woman sighed. "Two bachelors, all the time. It weighs heavy on my heart. Come. I will settle you."

"Mary is Sioux," Winthrop told Nicole. "And plainspoken. Too plainspoken, at times," he added, glaring at Mary's broad back.

Mary whirled with amazing speed for such a big woman and made some strange gestures with her hand. Winthrop's eyes gleamed. He made some back. Mary huffed and went up the long, smooth staircase.

"What did you do?" Nicole asked, amazed.

Winthrop looked down at her from his great height, his eyes faintly hostile but temporarily indulgent. "The Plains Indians spoke different languages. They had to have some way to communicate, in the old days, so they did it with signs. This," he added, drawing his hand, palm down, across his forehead, "for instance, means white man or paleface. The sign refers to this part of a man's forehead that was usually covered by a hat and so didn't get tanned like the rest of him. It was pale. This," he continued, rubbing two fingers in a long oval on the back of his left hand, "means Indian."

"Winthrop and Mary used to talk about the rest of us at the table —" Gerald chuckled, tugging affectionately at a short curl beside Nicky's ear "— using sign language. None of us could understand a word."

"It's fascinating," Nicky said, and meant it.

"If you ask Mary, she might teach you a little," Winthrop told Nicky, smiling with cool arrogance. In other words, that look said, don't expect any such favors from me.

She wondered how she was going to survive a month around him, but she did come from a long line of Irishmen, so maybe her spirit was tough enough to cope. She turned back to Gerald. "Do you want to work today?"

"No," Gerald said with certainty. "Today we both rest. Get on some jeans and I'll show you around."

"Great!" She ran upstairs, careful not to look at Winthrop Christopher. It was going to be imperative that she keep out of his way while she was here. He wasn't going to pull his punches, apparently, or accord her any more courtesy than he would have given to any other woman. Remembering what Becky had told her, it was even understandable. But it was going to make her stay here more uncomfortable than she'd expected. The fact that he disturbed her only added to her discomfort. Becky had said that Winthrop had been watching her the day he came to the office. And it was vaguely unnerving to think of those black eyes watching her in an unguarded moment. And why had he? Did she remind him of the woman who'd crippled him? She wasn't blond, of course, but perhaps her facial features were similar. She'd have to ask Gerald.

She was only sorry that she couldn't dislike Winthrop as forcefully as he seemed to dislike her. Quite the contrary; he disturbed her as no man ever had, scarred face, limp and all.

Chapter Two

The room Mary led Nicole into was delightful. It had pink accents against a background of creamy white, complete with a canopied bed and ornate mirror and even a small sitting area with pink, satin-covered chairs.

"This was their mother's room," Mary said. "Pretty, yes?"

"Are you sure I was meant to go in here?" Nicole asked hesitantly.

"Oh, yes, very sure. Mr. Winthrop said so." She winked at Nicole without smiling. "With his hands, you see."

Nicole shook her head. "He seems very . . ." She turned, shrugging as she tried to find words.

"His path has not been an easy one," Mary told her. Those dark eyes were sizing her up while she spoke. "Gerald was the favorite. He was a gentle, easy child. Winthrop was forever in trouble, always fighting, always in turmoil. He was the eldest, but not the most loved. And then came her. She with the blond hair and city ways, who was like a clear morning to me, and I saw through her. But Winthrop could not see through to the greed that motivated her. She crippled him and left him."

Nicole searched the smooth old face quietly. "He hides," she said perceptively.

Mary smiled. "You see deep."

"I know a survival instinct for what it is," came the quiet reply. "We all hide inside ourselves when we've been hurt." She met the dark eyes levelly. "I won't hurt him."

"I see deep, too," Mary mused. "He won't let you close enough to do harm. But watch yourself. He has no love for women. He might take out old wounds on you."

"I'm a survivor," Nicole said, laughing. "I'll manage. But thank you for the warning."

Mary only nodded. "Come down when you are ready. Are you hungry?"

"I could eat a moose," the younger woman sighed.

"Lovely idea. I have moose in the freezer. How would you like it? Baked, fried or in a stew?"

Nicole burst out laughing. "I love stew."

"Me, too." Mary grinned and left her.

Nicole put on a pair of faded jeans with a long-sleeved, gray knit shirt, because the air was chilly, and her pink sneakers and went downstairs without bothering to fix her makeup or comb her hair. She wasn't trying to catch any eyes, after all, so why irritate Winthrop by making it look as if she were making a play for him?

There was no one around, so she went outside and found a comfortable seat on the porch swing. It was peaceful. Birds twittered and somewhere a dog barked. Farther away, cattle were lowing. Nicole closed her eyes as the breeze washed around her. Heaven.

"I see you've found the swing."

She jerked upright as Winthrop came out onto the porch. He was bareheaded, still in the jeans and blue-checked shirt he'd worn to the airport. He'd taken time to shave, because his face was dark and smooth now, with the hairline white scar more visible without the stubble of a beard to hide it.

"I like swings," she said. Her pale green eyes wandered over him. He was terribly attractive without his jacket. Muscles rippled in his long legs when he walked, in his arms when he lifted them to light a cigarette. Despite his size, there wasn't a spare ounce of fat on him. He looked lean and fit and a little dangerous, despite the faint limp when he moved toward her.

"Deer come up into the yard sometimes," he observed. He dropped into a big rocking chair and crossed his long legs. "Moose, elk . . . it's still pretty wild here in the valley. That's why we attract so many bored Eastern sportsmen. They come here to hunt and pretend to 'rough it' but they've lost something that mountain people have all their lives. They've lost hope." He glanced down at her. "I hate rich people."

She felt as if he knew something, but she was afraid to bring the subject out into the open. "I'm not rich," she said, and it was the truth. "But I thought you were."

It was the wrong thing to say. His dark eyes kindled and his face took on the sheen of stone. "Did you?" he asked deliberately, and the mockery in his face was daunting. "Was that why you came with Gerald, or is it his money you're after?"

"You don't understand —" she began.

"I understand women all too well," he returned coldly. He moved away from her without another word, almost colliding with Gerald, who was coming out of the house as he was entering it.

"Sorry, Winthrop," Gerald murmured, curious about the expression on his brother's face. "I was looking for Nicky."

"I'm out here, Mr. Christopher!" she called.

"Oh, for God's sake, I'm Gerald here," he said shortly, joining her with a resigned glance over his shoulder as the door slammed behind Winthrop. He looked even younger in jeans and a pullover shirt. Nicky moved over to make room for him on the swing, and struggled to regain her lost poise. Winthrop was going to make her life miserable, she just knew it, and her stupid careless remark had provoked him. "Mr. Christopher was my father," Gerald continued, "and he was *Mister* Christopher, too," he added with a faint smile. "Our mother was on a camping trip up here. She wandered off and he found her. He nursed her back to health and she left, thinking that was the end of it."

"Was it?" Nicole asked.

Gerald laughed. "No. As a matter of fact, Dad followed her all the way to New York, found her at some social gathering, picked her up and carried her to the train station and brought her here. Eventually, to save her reputation, she agreed to marry him."

"I guess he was used to getting his own way," Nicky mused, and in her mind's eye she could see Winthrop doing exactly the same thing. Her fine skin flushed just a little at the unexpected thought.

"They were happy together," Gerald said. "She died one spring of pneumonia. He died six months later. They said it was a heart attack, but I've often wondered if it wasn't loneliness that did it." He paused for a moment, then said suddenly, "I'm sorry Winthrop's so inhospitable." He glanced at Nicole's quiet face. "You aren't afraid of him, are you? If you are, don't ever let him see it. He's a good man, but he's pretty hard on women."

"I'm not afraid of him," she said. And she meant it. She wondered if there was any chance that he found her as disturbing as she found him. That didn't bear thinking about.

"You must miss all this in Chicago," Nicole said, looking up at her boss.

"I miss this, and other things," he replied. He stared at a house far on a hill in the distance, his eyes narrowed and unexpectedly sad. "Sadie Todd lives over there," he said absently, "with her invalid mother. We'll have to go and visit her while we're here."

"She was nursing at the general hospital, wasn't she?"

"Yes. She had to give up her job and come home when her mother had a stroke. Mrs.

Todd is completely paralyzed on one side and doesn't seem to want to get any better. Sadie said she couldn't leave her at the mercy of strangers. Her father is dead."

She knew almost to the day when Sadie had left, because Gerald Christopher had withdrawn into a tight little shell afterward and seemed to walk around in a fog. He'd put enough pressure on himself thereafter to give him that ulcer. But it had surprised her that he wanted to come home, because he worked like a Trojan all the time lately. She was almost sure that Sadie was the reason he felt the need of a month's vacation in Montana. She smiled to herself.

"I'd like very much to go and see her," she said.

He smiled down at her. "You're a nice person, Nicole." He got up. "I'm going to make a few phone calls. Just sit and enjoy the view, if you like."

"Yes, sir," she promised.

He went inside, and she lounged in the swing until Mary called her to have a sandwich. She sat in the spacious kitchen, enjoying a huge ham sandwich and a glass of iced tea while Mary prepared what promised to be the world's largest moose stew. They talked about the ranch and the country and the weather, and then Nicole went out the back door and wandered down to the river, just to look around.

She could imagine this country in the years of the Lewis and Clark expedition. She'd read a copy of their actual journal, enjoying its rather anecdotal style, seeing the country through their eyes in the days before supersonic jets and superhighways. Trappers would have come through here, she mused, kneeling beside the river with her eyes on the distant peaks. They'd have trapped beaver and fox and they'd have hunted.

Kentucky had its own mountain country, and Nicole had been in it a few times in her life. It had been a different setting then. Elegance. Parties. Sophisticated people. Wealth. She sat down on a huge rock beside the river and tore at a twig, listening to the watery bubble of the river working its way downstream. She much preferred this kind of wealth. Trees and cattle and land. Yes.

"Daydreaming?"

She turned to find Winthrop Christopher sitting astride a big black stallion, watching her.

"I like the river," she explained. "We have one in Chicago, of course, but it's not the same. We have concrete and steel instead of trees."

"I know. I've been to Chicago. Even to the office, in fact." His eyes narrowed. "You don't remember me, do you?"

She did. Even that brief glance had stamped him onto her memory, but it wouldn't do to let him know that. She avoided a direct answer. "It's always hectic. I don't pay a lot of attention to visitors, I'm afraid."

"The morning I came, you were sitting at that computer with a stack of steno pads at your elbow and a telephone in your hand. You barely looked up when I went into Gerald's office." He smiled mockingly. "I was wearing a suit. Maybe I looked different."

"I can't quite imagine you in a suit, Mr. Christopher," she said, thinking, top that, cattle king.

"Winthrop," he corrected. "I'm not that much older than you. Eleven years or so. I'm thirty-four."

"How old is your brother?" she asked, curious.

He lifted his chin. "Thirty."

"Sometimes he seems older," she mused. "When they call the stockholders' meetings, for instance."

He glanced into the distance. "No doubt. I'm glad I don't have to deal with those damned things. That's Gerald's sole province now. I just run my ranch, and the only stockholder I have to please is myself. Gerald doesn't own enough shares to squabble over the decisions I make."

"You inherited the ranch, didn't you?"

He stared at her for a minute, and she swallowed hard, sure that he was going to give her some sarcastic financial rundown and chide her for asking. But, surprisingly, he didn't. He just nodded. "That was the way my father wanted it. He knew I'd hold it as long as I lived, no matter what. You'll find that Gerald isn't terribly sentimental. He'd just as soon have a photograph as the object itself."

She pursed her full lips and studied him. "I'll bet you saved bobby pins and bits of ribbon when you were a teenager," she said daringly, just to see what he'd say.

He blinked, then laughed, but it wasn't a pleasant sound. "I had my weak moments when I was younger," he agreed. His eyes darkened. "Not anymore, though, Kentucky girl. I'm steel right through."

She wouldn't have touched that line. She turned, glancing at the distant ribbon the river made running into those towering, majestic peaks. "I was thinking about Lewis and Clark," she murmured, glancing toward the horizon, so that she didn't catch the look on his face. "A man died during the expedition. What they described sounded just like food poisoning. They wouldn't have known, of course. How much we've learned in over a hundred years. How far we've come. And yet," she said softly, "how much we've lost in the process."

"The expedition went down the Missouri and Jefferson rivers," he said slowly. "We're on a tributary of the Jefferson, so they may have camped in this valley." He looked away. "They used to call it Buffalo Flats. The buffalo are gone, though. Like the way of life that existed here long ago." He shifted restlessly. "Where's Gerald?"

"Back at the house, I suppose," she said, bothered by the curtness of his tone. "He said he had some important phone calls to make. I would have stayed, but he said we wouldn't work today."

"Want a ride back?" he offered, and then seemed to withdraw, as if he regretted the words even as he was speaking them.

Some devilish imp made her smile at him. "Suppose I say yes?" she asked, driven to taunt him. "You look as if you'd rather sacrifice the horse than let me on him." And she grinned, daring him to mock her.

He felt a burst of light, but he wouldn't

44

give in to it. "Damn you."

She grinned even more. "I won't accept, if you'd rather not let me aboard. Anyway —" she shuddered with deliberate mockery and more sarcasm than he could know, because she'd practically grown up on horses "— I'd probably fall off. It looks very high."

"It is. But I won't let you fall off. Come on." He kicked his foot out of the stirrup and held down a long arm, giving in to an impulse he didn't even understand. He wanted her closer. He wanted to hold her. That should have warned him, but it didn't.

He had enormous feet, she noticed, as she put a foot in the stirrup and let him pull her up in front of him. He was amazingly strong, too.

She hadn't realized how intimate it was going to be. His hard arm went around her middle and pulled her back against a body that was warm and strong and smelled of leather and spice. She felt her heart run away, and that arm under her breast would feel it, she knew.

"Nervous?" he asked at her ear, and laughed softly, without any real humor. "I'm not dangerous. I don't like women, or haven't they filled you in yet?" She's a woman, he was reminding himself. Watch it, watch yourself — she'll sucker you in and kick you down, just like the other one did.

"Yes, I'm nervous," she said. "Yes, you're dangerous, and you may not like women, but I'll bet they chase you like a walking mink."

His eyebrows arched. "You're plainspoken, aren't you?" he asked, gathering her even closer as he urged the restless stallion into motion, controlling him carefully with lean, powerful hands and legs.

"I try to be," she said, still uneasy about the double life she'd led since leaving Kentucky. To a man who'd been betrayed once, it might seem as if she were misleading him deliberately. But the past was still painful, and she'd forsaken it. She wanted it to stay in the past, like the bad memories of her own betrayal. Besides, there was no danger of Winthrop becoming involved with her. He was too invulnerable.

She held on to the pommel, her eyes on his long fingers. "You have beautiful hands, for a man," she remarked.

"I don't like flattery."

"Suit yourself, you ugly old artifact," she shot right back.

It had been a long time since anything had made him laugh. But this plain-faced, mysterious woman struck a chord in him that had never sounded. She brought color and light into his own private darkness. He felt the sound bubbling up in his chest, like thunder, and then overflowing. He couldn't hold it back this time, and the rush of it was incomprehensible to him.

She felt his chest shaking, heard the deep rumble of sound from inside it. She would have bet that he didn't laugh genuinely very often at anything. But she seemed to have a knack for dragging it out of him, and that pleased her beyond rational thought.

The lean arm contracted, and for an instant she felt him in an embrace that made her go hot all over. What would it be like, she wondered wildly, if he turned her and wrapped her up in his embrace and put that hard, cruel mouth over hers. . . .

She tingled from head to toe, her breath catching in her throat. It shouldn't have been like this, she shouldn't still be vulnerable. She had to stop this, or it was going to be an unendurable month.

"Watch out, Miss White," he said at her ear, his voice deep and soft and dangerous. "Save the heavy flirting for Gerald. You'll be safer that way."

He let her down at the porch, holding her so that she slid down to the ground. For an instant his dark face was very close, so close that she saw his dark eyes at point-blank range and something shot through her like lightning. She pulled back slowly, her eyes still linked to his. What had he said? Something about flirting with Gerald. But why should she want to flirt with her boss?

"See you." He wheeled his stallion and rode off, and she watched him with mingled emotions.

Supper was an unexpectedly quiet affair. Winthrop was out when she and Gerald sat down to eat, along with the ranch foreman, Michael Slade, a burly man of thirty who seemed perfectly capable of handling anything.

"Boss said he wouldn't get back in time for chow," Michael told Gerald with a grin. "Had to go into Butte for some supplies he needed. I offered, but he said he had some other things to do as well."

"Odd that he didn't do it before he met us at the airport." Gerald sighed as he took his medicine and glared at his plate. The doctor had told him that they didn't treat ulcers with bland diets anymore, but Mary hadn't believed him. Amazing, how disgusting green pea soup looked in a bowl, and he did hate applesauce. He glanced at Mary, sighed and then gave in to her, as he had done even as a child. He picked up his spoon and began to sip the soup. "Oh, well, that's Winthrop. Unpredictable. How's it going, Mike?"

The foreman launched into grand detail about seeing to the winter pasture, fixing fences, storing hay, culling cows, doing embryo transplants for the spring calving and organizing other facets of ranch life that he'd expected would go right over Nicole's head.

"One of my family was into embryo transplants when it was barely theory," Nicole interrupted. "They had some great successes. Now there's a new system underway, implanting computer chips just under the skin to keep track of herds. . . ."

"Say, I've read about that," Mike agreed, and Gerald sat and stared while the two of them discussed cattle.

"Mr. Christopher must be feeling pretty proud of himself to have someone like you on the payroll," Nicole told the foreman when they reached a stopping point. "You know your business."

"Forgive me, ma'am, but so do you," Mike grinned, his ruddy face almost handsome with his blue eyes flashing. "I never knew a woman who could talk cattle before."

"I never knew a man who talked it as well," she grinned back.

"I thought you were from Chicago," Gerald sighed, shaking his head, when Mike had gone and they were sipping coffee in the living room. "Until you admitted that you were a Kentuckian, at least," he added. His gaze was warm and faintly questioning. "Amazing, that we worked together for two years and knew nothing about each other."

She smiled at him. "I guess most bosses and secretaries are like that, really," she agreed. "You're very nice to work for, though. You don't yell, like some of your vice presidents do."

He laughed. "I try not to. Winthrop, now," he said, watching her face as he spoke, "never yells. But it's worse that way, somehow. He has a voice like an icy wind when he loses his temper, which isn't often. I've seen him look at men who were about to start fights and back them down. One of our ancestors was a French fur trader up in Canada. Our grandmother used to say Winthrop takes after him."

"He has expressive eyes," she agreed, glancing at Gerald warily. "He doesn't want me here, you know."

His shoulders rose and fell. "He's buried himself up here for three solid years," he said irritably, staring into his coffee. "No company, except these hunting parties that he tolerates because it gives some variety to his life. No women. No dating. He's avoided women like the plague since Deanne left him. He uses that limp like a stick, have you noticed?" he asked, lifting troubled eyes to hers. "It isn't all that bad, and he could walk well enough if he cared to try, but it's as if he needs it to remind him that women are treacherous."

"I'd heard that he was something of a playboy in his younger days," she probed, curious about Winthrop in new and exciting ways.

"He was," Gerald agreed with a faint, musing smile. "He broke hearts right and left. But Deanne liked him because he was a new experience. I don't think she really meant to hurt him. She was young and he spoiled her, and she liked it. But when he got hurt, she had visions of being tied to a cripple for life, and she ran. Winthrop was shattered by the experience. His black pride couldn't deal with the humiliation of being lamed and deserted, all at once."

"Poor man," she said gently, and meant it.

"Don't make that mistake, either," he cautioned quietly. "Don't ever pity him. He's steel clean through, and if you give him half an opening, he'll make a scapegoat of you. Don't let him hurt you, Nicky."

She colored delicately. "You think he

might?"

"I think you attract him," he said bluntly. "And I have a feeling that you aren't immune to him, either. He doesn't like being vulnerable, so look out."

Hours later, when she went up to bed, she was still turning that threat over in her mind. She could picture Winthrop behind her closed eyes, and the image made her sigh with mingled emotions. She'd never felt so empty before, so alone. She wanted him in ways that she'd never dreamed she could want a man. She wanted to be with him, to share with him, to ease his hurt and make him whole again. She didn't quite know how to cope with the new and frightening sensations. Nicky had her own scars and she didn't want involvement any more than Winthrop did. But there was something between them. Something that was new and a little frightening, and like an avalanche, she couldn't stop it.

She was almost asleep when she heard slow steps coming past her door. She knew from the sound that it was Winthrop, and her heart beat faster as he passed her room. Odd, how deeply she could be touched just by his step. She wondered if he was as curious about her as she was about him, despite his understandably deep distrust of women.

He was like her, in so many ways, hiding from a world that had been cruel to him. They had more in common than he seemed to realize. Or perhaps he did realize it, and was drawing back because he didn't trust her. She closed her eyes as she heard a door close down the hall. In no time at all, she was asleep, secure because the master of the house was back, and she was safe.

CHAPTER THREE

Winthrop's horses attracted Nicole immediately, even though he'd given her a terse warning at breakfast about going too close to them. One of the happiest memories of her childhood was watching old Ernie at her home in Kentucky as he worked the thoroughbreds when they were ready to be trained.

Besides his saddle horses, mostly quarter horses, Winthrop had at least two thoroughbreds with unmistakably Arabian ancestry, judging by their small heads. All American thoroughbreds, she remembered, were able to trace their ancestry to one of three Arabian horses imported into England in the late 1600s and early 1700s: Byerley Turk, Godolphin Barb and Queen Anne.

Winthrop's horses had the exquisite conformation and sleek lines that denoted thoroughbreds, too. She'd watched them during her brief stroll around the stables and corral. One was a mare about to foal, the other a full stallion, both with sleek chestnut coats and exquisite conformation. She'd wanted to ask Winthrop about them over scrambled eggs and steak that morning, but he'd been unapproachable. Frozen over, in fact, and she knew why without even being told. He didn't want her too close, so he was freezing her out.

She'd finished her two hours in the study, taking dictation from Gerald, and now cozy and warm in tailored gray slacks and a white pullover sweater, she was lazing around the corral looking for the horses. The stallion was there, but she didn't see the mare anywhere.

A noise from inside the big barn caught her attention. She couldn't see inside, but it sounded like a horse's whinny of pain. It was followed by a particularly virulent curse from a voice she recognized immediately.

She darted into the dim warmth of the big barn, down the neat corridor between the stalls that was covered with pine shavings.

"Winthrop?" she called quickly.

"In here."

She followed his voice to the end stall. The mare was down on her side, making snuffling sounds, and Winthrop was bending over her, his sleeves rolled up, bare-headed, scowling.

"Something's wrong," she said, glancing at him.

"Brilliant observation," he muttered, probing at the mare's distended belly with tender, sure hands. "This is her first foal and it's a breech, damn the luck! Go get Johnny Blake and tell him I said to come here, I can't do this alone. He'll be —"

"The mare will be dead by the time I find him," she said matter-of-factly. She eased into the stall, ignoring Winthrop as she gently approached the mare, talking softly to her with every step. While Winthrop watched, scowling, she slid down to her knees beside the beautiful, intelligent creature, watching the silky brown eyes all the while. She sat down then, reaching out to stroke the mare. And slowly, she eased under the proud head and slowly coaxed it onto her knees. She drew her fingers gently over the velvety muzzle, talking softly to the mare, gentling her.

"She'll let you help her now," she told Winthrop softly, never taking her eyes from the mare's.

"Yes," he said, watching her curiously for a few seconds before he bent to his task. "I believe she might. You'll ruin that fancy sweater," he murmured as he went to work.

"Better it than lose the foal," she said, and smiled at the mare, talking gently to her all along, smoothing the long mane, cuddling the shuddering head, as Winthrop slowly worked to help the colt in its dark cradle. She knew instinctively that the mare would realize that she was trying to help, and not hurt her.

Minutes later, guided by patient, expert lean hands, hind fetlocks appeared suddenly, followed rapidly by the rest of the newborn animal. Winthrop laughed softly, triumphantly, as the tiny new life slid into the hay and he cleared its nostrils.

"A colt," he announced.

Nicole smiled at him over the mare, amazed to find genuine warmth in his dark eyes. "And a very healthy one, too," she agreed. Her eyes searched his softly, and then she felt herself beginning to tremble at the intensity of his level gaze. She drew her gaze away and stroked the mare again before she got slowly to her feet so that the new mother could lick her colt and nuzzle it.

"A thoroughbred, isn't he?" she replied absently, her eyes on the slick colt being lovingly washed by his mother. "The stallion has a superior conformation. So does the mare. He might be a champion."

"The stallion is by Calhammond, out of Dame Savoy," he said, frowning as he moved away to wash his hands and arms in a bucket of water with a bar of soap, drying them on a towel that hung over it. "How did you know?"

"Kentucky is racehorse country," she laughed, sidestepping the question. She didn't want to tell him how much she knew about thoroughbreds, although she'd certainly given herself away just now, and she'd have to soft-pedal over it. "I cut my teeth on thoroughbreds. I used to beg for work around them, and one of the trainers took pity on me. He taught me a lot about them. You see, one of the biggest racing farms in Lexington was near where I lived — Rockhampton Farms." Actually Rockhampton was her grandfather's name; her mother's people had owned the stables there for three generations. But it wouldn't do to admit that to Winthrop, because he'd connect it with Dominic White, who was her father and the current owner. He might even know Dominic, because he entertained sportsmen, and her father was one of the best.

"I've heard of it," Winthrop told her after a minute. He turned, staring hard at her with dark, curious eyes as he rolled down the sleeves of his brown Western shirt and buttoned the cuffs with lazy elegance. White. Her name was White. Wasn't that the name of that jet-setting sportsman from Kentucky who was coming with the Eastern hunting party? Yes, by God it was, and Dominic White owned Rockhampton Farms. He lifted his head. "The owner of Rockhampton is a White," he said in a direct attack, watching closely for reaction. "Any kin of yours?"

She held onto her wits with a steely hand. She even smiled. "White is a pretty common name, I'm afraid," she said. "Do I look like an heiress?"

"You don't dress like one," he commented, with narrowed eyes. "And I guess you wouldn't be working for Gerald if you had that kind of money," he said finally, relaxing a little. He didn't want her, but it was a relief all the same to know that she wasn't some bored little rich girl looking for a good time. He couldn't have borne going through that again. "I've been to Kentucky, but I've never been on the White place. My stallion and mare came from the O'Hara place."

"Yes, Meadowbrook Farms," she murmured. She could have fainted with relief. She didn't want him to know about her background. Of course, there was always the danger that he might someday find out that she was one of those Whites, but with any luck she'd be back in Chicago before he did, and it wouldn't matter anymore. Right now, the important thing was to get her boss well and not upset him with any confrontations between herself and Winthrop.

Winthrop had every reason to hate rich society girls, and he might be tempted to make her life hell if he knew the truth. And probably it would be worse because she hadn't told him about it in the beginning. Her character would be even blacker in his eyes for the subterfuge. For one wild instant, she considered telling him. But she knew she couldn't. He disliked her enough already. And it was suddenly important, somehow, to keep him from finding new reasons to dislike her. It did occur to her that someday he might hate her for not being truthful with him. But she'd discovered a tender streak in his turbulent nature while he was working with the mare, and she wanted to learn more about that shadowy side of him. That might not be possible if he knew the truth about her.

"I couldn't have managed that alone," he said quietly, watching her. "I'm obliged for the help."

"I like horses," she said simply. "And he's a grand colt."

"His father has been a consistent winner, but he was hurt in a race last year. I bought him to stand at stud rather than see him put down. I had a lot of money that was lying spare, so I developed an interest in racehorses. I've spent a good deal of time at racetracks in the past year."

Another chink in the armor, she thought, thinking about his compassion for the stallion as she looked up at him.

He saw that speculative gleam and it irritated him. She wasn't working out the way he'd expected. She had too many interesting qualities, and he didn't like the feelings she aroused in him. He'd buried his emotions, and she was digging down to them with irritating ease.

"You don't like me, do you?" she asked bluntly. "Why? Is it because I'm plain, or because I'm only a secretary . . ."

"You aren't plain," he said unexpectedly, his dark eyes tracing the soft oval of her face. Big green eyes. Pretty mouth. High cheekbones. Skin like satin, creamy and young. She was young. He sighed wistfully. "And I'm no snob. I just don't want women around."

"That's straightforward," she said softly.

"And I hope it won't offend you if I speak as bluntly. I know a little about what happened to you and why. I'm very sorry. But hating me and making my life miserable for the next few weeks isn't going to erase your scars. It will only create new ones for both of us. So can't we be sporting enemies?" she asked, her green eyes twinkling. "And I'll promise not to seduce you in the hay."

His eyebrows shot straight up. Unexpected wasn't the word for this little firecracker. He'd have to think up a new one.

"What do you know about seduction, Red Riding Hood?" he asked with blithe humor, and she got a tiny glimpse of the man he'd been before the accident.

"Not much, actually," she said pleasantly, "but that's probably in your favor, because it will save you a lot of embarrassing moments. Just imagine if I were experienced and sophisticated and out to sink my claws into you!"

Her earnestly teasing expression made him feel as if he were sipping potent wine. He had a hard time drawing his eyes away from her soft mouth and back up to her laughing eyes. Incredibly long lashes, on those eyes. Sexy. Like the rest of her. She was tall, but she wasn't overly thin. He liked the way she looked in tailored slacks and that white sweater. Both were thick with horsehair about now, and she'd smell of horse. . . .

"She'll want some water now," she reminded him, unnerved by that slow, bold scrutiny and hoping that it didn't show.

It did. His chin lifted just a little, in a purely male way, and his chiseled mouth twitched. "Nervous of me?"

"If all the gossip I've heard about you is true, I have good reason to be, and that isn't conceit on my part," she added proudly. "Playboys don't usually mind who they charm, because it's all a game to them."

The light in his eyes went out, like a cavern succumbing to darkness. "I don't play games with virgins, honey," he said unexpectedly, catching her chin with a lean, steely hand. "And you'd better remember it. I've forgotten more about lovemaking in my time than you've ever learned, but I'm not low enough to take out my hurt on you."

He was so close that she could feel the strong warmth of him. Her heart ran wild. She'd never had such a powerful, immediate reaction to a man before. Not even to Chase. This was new and wildly exciting, and she wanted more.

"How do you know that . . . about me?" she whispered, shocked that he could so easily discuss the most intimate subjects.

"I don't know," he replied quietly, searching her soft eyes. His blood warmed in his veins, and he felt his heartbeat slowly increase. Her scent was overpowering, drowning him, seducing his senses. He knew a lot about her, knowledge that only instinct could have supplied.

Her lips parted on a rush of breath. The dimness of the barn was warm and cozy, shutting them away from the world. Winthrop was closer than ever, towering over her, drowning her in a narcotic kind of hunger.

She took an involuntary step toward him. "I . . . don't understand," she whispered, her voice shaking. One slender hand went hesitantly to his chest and pressed against it, feeling the shock of warm muscle and a spongy wiriness that might have been hair underneath. She felt him tense, even before his hand came up to remove hers with abrupt impatience.

"Don't do that," he ground out, glaring at her. "I don't want your hands on me."

Her own forwardness shocked her more than his irritable statement. She turned away, feeling a rush of tears that she couldn't let him see.

"I'd better get back to the house," she said

quickly. "Your brother was going to make a phone call and then finish his dictation. I'm glad the mare's okay." She said it all in a mad rush and threw a vague smile in his direction before she went out of the barn as if her shoes were on fire.

He watched her go with mingled emotions. Anger. Irritation. Hunger. Frustration. He couldn't sort them out, so he didn't bother. He went back to feed and water the mare and see about the colt. Damn women everywhere, he thought, and limped more than usual as he went about his business.

Nicole made a point of avoiding her boss's unpredictable brother for the rest of the day. But there was no getting away from him at the supper table, and she had to fight not to look at him.

Cleaned up and freshly shaved, wearing a white shirt that suited his darkness, he would have drawn any woman's eyes. It was easy to see how he'd appealed to women when he was younger. He was still a striking man, and it wasn't just his looks. There was an indefinable something about him, a vibrant masculinity that was almost tangible and certainly overpowering at close range. Her hands trembled just sitting next to him at the long table.

Gerald was quoting figures on some real

estate he'd acquired, and Winthrop was listening with barely half his mind. He was watching Nicky while he pared his steak and chewed it deliberately, trying not to let her know that he was watching her. She was wearing that gray jersey dress that clung so lovingly to her curves, and the memory of the effect she'd had on him in the barn wasn't doing his appetite any good.

He finally grew impatient with her down-bent head and stopped eating and just stared at her intently while Gerald went on talking without realizing that he was talking to himself.

Nicole felt that intent stare and looked up into Winthrop's dark eyes. And her heart stopped beating.

Electricity danced between them. She couldn't drag her eyes from his, any more than his were willing to be tugged away. The look they exchanged was long and piercing and shattering in its intensity. It was as personal as a kiss, so steady and unblinking that she felt her body tremble in intimate response to his blatant interest.

His gaze held hers for a shuddering moment, and then it dropped to her mouth, and she felt her lips part helplessly for him.

"Winthrop, are you listening?" Gerald asked suddenly, breaking the silence when he discovered that his brother was apparently staring into space.

"What?" Winthrop turned back to him. "Something about real estate values?" he asked absently. He didn't like the way his body responded to that look in Nicole's eyes. He was going to have to do something. But what?

Nicole was having as difficult a time with her own body. She shifted restlessly and drank coffee that was, by now, hopelessly oversugared. While Winthrop's dark eyes had been openly making love to hers, she'd put six spoons of sugar in the black liquid. She took a sip and shuddered and left it in favor of the glass of water Mary had provided for each of them. So much for common sense. It was time to retreat.

For the next few days, she and Winthrop avoided each other — ignored each other — to the extent that everybody noticed, and Mary began asking gentle questions that Nicole smiled at and avoided answering. And that might have gone on for another week if she hadn't tripped on the steps coming in from a walk late one afternoon, to be caught by Winthrop in the gathering darkness.

He'd apparently just come in from the corral himself. He smelled of cattle and he needed a shave, but his arms in the sheepskin jacket felt strong and warm, and instead of pulling away like a sensible girl, Nicole had sighed and relaxed against his tall, strong body.

Winthrop muttered something, but he didn't push her away. His hard arms contracted, drawing her against him under the unbuttoned jacket, and he stood holding her in the dusky light, savoring her softness, his cheek against her dark hair.

It seemed so natural, somehow. So right. His eyes closed and all the reasons why he shouldn't allow her this close vanished. He didn't make a sound, and neither did she. The wind sang through the tall lodgepole pines, whispered through the aspen and maples, whipped her hair against her flushed cheek. She pressed closer with a tiny, inarticulate sound, too hungry for the contact to listen to the warning bells going off in her head. He was warm and strong, and it was sheer delight to be held by him. She felt her body tremble with exquisite pleasure.

"We could hurt each other badly," he whispered in her ear, his voice deep and soft and slow. "You don't have the experience to understand the risk, and I can't be sure that I wouldn't take out old hurts on you, even though I wouldn't do it consciously. This is crazy."

"Yes."

He nuzzled his cheek against her hair. "I mean it, Nicky."

She sighed, reluctantly drawing away from him. She looked up, curious, excited. "Afraid of me, cattle baron?" she asked softly.

"In a way," he agreed unexpectedly, but he wasn't smiling. He touched her cheek with the back of his fingers in a soft caress. "I don't like to start things I can't finish."

"Meaning?" she persisted. If it was digging her own emotional grave, she couldn't help it. She had to know.

He stared into her eyes for just a second, and then drew back, physically and emotionally. "You'll figure it out. Don't wander out of the yard when you go walking. One of the men thinks he spotted a wolf today. I don't want anything to happen to you, little Eastern girl. I may never be your lover, but I'll take care of you, all the same, while you're here."

And with that surprising statement, he turned and walked off. Nicole stared after him with eyes that brimmed with unshed tears. He was very protective of her, and she wondered if he realized it. He wasn't saying what he felt, but she knew instinctively that he shared some of the warm feeling that was growing inside her. But whether he'd ever give in to it was anyone's guess. As for Nicole, it had shocked her to realize that she had none of her usual defenses when he was near her. And that realization kept her quiet all through supper and beyond bedtime. What an unexpectedly complicated thing this vacation of her boss's had become. She hoped that she was going to be able to cope with the new and disturbing feelings that Winthrop had unearthed in her.

Life sailed into a pleasant routine after that. She and Gerald settled down to work, and Nicole spent her free time exploring outdoors or watching Mary in the kitchen. Winthrop was pleasant enough, but he kept things cool, although from time to time she found those dark, quiet eyes watching her in a way that excited her beyond bearing.

Two days later, she heard cattle bawling and excited male voices, and she succumbed to the need to see Winthrop. The cattle were massed at a makeshift corral just away from the barn and the stables, and Winthrop was on his horse, helping to drive cattle into a holding pen where they were apparently being vetted and vaccinated and examined and treated for diseases or infestation by grubs.

That weak leg didn't seem to bother the big man one bit on horseback. He could cut and rope with the best of them, and the wilder the horse, the better he seemed to enjoy himself. He laughed deeply and with obvious pleasure the whole time. She imagined that when he was in the saddle he could forget how ungraceful he was on the ground.

Not that a limp made him any less a man. He bristled with masculine sensuality. She could see quite easily how he'd gained a reputation in his youth as a playboy. He was devastating physically, and he had a voice that even in memory could make her flush with pleasure. Her heart hadn't been the same since that unexpected embrace on the porch. She could close her eyes and hear his voice all over again, as it had been that evening, and she could almost imagine it in a dark room, coaxing, deliberately seductive. . . .

Warmth coursed through her and she forced herself to watch the men and the cattle. Winthrop had climbed off the horse to help catch a calf, apparently one that needed doctoring. He looped his rope and undid it, lazily coiling it while one of the other cowboys threw the calf and began to do something to it. Winthrop was rubbing

his leg, and the limp was even more pro-
nounced when he turned, leading his horse
by the reins.

He saw Nicole at the fence, and he stood
very still for an instant. She could feel his
anger even at the distance, and made a
discreet and quick withdrawal. He was
headed in her direction, so she changed it
and walked quickly into the forest that
encircled the house.

Why she should have been embarrassed,
she didn't know. But she knew he was
angry, even before he caught up with her
minutes later.

She stopped, catching her breath. He was
right behind her, still leading the horse. As
he walked, he favored that right leg.

"Running away?" he taunted. "Why?"

She stared at him. It was silly to be so ill
at ease with him, but his expression wasn't
at all welcoming. "I don't know," she said
quietly. She was wearing jeans and a long-
sleeved yellow sweater. He had on a shirt
the same shade of yellow and brown as his
jeans, and she thought illogically how well
they matched.

He lifted his dark head. "Don't you? What
are you doing — spying? Did you want to
see if the cripple could still throw a calf?"

She went forward without thinking and

put her soft hand over his mouth. "Don't," she said softly. "Don't do that to yourself. You're not a cripple. You're a man with a limp."

The feel of her fingers shocked him. The gesture was unexpected and it threw him off balance. He caught her smooth hand, holding it near his cheek as if he couldn't quite decide what to do with it.

He stood over her, breathing roughly, his eyes dark with pain and anger as they searched hers. His fingers contracted absently around hers, bruising a little, but she didn't protest.

"I don't want you here," he said quietly, his eyes narrow, piercing.

"Yes, I know." She moved her fingers experimentally, and he let them go. She touched his cheek, tracing the long scar down his jaw, into the dimple in his chin. It was incredible how secure she felt with him, and not the least bit afraid. She sensed something in him, something vulnerable and tender, and she wanted to reach it. She needed to reach it, although she didn't understand why. "You don't talk about it, do you? Not ever."

His broad chest rose and fell. He was very close. Too close. She could feel the muscles ripple when he moved, feel him breathing, feel the warmth of him in the chill air.

His fingers slid into her hair, hesitantly, feeling the curls as he moved his hands to her nape and turned her head up with firm gentleness.

"It's been one hell of a long time since I kissed a woman," he said half under his breath, looking down at her coldly. "Don't you realize that you've been inviting that for days? I'm not a boy, and I've gone hungry in recent years. I can't play games, I even told you so. You could start something that would ruin both our lives."

She let him pull her head back. She looked up at him unafraid, her eyes soft with understanding and compassion. "I'm not afraid of you," she said softly.

"I could make you afraid, Nicole."

His voice was velvety soft and deep. Her lips parted, because it was as sensuous as she'd imagined it would be. She liked being close to him. She wanted his mouth and her lips parted in subtle invitation. She might have imagined herself in love with Chase James, but never in her life had she felt anything as sweet as this.

He looked down at her soft mouth, seeing it open, and something in him snapped. He bent quickly, covering it with his hard lips. He wanted to hurt her. She was a child, playing at sensuality, and he wanted to make it so rough that she'd stop tormenting him with emotions he never wanted to feel again. . . .

She yielded completely, no thought of fighting him. His mouth was hard, warm and tasted of tobacco and it was only then that she realized how expert he really was. He made no allowances for her youth, and despite her small experience with Chase, this was her first real taste of passion. It was devastating, this helpless feeling he caused in her. She sighed hungrily, letting him draw her completely against the powerful hard length of his body, letting him crush her against it. Her mouth yielded eagerly to his insistent lips, tasting the tobacco tartness of his tongue as it pushed into her mouth, penetrating her in a silence that blazed with kindling sensations.

Her hands grasped his shirtsleeves, holding on, because her knees were getting weak. His arm at her back arched her, the hand at her nape tangled in her curly hair. He made a sound deep in his throat and lifted his head, his eyes black and blazing as they probed her dazed ones.

"Aren't you going to fight me?" he taunted with a faint, mocking smile as his mouth poised over hers.

"No." She reached up, sliding her arms around his neck. Her mouth was soft, parted and waiting, tempting his. "Oh, no, I want it, too!"

"Nicky . . ."

It was a groan, her name on his lips. He bent, half lifting her up to him. But this time, he didn't try to hurt her. This time, he was achingly gentle. His hard mouth slowed and softened on hers, and he kissed her with a subdued passion that aroused all her protective instincts. Poor, tormented man, she thought. So much love in him, all wasted on the wrong woman. And now he was driven to hurt back, out of fear that it was going to happen again. But it wasn't, she thought, her heart blazing with compassion. It wasn't, because she'd never hurt him.

She closed her arms tight around his neck and opened her mouth for him, drawing it over his as she was learning he liked it. Her tongue teased at his full lower lip and he made a sound that corresponded with the tautening of his body.

"I'm sorry," she whispered against his lips. "I don't . . . know much about this. I'm sorry if I did it wrong."

He lifted his head again. He was breathing roughly, and his eyes had a haunted look. The hand in her hair caressed gently. "You really are a virgin, aren't you?" he murmured with a tenderness he wasn't aware of.

"I guess it shows," she whispered dryly. She looked down at his shirt, missing the sudden shocked delight in his eyes. "I haven't had a lot to do with men in the past few years."

He brushed the curly hair away from her face, touching her with pure wonder. Yes, this was what he'd been uneasy about, this vulnerable side of her that attracted him. He'd tried so hard to avoid this confrontation. Ridiculous, really, when it was inevitable that he was going to feel her warmth in his arms, savor the soft nectar of her mouth. He'd known she was nearby, back at the corral. He'd sensed her somehow. "Why were you watching me?" he asked.

"I don't know. I needed to." She shifted, burying her face against his broad shoulder. "You disturb me," she whispered shakily. "It frightens me."

"It shouldn't." He held her, rocked her. His mouth touched her forehead in a kiss as gentle as the arms that held her. "I won't hurt you again."

She nuzzled her face against him. "It's very exciting, being kissed like that," she whispered shyly.

He smiled. "Is it?" He tilted her chin up and searched her eyes. "Then let's do it again," he whispered into her open mouth.

It was wilder this time, hotter, more unbearably sweet. She gave him her mouth and melted into the hard contours of his body with a soft moan. It wasn't until she felt the tautening, felt the sudden urgency in the mouth devouring hers, that she realized things were getting out of control.

She put her hands against his wildly thudding chest and pulled her lips away from his. "No," she said shakily.

He bit at her lower lip, his head spinning. "No?"

"You're a man . . . and experienced," she whispered. "I've never . . . and I can't. I'm sorry."

He was breathing roughly, but he didn't seem to be angry. He brushed his mouth over her eyes, closing her eyelids. "Do you want to?" he whispered, smiling.

"What a ridiculous question. I expect you know the answer," she said dazedly.

"I suppose I do, at that." He sighed, wrapping her up against him. "Hold tight. They say it passes, eventually. I can't vouch for it, of course. I'm not in the habit of drawing back at this point."

"Oh, I'm sorry," she moaned.

"I won't die." He nuzzled his cheek against hers, rocking her. His arms had a faint tremor, but his breathing was calmer now and his heartbeat had stopped shaking them both. "What a potent little package you are. I didn't plan this. I meant to . . . hell, I don't know what I meant to do. Scare you, maybe."

"You did."

He laughed. "Like hell I did, you were with me every step of the way. I could have laid you down in the grass and —"

"Hush!"

He drew back then and looked down at her, frowning, his eyes wary and searching. She was flushed, and her eyes had an unnatural brightness, as if she were holding back tears.

"What are you so afraid of?" he asked quietly, touching her eyelid gently to release a long, silver tear. "It was passionate, but still just a kiss. I didn't even try to touch you in any way that would have offended you."

"It isn't fear," she whispered. She lowered her eyes. How could she explain to him the intensity of her feelings, the aching tenderness she was beginning to feel for him?

"Are you afraid of intimacy?" he asked

very quietly.

She lowered her eyes to his chest and closed them. "I'm afraid of getting involved. Just as afraid as you are," she added. And it was true. She'd given her heart to Chase — she'd almost given her body to him. And he'd betrayed her trust. How could she risk it again?

"Why?"

She looked up at him. "Why are you?" she countered, searching his quiet eyes.

He bent and touched her forehead with lips that were breathlessly gentle. "I loved her," he whispered, "in my way. It was the first time I'd ever felt more than a physical hunger for a woman. When she walked away from me, I wanted to die. I swore I'd get over it, but I don't know that I really have. The scars go deep."

She touched his face gently, running her fingers slowly along his hard cheek. Amazing, how exquisite it was to be near him.

"I got thrown over by my fiancé," she confessed. "He decided he wanted a rich girl, and I wasn't . . ." She almost added "anymore" but she caught the word in time.

He searched her soft green eyes. "You didn't sleep with him," he said, gazing at her intently.

"That's hard to explain." She stared at his

top shirt button. It was undone, and thick dark hair peeked out against his tanned skin. "I wanted the first time to mean something. What hurts the most is that I never felt that way about him. I thought I loved him, but I never thought about sleeping with him."

That was the truth. Seeing how fast living had ruled her parents' lives had soured her on that part of life. Intimacy had become to them as careless as handshakes, and Nicole had determined that it would be treated more reverently in her own life. Perhaps, in retrospect, that was one of the reasons Chase had left her. He'd pushed her toward intimacy more and more after their engagement, but she'd resisted stubbornly. And now, standing close in Winthrop's arms, she was savagely glad she'd resisted.

There was more to it than that, he knew, but she wasn't volunteering any more information. He studied her quietly, thinking how much like him she was. He ran his finger down her cheek. Secretive, too, but he'd get more of an explanation eventually. It was insane to be so pleased that she was still innocent. It excited him, as sophisticated women never had.

"I could eat a moose," he said conversationally. "Why don't we rush back to the house and raid the freezer? Can you cook, in case Mary decides to try out for the Rockettes one day?"

She laughed at him. His humor had surprised her. Was this the real man? Had that cold veneer finally melted away? "Yes, of course I can cook. Why would Mary want to try out for the Rockettes?"

He shrugged. "She threatens it once or twice a winter. She saw them on television once and was sure she was just the right height, even though her legs were a bit large. I haven't taken her seriously in past years, but as I get older, my stomach worries."

"Don't you worry, Mr. Christopher, I'll take care of you," she murmured and turned toward the house. "Are you walking or riding?"

He sighed and grimaced. "I guess I'm riding," he muttered. "Damned leg hurts like hell."

She had a feeling he wouldn't have admitted that to anyone but her. It was the best kind of compliment. She smiled and shook her head when he offered to let her ride with him after he'd painstakingly mounted the horse and was sitting regally on its back.

"It wouldn't do your leg much good," she reminded him. "I'll just walk alongside and look up at you adoringly, if you don't mind."

"That'll be the day," he mused.

She looked up. "What happened to your leg?" she asked softly.

"Bone damage and torn ligaments. I was pinned in the car when she wrecked it," he said simply. "The surgeons repaired it as best they could, but there were complications. I'll always limp. And when I overdo, I'll always hurt." He glanced at her. "I had a choice between limping or giving up the leg. I came in with a matched set and I intend to go out the same way."

She pursed her lips, feeling mischievous, and almost asked an outrageous question. Then she blushed wildly and turned away.

He guessed the question and burst out laughing. "No," he murmured. "It doesn't cramp my style in bed."

She gasped, glaring at him. "I never —"

"You might as well have written it in twelve-inch letters on canvas," he retorted.

Her mouth opened and then closed while she thought up searing retorts, none of which came to mind. Later, she'd think up hundreds, she was sure. But the thought of him in bed with another woman made her feel jealous and angry. And it showed.

He stopped, fingering the reins in one lean hand and waited for her to look up at him. His dark eyes, shadowy under the wide brim of his hat, watched her. "I'll qualify that," he said after a long exchange of eyes. "I don't think it will cramp my style. I haven't been with a woman since it happened."

Her breath caught, but she didn't look away. It was such an intimate thing to know about him, and she struggled to think of a suitable reply.

"That wasn't fair, was it?" he asked with a slow smile. "And I can't tell you for the life of me why I wanted you to know that. But I did. We'd better get home. It's getting dark."

She lowered her eyes to the trail that led back to the house. His revelation shouldn't have mattered to her, but it did. She smiled softly to herself, unaware that he saw the smile, and understood it.

He lit a cigarette and rode along beside her with a carefully hidden smug expression while he smoked it. "How about dinner tomorrow night? I'll drive you into Butte."

She felt chills to the tips of her toes and a wild excitement that was new, like the sudden tenderness between herself and Winthrop. "If Gerald doesn't need me, I'd love to," she said.

He hesitated. He looked down at her curiously, but he didn't speak. "Okay."

She wondered about the reason for his withdrawn expression and the odd silence the rest of the way to the house. That was good, because it kept her from thinking about the way he'd kissed her. She'd never felt more threatened in her life, and the worst of it was that she wasn't even afraid of what might happen between them.

He glanced at her just once, shocked by the surge of jealousy he felt at her remark about Gerald. It was that, too. Jealousy. He was afraid that there was something between this woman and his brother, and his own sense of honor and family wouldn't allow him to trespass on Gerald's territory. He wanted her to be heart-whole. He wanted that desperately. Could she have kissed him that way and still belong to Gerald? Surely not!

He pulled his emotions up short. It wouldn't do to give in to this unexpected yen for her. He was playing with fire, and God forbid he should get burned a second time.

Nicole, unaware of his thoughts, was having some difficulties of her own trying to figure out his taciturn somberness after the new and delicate camaraderie between them. She guessed, rightly, that he was holding back out of apprehension, and she even understood. But she didn't want him to leave her alone. She was beginning to love him, and it was only when she admitted it that she realized how desperately she wanted him.

CHAPTER FOUR

Winthrop wasn't at the supper table. Nicole didn't really expect him to be, because it was early November now, and according to Gerald, the boss was getting his management program in gear for winter. That included culling cattle; weaning, preconditioning and delivering calves; making the initial selection of replacement cattle and starting them on feed; and all the veterinarian-related chores that that entailed. With the sheer immensity of the cow-calf operation, it was a full-time job for the boss to keep up with what was going on. Mike, the foreman, relieved Winthrop of a lot of headaches, but even with a firm of accountants to do the paperwork, Winthrop still had to make the big decisions. No wonder he was putting in so many late hours, Nicole thought after Gerald had explained his absence.

Later that evening, Gerald had some correspondence for her. They went into the study to work. The room had Winthrop's personality stamped all over it. There was a bear's head on the wall, and burgundy leather furniture. The rugs were Indian, and the huge stone fireplace was made of native rock in comparable colors. The desk was oak, the chairs man-size and comfortable. There was a copper kettle on the hearth, and it reminded Nicole of the huge copper mining operation she'd seen as they came through Butte on the day they'd arrived. On the wall was a portrait of a man in buckskin, and she wondered if that was the French trader who was an ancestor of the Christophers.

"By the way, Sadie's invited us for dinner Friday night," Gerald said as he sorted out his mail, which had been forwarded from Chicago that afternoon. "Is that convenient for you?"

"That's fine," she said. "I look forward to meeting her again." She sat poised with her steno pad on her lap. "Uh, Winthrop asked if I'd go into Butte with him tomorrow night. To a restaurant."

Gerald pursed his lips and smiled mischievously. "I see," he mused. "So Winthrop's out to take my girl away from me, is he? I'm not sure if I like that."

It was an old joke between them, dating from her first six months as his secretary when two of the vice presidents had tried to steal her out from under his nose. She laughed and he was smiling. But the man out in the hall, overhearing him, didn't see that. Winthrop was within reach of the doorknob, but his lean hand faltered.

"He's not likely to try to take me away from you, so you can stop worrying," she said, tongue in cheek. "Anyway, he couldn't do it, you're quite unmatchable. Are you reassured?"

"I am." Gerald sighed theatrically, his brown eyes playful. He wasn't at all bad-looking. He just seemed very young beside his brother. "What a frightening thought!" he added with a mock shudder. "That I could lose you to my own brother. But Winthrop is too much a gentleman to steal from people, so I can relax. Now, suppose we get down to work?"

Winthrop turned and walked out the front door. His footsteps were so soft, and the closing of the door so quiet, that the occupants of the study didn't hear him.

He hadn't expected Nicole to be like that. He'd been sure that her ardor was real, that she'd felt the same tenderness he had. And here she was telling Gerald that there was no chance Winthrop could turn her head. He felt sick to his stomach and furiously angry. He couldn't bear the thought of being near her anymore, not after hearing her conversation with Gerald. What a close call, but at least he'd been spared. His face hardened as he began to work out what he was going to do. Thank God, she'd never know just how close she'd come to getting under his skin.

There was no sign of Winthrop for the rest of the evening, and the next morning, Gerald found a note waiting for him when they sat down to breakfast. He read over it, obviously puzzled.

"Winthrop," he said, waving the slip of paper. "He's gone to Omaha, God knows why. Something about a cattle deal. He said he's sorry about this evening, but he'll have to take a rain check on your dinner date."

"That's all right," she said, hiding her disappointment. "I'm sure he couldn't help it."

Gerald, who knew his older brother a little better than Nicole did, was uneasy. Winthrop hadn't offered to take a woman out to dinner since that blond barracuda did him in. Nicky had touched something in him, something cold and dormant, and now Winthrop seemed determined to fight it to the last breath. Gerald studied Nicky, wondering if she had any idea how disturbing Winthrop must find her. Probably not. She was a sweet person, a little reserved most of the time. Gerald was fond of her, in a brotherly way, and he felt responsible for Winthrop's unexpected coolness toward her. Knowing how his brother felt, Gerald should have been more wary of bringing a woman to the ranch. But it had been Winthrop who'd mentioned bringing Nicky. Come to think of it, Winthrop had asked a lot of questions about her after he'd seen her that day at the Chicago office. He pursed his lips. Well, well. Big brother had an Achilles' heel, it seemed. He smiled as the thought warmed his mind. And now that Winthrop had the quarry near the hook, he was going to play her for a while, was that it? Or had he gotten cold feet and was now running?

"You're very quiet," Nicole said hesitantly.

"I'm just thinking. By the way, with Winthrop gone, would you rather spend tonight at Sadie's?" he asked with old-world politeness.

She smiled. "You're a nice man. Would you mind?"

"Heavens, no," he murmured. Besides, it would give him an excuse to see Sadie again

91

the next day, when he went to fetch Nicky. And it would kill any potential gossip stone dead. Winthrop might appreciate that one day.

They went that night to have dinner with Sadie. She was a tall woman with blond hair and soft brown eyes. Nicky had always liked her, and the two of them found plenty to talk about when Sadie had come by the office to wait for Gerald.

"I'll be delighted to have you stay the night," Sadie told her enthusiastically. "It gets lonely with just me for company. Mother likes people."

"How is she?" Gerald asked gently.

Sadie sighed and shook her head. "No better. No worse. She just lies and looks at the wall and begs to die." She bit back tears. "Here, Nicky, help me get the food on the table, will you? Gerald, would you like to go in and ask Mother if she needs anything?"

"Certainly," he agreed, and paused to exchange a look with Sadie that was long and bittersweet.

Sadie watched him leave the room, her eyes wandering over his tall figure in the becoming tan suit.

"I'm hopeless," Sadie sighed, smiling shyly. "I love him to death, but there's not a thing I can do about it. I love Mother, too. I can't leave her."

Nicky studied the wan face. "He hasn't been well, either," she said.

Sadie glanced up. "Oh, dear."

"An ulcer," Nicole said. "Just an ulcer. But he pushes so hard."

"He always has. Competing, you know," she added with a loving smile. "He feels he has to come up to par with Winthrop."

"That would be a tall order," Nicky said without thinking as she laid the table.

Sadie glanced at her as she filled cups with steaming black coffee. "He's a cold man."

"Not really," Nicole replied softly. "He's just hurt, that's all."

The older woman pursed her lips. "How did you wind up on the ranch?"

"Mr. Christopher wanted to come home for a month to rest and work. I have car payments, furniture payments, payment payments . . ." She grinned. "I couldn't afford to lose a month's pay, so I came, too."

"And now Winthrop's done a vanishing act. Why?"

"I don't know," Nicky said honestly. "He asked me out to dinner tonight, and then this morning he left." She shrugged. "He's very difficult to understand."

"He always was. I've known the two brothers for years. I went to school with

Gerald." She filled the coffee cups and then placed them in their lovely china saucers on the linen tablecloth. "Winthrop was always a loner, although he was something of a rounder in his younger days. He broke hearts . . ."

"I'll bet he did," Nicky murmured. She looked up. "Did you know about the blonde?"

"Everybody around here knew about the blonde," Sadie replied. "It was a nine-day wonder. The gossip went on forever, as it does in small communities. Winthrop got back on his feet and lived it down, but I imagine he hasn't really gotten over it. She was a first-class barracuda. She'd have cut him up like fish bait if they hadn't been in that wreck. She'd have taken him for everything he had, and left him bleeding without a backward glance. She married an oil millionaire, you know. They say she's got a closet full of mink coats."

"How sad," Nicky said genuinely, her green eyes full of bitterness. "So many people marry for money. Or try to."

"I'll bet you never would," Sadie said unexpectedly. "Gerald always did like you. I'm a bit jealous of you."

"Me?" Nicky grinned. "Thanks, but he's too nice a man to make a play for his secretary. I'd do anything for him, but only in the line of duty. I'm shy that way. Most men don't appeal to me physically."

"Does Winthrop?"

Nicole flushed and flapped around while Sadie burst out laughing.

"I'm sorry, but your guilty secret is safe with me," Sadie said with a laugh. "Oh, Nicky, what a man to get hot and bothered by. The iceman!"

"It could be worse. I could develop a case for some married man with twenty kids."

"True, true." She put the finishing touches on the table arrangement. "Come and meet Mother, and then I'll show you where to put your overnight case."

"You're nice to let me stay," Nicky said. "You and I know that nothing would go on, but people talk. I don't want any gossip about my nice boss."

"Neither do I, and I'm glad you're old-fashioned." The nurse narrowed her eyes. "You really are old-fashioned, aren't you?" she asked with startling perception.

Nicky cleared her throat. "I always thought . . . well, marriage is nice. They say white only means it's your first marriage, but it means a lot more than that to me. I had old-fashioned grandparents."

She didn't add that she had wildly liberated parents and a succession of step-parents, or that her grandparents had gone to court to save her from the glitter.

"Good for them," Sadie said. "Her room's through here."

Sadie's mother was small and withered and very quiet. She looked like a little doll lying there, white hair and pale blue eyes and a beaten look about her. She could only move one side of her body — even one eye and part of her mouth were affected. It must have been a massive stroke.

"Mama, this is Nicky," Sadie introduced her.

Gerald moved. He'd been sitting on the bed beside the little old woman, holding her hand. He got up so that Nicky could sit and take the wrinkled little fingers in hers.

"Hello, Mama," Nicky grinned. "Or should I call you Mrs. Todd?" She raised her eyebrows.

"You may call me Mama if you like," Sadie's mother said, with the first hint of a twinkle in her eyes.

"That would be nice," Nicky said, smiling. "Mine died a long time ago. I don't have one. So if Sadie doesn't mind, I can share you. It's a pretty big deal," she added with mock solemnity. "I live on a tight budget, so working another person into my

Christmas shopping list is a great honor. I give Godiva chocolates as presents," she whispered.

The old lady actually laughed. Her thin fingers tightened on Nicky's. "Do you?" she whispered.

"Do you like chocolates?"

Mama managed to smile. "I love them!"

"Lucky you, to have just adopted me," Nicky said. She searched the tired old eyes. "I'll bet you were as beautiful as Sadie, at her age," she mused.

"Yes, I was," the old woman said emphatically. "Sadie . . . show her."

"This was Mother at my age." Sadie held up a small portrait study. The woman in the photograph was standing beside a tall, dark man, and she was the image of Sadie.

"Weren't you a dish?" Nicole sighed, studying it. "You're still a dish," she added, glancing down at the smiling woman. "What can we bring you to eat? I saw roast beef and mashed potatoes and a salad. . . ."

"Mashed potatoes and gravy," the woman replied eagerly. "And is there pudding?"

"Yes," Sadie said quickly, although there wasn't and she'd have to rush back and make one.

"I'll have pudding, too," came the pleased reply. "Now go and eat," her mother said.

"Then Nicole can visit with me while you and Gerald put everything away."

"Nicky's staying the night. Winthrop's away," Sadie explained.

"If it's all right," Nicky asked.

"It's all right," the old woman said fiercely. "Go and eat, child. If I adopt you, you must be fattened up. I don't want any thin children."

Nicky laughed, her green eyes sparkling in her elfin face as she got to her feet. "I'll double up on portions. And I'll bring your pudding myself."

Sadie just shook her head when they were back in the dining room. "Never," she whispered, smiling. "I've never seen her so animated. She just lies there and hates it. Tonight, for the first time, she came alive. Nicky, what did you do?"

"I stirred her up," Nicky said with twinkling eyes. "That's all. People need stirring up now and again, especially when they're bitter."

"You should see what Nicole did to Winthrop," Gerald mused. "He left home."

"That wasn't my fault."

"Tell me about it," Gerald invited, a mischievous twinkle in his dark eyes.

"It wasn't. All I did was . . ." She hesitated, her face turning red as she thought about what she'd done and the way she and Winthrop had kissed so hungrily in the woods.

Gerald raised an eyebrow and exchanged a glance with Sadie.

"Is everything on the table?" Nicky asked quickly, sitting down.

With the subject safely changed, they took their places and began to eat. Watching Gerald and Sadie, she could easily see that they felt something for each other. Nicole's gentle heart went out to them, because it was obvious that they couldn't have any kind of future together in this situation. Putting Mrs. Todd in a nursing home would be condemning her to death. And Nicole had a feeling that she was very possessive about her daughter, perhaps without realizing it. Sadie was shy and so was Gerald, to a large extent. It was a difficult situation.

Sadie made a vanilla pudding and when it was dished up, Nicole took a tray to Mrs. Todd's room.

"I haven't enjoyed anything so much for a long time," Mrs. Todd sighed when she finished. "It's so hard to bear, being like this. I was always active, able to do as I pleased. And now . . ."

"Won't you get better?" Nicole asked quietly.

"I don't know. The doctors said I might.

But that was a year ago; I think they've given up now."

Nicole put the tray to one side. "That's a nice bird feeder outside the window," she remarked, glancing at the elaborate chrome and glass affair.

"I love birds," the old lady explained. "I can watch them."

Nicole pursed her lips. "Do you have any binoculars?"

Her eyes gleamed. "No."

"I'll get you some. How about a book on birds, so you can identify them?"

The old eyes got brighter. "I'd love it!"

"Done. Just give me a few days. Now, how about a good murder mystery? There's one on television, one of those Agatha Christie ones, and I won't even tell you who done it."

Mrs. Todd actually laughed. "You should be with the young people, Nicole."

"The young people are — what did you flappers call it — spooning," she whispered conspiratorially. "At least, I hope they are. Gerald's very shy, and I think your daughter is, too."

"Yes, she is, poor child. She's such a good girl, and she's been so sweet to come and look after me. A lot of children would have turned their backs, or put me in a nursing home," Mrs. Todd said worriedly. "She hasn't said anything about it, but I know she's lonely here."

Nicole patted the old hand. "She loves you."

Mrs. Todd looked up. "And that young man . . . is he yours?"

She shook her head. "But I think he might be Sadie's. Would you mind?"

Mrs. Todd thought about it for a minute. "Well, no. He's a good boy. Not a patch on Winthrop, mind you, but the Christophers are fine people. I knew their mother. She was a dream girl."

"I hear their father was a nightmare man," Nicole said, fishing for information.

"Oh, no. He was a dynamo. We were all so jealous when he went to New York after Margaret. She didn't want to come, they'd had some terrible falling out. But he made her, kept her down at that house a virtual prisoner, until she agreed to marry him. Just between you and me, I think he took unfair advantage, too, but she loved him like a tigress. They were very happy."

"Did he look like Winthrop?" Nicole asked softly.

The old eyes seemed suddenly young. "Yes."

"A big man?"

"Body and heart. How is Winthrop? Is he getting over that woman?"

"I don't know him that well."

"Of course you don't, but you light up when I mention him, all the same. Turn on the television, child, and save your blushes. And then why don't you say good-night to the young lovers for us both and we'll hope something nice develops."

Nicole laughed delightedly as she followed the smug instructions. She tiptoed down the hall. It was unusually quiet, and when she reached the hall door, she saw why. Gerald, who seemed such a quiet and shy man, had Sadie in an embrace that spoke volumes and the way they were kissing said everything. Nicole tiptoed back and shut Mrs. Todd's door.

"Did you say good-night?" she asked Nicky.

Nicky said no with a straight face. "They're having a lively discussion. I expect it will be some time before we hear from them."

Mrs. Todd settled back against her pillows. "Lovely. I think it would do Sadie good to have company more often."

Nicole just smiled and settled down to watch the movie.

■ ■ ■ ■

It was late the next morning before Nicole heard the sound of a vehicle coming up the driveway. That would be Gerald, she thought and she smiled at Sadie.

"I've had a lovely time," she told the other woman. "Thanks for letting me stay."

"I'm glad you did," Sadie mused. "Mother hasn't enjoyed herself that much since the stroke. You were just what she needed to shake her out of her lethargy. And now that I know you aren't making eyes at my Gerald, I'll be your best friend."

Nicole's eyebrows arched in surprise. "You didn't think that?"

"Of course I did," Sadie replied, amused. "So did everybody else. Gerald isn't the kind of man who brings women home, even secretaries, unless they mean something to him. Or at least, that's what we all figured."

Nicole wondered then about Winthrop's strange behavior, and if he could have thought the same thing. She went back over her easy friendship with her boss and began to see what an outsider might have seen.

"He's a very nice man," Nicole began quietly, "but . . ."

"That 'but' saved your life," Sadie whispered conspiratorially. She looked up as a knock sounded on the door and she went to open it with wide, bright eyes. But it wasn't Gerald standing outside. It was Winthrop.

CHAPTER FIVE

Sadie's face fell, although she tried not to let her disappointment show. "Oh, hello," she faltered. Winthrop's expression didn't encourage any pleasurable outbursts. He looked out of humor and unapproachable. Nicole, watching him, thought that he'd had time to build walls again, and he'd done it with enthusiasm. So much for her optimistic outlook on the future; the iceman had frozen over.

"Where's Gerald?" Nicole asked hesitantly. Her question made the situation even worse.

He positively glared at her. "He's at home on the phone, coping with some office disaster that one of his vice presidents is in the middle of. He's drinking buttermilk by the gallon, eating antacid tablets by the handful and generally getting sicker by the minute."

"Winthrop, you should have disconnected

the phone," Sadie sighed.

He smiled at Sadie. "How's your mother?"

"Doing better, thanks, and all because of Nicky. She built a fire under Mama," Sadie grinned.

Winthrop stared at Nicole speculatively. "She's good at starting fires, all right," he said, but it wasn't a compliment. He was spoiling for a fight.

Nicole glared back. He was wearing jeans with a chambray shirt and the familiar sheepskin jacket, and a wide-brimmed hat shadowed his cold face. He looked very Western and deliciously sexy. Nicole wondered why he always seemed to button his shirts up almost to the throat, and found herself unexpectedly curious about what was underneath. Hair peeked out at his throat, and she remembered the springy feel of his chest under her hands that evening he'd caught her on the steps. . . .

Winthrop was telling Sadie something about a party.

Nicole snapped back to the present. "A party?"

"Gerald thinks you're getting bored without some fun, buried out here in the sticks," Winthrop told her. "He wants to give a party. There'll be a band and all the neighbors will come. You too, Sadie. I'll drive

Mary up to sit with your mother."

"I haven't been to a party in a long time," Sadie confessed wistfully.

"Neither have I, but I guess we'll have to make the best of it," Winthrop said with unflattering resignation. "It'll be Friday night, around six. I'll drive Mary up and fetch you."

"Couldn't Gerald?" Nicole suggested.

Winthrop openly gaped at her. "What?"

"He'll have to welcome his guests and so will you," Sadie reminded Nicole.

Nicky sighed. "I guess so." She picked up her case, which Winthrop promptly took away from her, and followed him out to the truck with a rueful wave at Sadie.

He got in under the wheel, threw up a hand at Sadie and reversed the pickup with deft, controlled movements. He didn't speak until he had it headed down the long, winding road toward the ranch.

"I didn't expect to find you here," he said curtly, lighting a cigarette as he drove. The wind was fierce and the truck lurched. It was getting dark against the horizon, heavy blue clouds building over the peaks.

"It wouldn't have looked right, to have Gerald and me under the same roof alone," she faltered.

He glanced at her. "Then, my God, how

does it look to have the three of us under one roof?" he shot back.

She hadn't thought about that. She flushed scarlet and moved her gaze out the window. "How was your trip?"

"Fine."

"When did you get back?"

"About an hour ago."

She stared at her hands in her lap. She'd felt her heart soar when he walked into Sadie's living room, but now all she felt was miserable. He'd left town because he didn't want to take her out, and now he was as remote as the clouds. She felt abandoned.

"Don't look like that," he said abruptly.

"Like what?" she muttered.

"Lost. Wounded."

She studied her hands in her lap, twisting the small emerald ring she wore on her right ring finger. "You've been spoiling for a fight ever since you came in the door."

"And you don't know why?" he taunted, and his eyes cut at her. "Or hasn't it occurred to you yet that I want you?"

It had, but only in a vague way. She felt her face flush at hearing it put into words, and so bluntly. She couldn't even look at him. She was feeling a tenderness she'd never experienced, and he'd reduced it to something casual and physical and faintly irritating.

"That's plain enough," she said in a soft tone, forcing herself not to react violently when what she wanted most to do was push him out the door and down a sharp ravine.

He wouldn't back down, he told himself, no matter how miserable she looked. His jaw tautened as he wheeled the truck around a sharp curve, scattering dirt and gravel on the unsurfaced road.

"You get under my skin," he said abruptly. "I don't like it."

Her heart shifted uncomfortably. She stared out at the tall trees in the graying horizon. "You have the same effect on me," she said curtly, "and I don't like it, either."

"Then suppose we keep out of each other's way," he suggested. "You won't be here that much longer."

"That might be wise."

He drew on his cigarette, and then he turned and looked at her just as she lifted her eyes to his. The truck almost went off the road. He braked easily enough to stop the truck, but his gaze didn't waver. Her eyes were greener than new leaves on spring trees, he thought absently, his own narrowing with kindling hunger. She was young and soft and sweet and she made him ache as he had in his youth, made him feel invulnerable and all male.

Her lips parted, but she couldn't look away. It was like holding a live wire in bare hands. Her breath shuddered out of her throat and she felt throbbing fire in her blood.

"If I touched you now, there wouldn't be any stopping for either of us," he said in a deep, slow tone. His broad chest rose and fell heavily, and his eyes were narrow, dark. "You knock me off balance."

"You said yourself," she whispered, trying to be rational, "that you'd been away from women for a long time."

"And you think it's proximity that's causing my reaction to you?" he asked with a mocking smile. He reached out a lean hand and idly linked her fingers into his with a caressing pressure that was as arousing as a kiss. Her heart began to race, and her breath came in smothered whispers that she tried not to let him see.

"That," he whispered, "is chemistry. It doesn't have anything to do with proximity, or age, or sanity. I touch you, and my body aches. And if the way you're breathing is any indication, Kentucky girl, you're on fire for me."

She bit her lip, hard. But the tremors wouldn't stop. She tugged her hand away from his and he released it with careless indifference and went back to smoking his cigarette.

"Don't worry," he said with cool mockery, "I won't tell your boss. I love my brother. His happiness comes first."

She frowned slightly. "I don't understand."

"Don't you?" He turned back to the steering wheel and put the truck into gear without another word.

She rode beside him in an uncomfortable silence. She wanted to tell him that he'd gotten it all wrong, that she and Gerald were only boss and secretary. But he looked too unapproachable and she wasn't sure of him. Her feelings for Winthrop were new and a little frightening. She didn't want to have to face them.

When they got back to the house, he got out to carry her bag up to the front porch, all bristling masculine humor. He limped more than he usually did, too, and she wondered if it was due to his bad temper or if he was in pain from the walking he must have had to do on his trip.

"I don't understand why you're so angry at me," she murmured as she joined him on the porch. "I haven't done anything. . . ."

"This is why," he said quietly. He looked down at her from his formidable height and, aware of Mary standing just inside the door, he did something with his hands, in sign language — first a movement like someone drinking out of a cup, and then an odd movement with his elbows and closed fists. "See if you can get Mary to translate that," he chided, turning. "And you'll know it all."

She stared after him wistfully, loving the lines of his elegant body, the muscular fitness that emanated from him despite that limp. He was the most attractive man she'd ever known. And if he'd looked back, and seen her standing there watching him, it might have erased some of the ill humor from his dark face. But he went away without a backward glance and Mary seemed to vanish into thin air as Nicole went inside with her overnight case.

"There you are," Gerald moaned, rubbing his stomach as he appeared in the doorway of Winthrop's study. "My ulcer is killing me. Have Mary pour me some buttermilk, will you? Then we've got to get some paperwork done and see if we can sort out this mix-up in taxes. Hurry, Nicky!"

"Yes, sir!"

She got the milk from the kitchen, curious about Mary's oddly smug look.

"There's something I want to ask you." Nicole hesitated. "Those signs Winthrop made on the front porch — you saw them. What did they mean?"

Mary grinned, showing even white teeth. "Interesting things."

"What did he say?"

Mary folded her arms over her ample bosom. "Much."

"Well?"

"Hard to translate into English," Mary continued. "Many Indian signs have no equivalent in English."

"Yes, but you must have some idea what he said," Nicole persisted.

"Good idea, all right, but I must give thought to the proper manner of expressing it to you." Mary turned back to making a thick-crusted apple pie. "Some time soon, I will translate it for you." Then she grinned again over her shoulder and giggled.

Nicole, no wiser than before, sighed and carried the milk to Gerald.

The tangle took time to straighten out, especially over the phone, and by the time it was done, Nicole was too tired to do any-thing except eat a light supper and go to bed. Winthrop, as usual, was out working, so she didn't have to worry about keeping peace with him.

During the next few days, as she helped

113

Gerald plan the party in her honor, Nicole puzzled over Winthrop's cool behavior and Gerald's continued stomach pain. Gerald and Sadie had gotten off to such a great start, and now he seemed morose and moody and worried.

Nicole had planned a menu of hors d'oeuvres and finger foods for a buffet, and arranged for a local band to play. Gerald had called the neighbors to invite them.

"This will be fun," he said as he finished. "There hasn't been any music in this house since Winthrop announced his engagement." He seemed far away for a minute and wistful. "There was music that night, and the neighbors came over, and we danced until after midnight. Mrs. Todd was fit as a fiddle back then, and she danced, too." He glanced at Nicole from his comfortable armchair. "Winthrop hasn't allowed music in the house since, although I can't blame him. He won't go near a party, either. He says he can't dance because of his leg, but I think the memories are stopping him more than any physical pain."

"I guess he really loved her," she said, remembering what little Winthrop had told her about his feelings at the time.

"It's been three years. He should be healing, mentally at least."

She didn't like to think about Winthrop's broken heart, or the cause of it. Her feelings were too turbulent, and jealousy was still topmost.

"Will he even come to the party?" she asked.

"He'll have to," he chuckled. "Or the neighbors will talk about him. He hates gossip more than he hates music. At least, he does since the accident. It never used to matter in the old days."

"We haven't heard from Sadie lately," she said with deliberate casualness.

He looked uncomfortable. "Her mother hasn't been well."

She studied his wan face. "Hasn't she?"

He shifted restlessly, crossing his legs. "She doesn't want to lose Sadie," he said curtly. "She's afraid of being alone, or at the mercy of strangers in some nursing home. I can't blame her, Nicole. It's just that Sadie's so young to be buried alive like that."

"Couldn't Mrs. Todd get better if she had more interest in life, in living?"

"Perhaps," he agreed. "But it's very hard to keep that interest going. You made a good start with her. Unfortunately, she's only enthusiastic when people are around. The minute they leave, she goes back to brooding."

"Doesn't she have relatives besides Sadie?"

"She has a sister in Florida," he murmured. "Ten years her junior and a live wire. She wants Mrs. Todd to come and visit, but Mrs. Todd is terrified to leave here. She has some idea that she'll die if she does. Meanwhile," he sighed, "Sadie is trapped. She loves her mother, you know."

"And you love Sadie," she said quietly.

He started to deny it, and then he saw the gentle compassion in Nicole's green eyes. "Yes."

"Give it time," she said. "And we needn't rush back to Chicago," she added with a faint grin.

"Even if that means watching Winthrop do a job on your nerves?" he probed. "Because he's wearing them down, isn't he?"

"I bother him," she said, then looked up at Gerald. "He bothers me, too."

"Good. You both need a little shaking up," he said with a smile. He got to his feet, grimacing. "I need some more buttermilk."

"And your tablets," she added.

"And my tablets. But you're good medicine, Nicky."

She smiled. "Thank you. And thanks for

the party, too. It was a nice thought."

"I hope you enjoy it."

"Oh, I think I will," she said. She was already thinking about breezing down the staircase in a billowy white gown, dragging a black mink coat behind her, dripping diamonds so that Winthrop would fall at her feet. Of course, she didn't have a white gown or a black mink or any diamonds. It would be the gray jersey dress and he'd be too out of humor about the whole thing to notice if she waltzed down the staircase stark naked. She sighed and went back to the typewriter.

The night of the party, Nicole dressed carefully in the hated gray jersey and did her face with a minimum of makeup. The band, a very good country and western one, was already in full swing when she went to answer the door with Gerald.

Winthrop came in behind Sadie, glaring at Nicole and Gerald with coal dark eyes. He was wearing a white shirt with dark slacks and a leather jacket, a creamy dress Stetson atop his neatly combed straight hair. He and Nicky had barely spoken in recent days. He'd commented that a party was just what he needed the night before his group of Eastern hunters arrived — which they were scheduled to do that Saturday. But Gerald had made soothing noises to the big man and he'd calmed down.

But only temporarily. His eyes were already promising retribution on Nicky's poor head.

"Good evening, Winthrop," she drawled softly as Gerald led Sadie off to the punch bowl, since she was the last to arrive and there were no more guests to receive.

"Good evening, Miss White," he replied. His dark eyes ran down her body like exploring hands, slow and very thorough. "I gather that you only brought one dress with you?"

"I didn't think I'd need more than one," she explained quietly. Her pale green eyes swept over his dark face and she felt tingles of pleasure from just looking at him. "It isn't too drab, is it?"

"You know you look lovely in anything you wear," he said suavely. He took off his Stetson, settled it on the hat rack, then hung up his jacket.

Watching the muscles ripple under the white shirt he wore with a blue patterned tie, Nicole wanted to stand in his arms and feel him holding her. It was a hunger that bordered on obsession. She moved closer to him as the band swung into a slow dance tune.

"I want to dance," she said quietly, aware of the guests watching them. Nobody was dancing yet; everybody seemed to be waiting for someone else to get things started.

He stared her down. "I don't dance anymore," he said coolly. "I can't. My leg won't hold me up under sudden turns and dips."

"It would if you danced slowly," she said. She moved even closer, her perfume floating up into his nostrils, her warmth teasing, seductive. "Hold me, Winthrop," she whispered, laying both palms slowly, hesitantly, flat down over the hard muscles of his chest.

He shuddered a little, and his chiseled lips parted. "I won't, damn it," he bit off.

She laid her head against his shoulder. "You want to," she whispered, "and I want to. Everybody's watching." Her own forwardness was beginning to embarrass her, but the need to be held by him was so strong that she fought down the urge to give in.

"No!" he bit off.

He started to turn, but she blocked his path. Everyone stopped talking, and she held her breath while he decided.

With a glance behind them and a muffled curse, he pulled her into his hard embrace and began to move very carefully to the slow rhythm of the music.

Gerald and Sadie watched the tall man's slow, hesitant movements with quiet smiles, amazed that Nicole had been able to manage such a small miracle. Winthrop was giving in, at least for the moment. His dark face was threatening, but he was holding her with such tenderness that it was almost tangible despite his temper.

Nicky savored her small victory, closing her eyes in wonder. Dancing with him was as sweet as she'd imagined it would be. He might hate her for it, but right now it seemed worth every expected bit of pain. He was tall and strong and warm, and he smelled of spice and soap. The lean, sure hand that held her made her feel safe and protected. She sighed with pure delight.

He felt that soft yielding and was furious at her for making a spectacle of him, for drawing everyone's eyes to his disability. Damn her, what was she trying to do to him?

He gave in with ill-concealed irritation and drew her slowly against him, one lean hand possessing hers. He began to move to the rhythm, a little clumsily at first, but quickly with more and more confidence. She melted into him, then, careful not to knock him off balance, she smiled against his shoulder.

"There," she mumbled happily, "I knew you could."

"I could wring your neck," he said, forcing himself to smile at her while all around them other people were finally joining them on the dance floor.

"It's your house," she reminded him. "The host is supposed to open the dancing. There are rules about that kind of thing."

"I can't dance with this leg," he said through his teeth.

"You're doing it, aren't you?" She drew back a little and looked up into his darkly glittering eyes. "But if you're sure you can't do it, then why don't you fall on the floor or something?"

"Lady," he breathed through his teeth, "you're brave in company."

"If we were alone, what would you do to me?" she asked with open curiosity, her green eyes wide and twinkling.

The look in them softened him, just a little. She was a handful, but her heart was in the right place. She wouldn't let him feel sorry for himself, or slide into thinking he had to give up living because he had a bum leg. And until now, he hadn't even realized how much he'd used that leg to keep him away from people. It had become his excuse for being a recluse, his excuse for avoiding involvement.

His fingers edged between hers and caressed them as he turned her with amazing flexibility. He smiled then, the cold anger in his eyes melting into reluctant pleasure.

"You danced before the accident, didn't you?" she asked, smiling. "You loved it, too. You're very good, despite that leg. You move with such grace for a big man."

"And what would you have done, Pollyanna, if I'd gone down on the floor with the first turn?" he asked.

"Oh, I'd have made sure I went down with you," she said matter-of-factly, "so that everyone would have thought I tripped you."

He felt his heart start pounding. Something stirred in him that he hadn't felt since his youth, something young and daring and utterly reckless. He pulled her against him and stood there for one long minute, fighting the urge to kiss her in front of everyone. He liked the way her body melted into his when he drew her close, he liked the faint trembling of her legs against his. She was his the minute he touched her, and he especially liked that. His eyes narrowed as he remembered the feel of her soft mouth, the exquisite pleasure it gave him to kiss her. She'd been engaged once, she'd told him. He felt a sudden heat of unreasonable jealousy. What had the man been like? Why had he jilted her? Was there some secret in her past that she was afraid to share with him?

"Are we doing statue imitations?" she asked breathlessly.

His lips pursed. "I'm trying to decide whether to kiss you."

"Not in front of all these people, for heaven's sake," she burst out.

"These people — or Gerald?" he asked softly.

Her eyebrows went straight up with surprise. "Well, come to think of it, I'm not sure how he'd react to it," she had to admit. Gerald hadn't said anything about her interest in Winthrop, and she didn't think he'd fire her over it. But, then again, she wasn't sure. . . .

Winthrop sighed, and drew her back against him. "Never mind, daffodil. Just dance."

"Why did you call me that?"

He smiled against her temple. "There's nothing more full of hope than a daffodil. It comes before the last snow is gone, fluffing up yellow and pretty and optimistic in the middle of all that freezing white. It takes a lot to kill a daffodil. They're glorious."

Tears stung her eyes. He could call her daffodil forever, if he liked. She snuggled closer. "What a nice compliment," she said.

"I meant it."

"I know. You're not the kind of man who spouts insincere flattery."

"Perceptive of you, Miss White."

"You bet, Mr. Christopher."

He was quiet then, circling the floor lazily with her soft weight against him, feeling his head whirl with delicious sensations. His leg was beginning to throb from the unfamiliar strain, but he'd have fallen on the floor before he'd have given in to it now. He didn't want to let go of her. He wanted to pull her closer, and bend his head and take her soft mouth fully under his. . . .

All too soon the music stopped, and Gerald was there, waiting.

"My turn," he grinned. "Sorry, big brother."

Winthrop stared at his brother for a long minute, searching the younger man's eyes curiously. And for just a minute, he thought about refusing. Then he came to his senses. She was just a woman, for God's sake, and women were treacherous. He wasn't going to fight with his brother. If Gerald wanted her, he could have her, Winthrop thought angrily. He smiled, but there was no humor in it. He nodded with a mocking smile at Nicole and then walked slowly away to the punch bowl, pausing to talk to some of the other men on the way.

"You angel," Gerald said, hugging her. "At first I thought he was going to breathe fire at you."

"So did I, but I bluffed him out. Doesn't he dance beautifully?" she murmured dreamily, staring past Gerald at Winthrop.

"Indeed he does, with the right partner." He whirled her around. "You've brought him back to life. I'd given up hope that he was ever going to put things into perspective. You're very good for him."

"Where's Sadie?" she asked.

"Phoning Mary to make sure Mrs. Todd is all right." He slowed down a little. "I wish I could decide what to do about it."

"Why don't you do what you want to and solve all your problems when the time comes? You can't cross a bridge until it's in front of you."

"Where did you learn so much?" he asked curiously. "You're not at all what you seem."

"I've had plenty of practice," was all she'd admit. And then that dance, too, was over, and she went from partner to partner for the rest of the evening.

Winthrop didn't dance with her again, but

she felt his gaze on her wherever she went. Her eyes were on him just as much, when she thought he wasn't looking. He was so good to look at. Dressing up suited him. Even in a simple white cotton shirt and dressy tie, he looked elegant. It made him seem darker than ever, more sensuous. She wasn't even surprised to discover that she loved him. That seemed as natural as breathing.

All too soon, the guests were leaving. Nicole had the crazy idea of being alone with Winthrop while Gerald took Sadie home. But he looked in her direction with an expression on his face that chilled her to the bone. It was as if he hated her, and perhaps he did for what she'd done to him. Dragging him onto the dance floor in front of all the neighbors might not have been the way to his heart, she realized. And because she was confused and a little hurt by his coldness, she asked if she could ride with Gerald and Sadie. They took one look at her face and agreed without protest.

When they got to Sadie's house, Mrs. Todd was asleep, and Mary was watching a gory horror film on television. It was just ending and Mary sat with a big bowl of popcorn on her ample lap, refusing to budge until the last drop of blood was spilled.

"Good movie," she enthused, walking out with Nicole while Sadie and Gerald said a lingering good-night indoors. "You like horror films?" she asked.

"I like vampire movies," Nicole said. "But I like science fiction better."

"You and Winthrop," she shook her head. "Those films are noisy. Too noisy. I like quiet movies."

"With screaming and lots of victims," Nicole chided.

Mary stared at her, stone-faced. "Beats all those noisy machines."

Nicole laughed delightfully. "I guess so. How did Mrs. Todd do tonight?"

"Done fine. We had pudding. I like pudding."

"So do I," Nicole said, smiling. "It was a good party. Winthrop and I started the dancing."

Mary's eyes widened. "Winthrop was dancing?"

"Yes. He does it very well."

"He used to," Mary agreed. "But I have not seen him dance since the accident. How did you manage it?"

Nicole chewed her lip a little and peeked at Mary. "I stood in front of him on the dance floor and wouldn't move."

Mary laughed. She did it seldom, but

when she did, it was wholeheartedly. "Good medicine," she told the younger woman. "We should bottle you."

"I'd most likely ferment and become illegal. There's Gerald."

He joined them, looking a bit hot under the collar and flustered. He grinned. "Ready to go?"

"Been ready quite some time," Mary said. "Long past my bedtime."

"There, there, too much sleep can kill a good woman," Gerald said soothingly. "Think of how I'm saving you from certain death."

"Saving me from much needed rest," Mary countered, climbing into the pickup between him and Nicole. "Winthrop danced, she tell you?"

"She didn't have to. I saw it with my own eyes," he volunteered, grinning past her at Nicole. "I wish I could have taken a picture. Nobody will believe it."

"Isn't it cloudy tonight?" Nicole was trying to change the subject, but it really did look cloudy, and it was getting colder.

"Snow clouds," Mary said. "We get buried in snow pretty soon."

"Not in November," Nicole said.

"This is Montana. Snow comes early and late — you can't predict mountain weather.

And snow in November is pretty routine," her boss informed her. "Lord, I hope we don't get shut up with that horsey set from back East. They'll be here tomorrow." He glanced at Nicole. "By the way, one of Winthrop's guests is from Kentucky, an expert on thoroughbreds. Winthrop wants him to take a look at the colt and give him an opinion. He wouldn't be able to race it for a couple of years, of course, but he's thinking along those lines."

Nicole knew a number of people in the horsey set. She was afraid of meeting someone from her old life, someone who knew her father, who might tell him where she was and what she was doing now. She didn't want him to know anything about her new life. There were deep scars from those young years. She wanted nothing to do with the man who'd driven her mother into a succession of lovers, followed by a fatal accident. Nothing at all.

"Did he tell you the man's name?" Nicole asked quietly.

Gerald glanced at her. "As a matter of fact he did," he replied. He grinned ruefully. "But I was on the phone at the time and I didn't catch it. There's a Murdock woman, and a couple of brothers named Harris. But I don't think the Harrises know much about horses."

Nicole consoled herself with the thought that there must be hundreds of horsey sportsmen in the world besides her father. She only nodded, closing her eyes as they went back to the Christopher ranch.

The house was quiet when they got there. If Nicole had hoped to see Winthrop again, she was disappointed. He was nowhere in sight. She said good-night to Mary and Gerald and went reluctantly to her room.

She didn't sleep. She lay awake staring at the ceiling for what seemed hours. Finally she got up and decided to make herself a cup of hot chocolate. Perhaps that would do the trick; she really couldn't stay awake all night.

Since the household was asleep, she didn't stop to fumble through the closet for a robe. Besides, her long flannel pajamas were more than decent, with their pale-pink rose pattern. She looked very young without her makeup and barefoot, as she went down the long, dark staircase. She hoped the house didn't have ghosts, she didn't fancy meeting one.

The kitchen light was on. She opened the door and paused, stopping dead at the sight of Winthrop bending over the stove. He was wearing pajama bottoms, nice brown striped ones, but no top. His chest was . . . incredible. Broad and bronzed and thick with a wedge of hair that covered his rippling muscles.

He turned, his dark hair tousled, and stared at her. "Looking for someone?" he asked.

"For some hot chocolate," she confessed. "I can't sleep."

"I'm making some," he said. "Come in and find some mugs."

She stared at herself. "I should get a robe . . ."

"Why?" he asked, glancing at her. "You're covered up in all the right places, and I'm hurting like hell. I'm not in any condition to lay you down on the kitchen table with evil intent."

She smothered a giggle, went in and closed the door behind her. "How savage sounding," she mused as she searched the cupboard for cups. "Think of the splinters!"

"A nice girl like you. Shame on you." He took the hot chocolate off the stove and poured it into the mugs before he put the pan in the sink to soak. He was limping rather badly, and she grimaced as he sat down with a hard wince.

"That's my fault, isn't it?" she asked gently. "I made you dance when you didn't want to, and you hurt it because of me. I'm sorry."

"Nobody makes me do a damned thing," he said curtly. He had two pills. He took them, swallowing them down with a sip of the hot chocolate. "I could have walked away from you if I'd wanted to."

"But you didn't."

He turned, his dark eyes holding hers. "I didn't want to. I like holding you. The excuse isn't particularly relevant."

Her face colored, and he smiled slowly.

She lowered her eyes to her cup and lifted it quickly to her mouth. She sipped at it for a long time, her mind hungry with sweet longings, her eyes darting to his broad, bare chest and back to her cup. He was through with his chocolate, but he sat back, quiet and faintly threatening and just looked at her until her body began to tremble.

"Did you wonder what I looked like under my shirt, Nicky?" he asked with blatant seduction in his voice.

Her lips parted on a husky sigh. She couldn't quite meet that searching gaze. She clung to her empty mug as if it were a life jacket. The silence was suddenly too sweeping, the loneliness of the deserted room staggering in its implications. They were alone. And he wanted her.

She felt him move before she saw him. He took the mug out of her hands and drew her up in front of him, holding her gently by her upper arms.

"There's nothing to be afraid of," he whispered. "Nothing at all."

He bent his head and she saw the shadow of his face, felt his chocolaty breath as his mouth brushed against hers. She relaxed then, because he was very slow and sure of himself. He wasn't in any hurry, and the leisure of his movements stopped the panic inside her. She began to unwind, feeling the softness of his mouth along with its hardness, liking the delicate probing of his tongue just under her upper lip. Amazing, she thought, how sensitive her mouth was to that light touch.

She lifted toward him a little, and heard his breath catch. She couldn't know that he was on fire with need, that he was in agony trying to hold back enough to keep from frightening her.

"Sweet," he whispered against her lips. "You're so sweet."

He had a lover's voice, she thought, very deep and seductive. She loved to hear him talk anytime, but particularly like this, in hushed whispers. She put her hands against him and felt them tingle where they touched the thick hair that covered him. It was wiry against her palms, deliciously abrasive when she began to draw them over his broad chest, disturbing the muscles so that they rippled under her fingers.

His breath caught. He stopped and suddenly moved back. His eyes held hers, searching them. "I want more than this," he said tautly.

She couldn't look away. "How . . . how much more?"

His eyes went to her pajama jacket. "Nothing terribly indiscreet," he said quietly. His hands followed his gaze. He hooked his index finger into the V neckline of her pajamas and tugged her toward him. "Don't panic, okay? I promise I won't let it go too far."

She wanted to protest. But her eyes went down to his lean fingers working the buttons with such deftness, and she couldn't look away. He undid them slowly, and then drew the fabric back from her high, pink breasts with a leisurely expertise that hypnotized her.

Then his gaze was on her, looking at her with blatant possession. Winthrop was a man with an eye for beauty, and the expression in his dark eyes told her that he found her beautiful. Her nipples went hard under his scrutiny, and she was embarrassed and tried to cover them. But he stopped her, shaking his head gently.

"It isn't sordid or shameful to let me see you," he said quietly, his voice very slow and deep. "God never made anything more beautiful than a woman's breasts."

Her breath stopped in her throat at his words. She looked up at him, her gaze sharing secrets with him. Then he smiled, and it was like the sun coming out.

He touched her cheek, gently tracing it. "Come here and let me hold you, Nicole," he breathed, drawing her. "Feel my body and let me feel yours. Let me teach you how beautiful it can be to touch skin against skin."

She let him draw her close, feeling the sting of tears as she went into his arms. Her eyes closed at the first contact with his warm, hard body, and she cried out as her nipples stabbed into his skin, burying themselves in the damp, abrasive mat of hair that covered the hard muscles. "Winthrop," she murmured.

"Yes." His hands spread against her silken back, under the pajama top. He drew her very close, closing his own eyes as her soft body melted into him. He was aroused, and she knew it. He felt her stiffen as her legs came into contact with his.

"Don't flinch away from me," he murmured at her temple, coaxing her back against him. "This is natural, too, and good and sweet and right between a man and a woman. Don't be afraid of it."

"It's so intimate," she whispered shakily against his warm, broad chest. His skin tasted of cologne and soap. Masculine smells. Good smells.

"Intimate," he agreed at her ear. "Yes, it's that. It's exquisitely sweet, having you close to me this way." His arms tightened and trembled a little. So did his tall, fit body. "Nicky," he breathed on a groan, bending his head over her. He began to rock her, fostering a new kind of intimacy between them, one that should have shocked her but was strangely familiar now. She clung to him, letting him hold her, yielding to his strength.

"Your leg . . ." she said a long minute later.

"What leg?" he murmured.

She drew in a long breath, and he shuddered as he felt her breasts swell against his skin.

"It's scary, isn't it?" she whispered. "Holding each other like this."

"Scary enough," he agreed on a bitter laugh. "You can't possibly imagine the thoughts going through my mind."

"I'll bet I can, too," she said. She nuzzled her cheek against him, loving the rough feeling of the hair over his chest. "Do you like that?"

"Can't you feel how much I like it?" he asked with blatant mockery. "Give me your mouth."

She lifted her lips to meet his, her hands sliding around him to his back, loving the feel of him, the vibrant masculinity of him. He kissed her slowly, warmly, and even that was intimate, his tongue probing softly in her mouth.

He shifted her a little so that his hand could find the soft curve of her breast and tease it into arching toward those tormenting fingers.

"Do you want me to keep going?" he whispered at her lips.

"Yes," she whispered back, her voice breaking. She wasn't old enough or sophisticated enough to hide her hunger.

"Like this?" he murmured, with a teasing touch around the nipple, his fingers faintly callused and deliciously abrasive on her soft skin. "Or like this?"

His thumb rubbed suddenly at the tiny hardness and she cried out, a whimper of sound that worked on him like a narcotic.

His hand covered her breast and he lifted his head to look into her misty eyes while he caressed her.

"I'm on fire," he whispered. "Burning."

"So am I," she moaned. "Winthrop . . ."

His head bent to her body, and as she watched, fascinated, he arched her and opened his mouth and put it completely over her breast.

She thought that as long as she lived, she'd never get over the sensation. It went on and on, tearing at her, shaking her, making her too weak to move, to breathe, to think. She was an instrument, and he was playing her with an expert touch, teaching her things about her own body that she'd never known.

She arched farther, her hands in his dark, cool hair, inciting him, begging him. His mouth slid from one breast to the other, and she moaned like a wounded thing, feeding on the sweet ardor of his mouth, living only through him.

Dazed, shuddering with sensation, she barely felt him move. And then she was on his lap in the chair, and he was holding her, cradling her while she cried. She hadn't even been aware of the intensity of her emotions until she felt the tears like rain on her face.

"Shh," he whispered gently, his mouth

soothing her now, touching her hot cheeks, her wet eyelids and eyelashes, her nose and mouth and chin. "It's all right. Hush, darling, it's all right now."

"Winthrop," she whispered tearfully.

"Nicole," he breathed, wrapping her up in his arms. He rocked her against him hungrily, laughing a little at her headlong response even now. "Wildcat! Never in my life, not ever . . . You damned near pushed me over the edge with those little cries you made."

"I couldn't help it," she said, hot-faced. "It was what you were doing to me . . ."

"I couldn't help that, either," he murmured dryly. He kissed her gently. "You have exquisite breasts, Miss White," he breathed huskily. "As soft as satin, as warm as velvet. I'd rather cut off my arm than cover them, but if I don't, you and I are very likely to become lovers within the next few seconds, right here on the floor."

And while she was getting over the shock from that statement, he sat her up on his lap like a big doll and proceeded to do up the buttons on her pajamas. When she was covered again, he drew her back down, holding her lazily while he pressed tender, undemanding kisses on her damp face.

"You're very quiet," he remarked finally.

"Why? Are you shocked? Outraged? Embarrassed?"

"I don't know," she confessed, snuggling closer. "Not outraged or ashamed, although I suppose I should be embarrassed. I'm not in the habit of . . . behaving this way with men."

"I know that." He brushed the damp hair away from her cheeks. His dark eyes held hers. "Is this all new to you?"

It wouldn't do to lie to him, she supposed. She searched his dark eyes. "Yes," she said quietly. "My fiancé . . ." she said quietly. "He wanted me, but I could never give in to him. I . . . didn't like it when he tried to touch me." She lowered her eyes to his broad chest. "And when I found out what he really wanted, I felt used and cheap and ashamed. I don't feel any of those things with you." She lifted her eyes again, because it was important to make him understand. "It isn't like a physical thing with you, however silly that sounds. It's . . ." She searched for the right words. "It's . . ."

"Beautiful," he said for her. "Poignant. Profound."

"Yes." Her pale eyes lit up, making her beautiful.

He kissed her very tenderly. "Any other woman I'd have in bed by now," he mur-

140

mured. "But you aren't the kind of woman who can play around with sex. Not even in the throes of an urgent need."

"Nevertheless," she said slowly, choosing her words, "I wouldn't refuse you."

"I know. That makes it worse. I can't take the responsibility alone." He touched her mouth with a gentle finger.

"Responsibility?" she whispered.

"I could make you pregnant," he said gently.

Her body felt wildly hungry. Her lips parted and the look in her eyes made him want to throw back his head and scream.

His fingers trembled as they touched her face. "Nicky," he whispered.

"Do you want a son?" she asked in a husky, loving tone.

"Yes," he bit off. "I want one with you. . . ."

Her body shuddered. She looked into his eyes and knew that she was lost, that she couldn't stop, that he couldn't. In his eyes, she saw the coolness of white sheets and the outline of two bodies in the darkness. . . .

And all at once, she was standing and he was five feet away from her with a burning cigarette in his hand.

She was so numb she could hardly feel.

Her eyes traced him, saw the faint shudder of his long legs.

"Go to bed, sweetheart," he said without looking at her.

"You aren't angry?"

"No," he said, his voice deep and slightly choked. "I'm not angry."

She turned toward the door, only half understanding. She paused with her hand on the knob and glanced back. "Winthrop, are you all right?" she asked, her tone exquisitely gentle.

"Team sports and cold showers will save me," he said on a husky laugh. "Go to bed."

She flushed because that explained it all. "I'm sorry," she said. "Really sorry."

"For what?" He glanced at her finally, and she was shocked at how pale and drawn his face was. "Nicky, you were in as deep as I was. I'm a little shell-shocked, that's all. But we can't stay here. Things are getting out of hand. I don't want anything to happen that we might regret."

She smiled at him. "I wouldn't regret anything."

"I can't be sure of that. It's easy to lose sight of things in the darkness. I want you very badly. I know you want me just as much. But let's stop and think before we commit ourselves that completely. I can't take you to bed one night and walk away from you the next morning. At my age, sex is a commitment, not a toy."

Her face colored. "I guess it is, when you start talking about making people pregnant," she murmured dryly.

"That, Miss White, I would enjoy," he said lazily, and his dark eyes glittered playfully. "And so would you; I'd make sure of it. So suppose you go up to bed and give it some thought. And tomorrow we'll discuss terms."

"What kind of terms?"

He smiled slowly. "That would be telling."

She turned back to the door. "If it means I get to live with you, I'll agree to most anything," she said and ran for it. Behind her, she heard rich, thunderous laughter, and by the time she got to the top of the staircase, she was laughing, too. Life was sweet and Winthrop had to feel the same way she did, because he was hinting at a lot more than a brief affair.

If he trusted her that much, it must mean that he loved her. And God knew, she loved him with all her heart. She was so preoccupied dreaming about Winthrop's arms holding her in the darkness, and little boys and never leaving this exquisite valley as long as she lived that it was hard to fall asleep.

For an instant, she had a twinge of guilt about not sharing her past with him. But there was still time, she told herself as she snuggled under the covers. Plenty of time, to explain why she'd kept it a secret, to show him that she loved him, that she'd never betray him. Yes, there was time.

CHAPTER SIX

When Nicole woke up the next morning, it was to an odd kind of silence. Although she was used to that particular stillness in winter, it was unfamiliar in autumn. But usually it meant snow.

She threw off the covers and ran to the window. Sure enough, the lacy white flakes were coming down like cotton out of the clouds, gently blanketing the trees and the grass. She sighed, vividly remembering last night and the newness of what she'd shared with Winthrop. Like a daydreaming child, she propped her elbows on the windowsill, put her face in her hands and mused about how it would be if she and Winthrop had been snowed in together, just the two of them.

Her daydreams were rudely shattered by the loud noise of an approaching vehicle — a four-wheel-drive vehicle, at that.

A huge Cherokee wagon came into view

with Winthrop at the wheel, and several passengers. They must be the hunting party, she guessed. The group didn't look too bad. There was a willowy redhead dressed from head to toe in white fur, followed by two older men, one in a wool plaid coat, the other in leather. And there was one more passenger, a big, white-headed man with an imposing nose, wearing tweeds. . . .

Nicky came away from the window feeling sick. She'd go back to Chicago alone, right now. She'd pack her things and get out while she could. The memories came back hauntingly. The loud arguments, the fights that never seemed to end. Her father apologizing halfheartedly for his latest infidelity, her mother's mocking laughter. She put her hands against her eyes, feeling all over again like the little girl who used to run into the kitchen and hide her face against Lalla's ample bosom and cry her eyes out until the argument ended.

"Nicky!" came Gerald's voice outside the door. "Nicky, come down! Guess who one of our visitors is? It's your father!"

Along with that horror came a new one. She hadn't told Winthrop who her father was, or that she'd renounced her inheritance. What was he going to think?

"I'll be right down," Nicky called back.

She got dressed in a daze, pulling on her gray slacks and white sweater, the ones Mary had miraculously cleaned. She'd been wearing them the day she'd helped Winthrop deliver the colt. Perhaps that memory, if her clothing triggered it, would make the next hours easier.

She ran a brush through her hair and smoothed on some lipstick. She looked pale and haunted, but that couldn't be helped. Why did it have to be her father, she wondered miserably. Of all the sportsmen in the world, why him? She'd suspected it, of course, when Winthrop had mentioned that he'd been to Kentucky and knew Rockhampton Farms. Since her father was a well-known sportsman, it wasn't far-fetched to imagine that he might enjoy hunting in Montana.

There were voices in the living room when she went downstairs, but the only face she saw immediately was Winthrop's. The tender lover of last night might have been a dream. His expression was hard, ice-cold. He barely looked at her before he turned back to his guests, a cup of coffee in one lean hand.

"Here she is," Gerald said with a grin, coming to meet her. His hand on her arm gave her the strength to walk into the room. "Look who's here," he added, pulling her toward the big white-haired man in tweed.

"Hello, Nicky," her father said coldly. "Long time, no see."

"Not long enough," she replied, and the bitterness of the past was in her eyes.

Winthrop frowned. It wasn't the reunion he'd expected to see at all.

Dominic White stood up, but he didn't approach her. His careless green eyes swept over her wan face and dismissed it. "This is Carol Murdock," he said, introducing the willowy, very young redhead in ski pants and a mohair sweater under all the fur. "She's visiting with me for a while."

"Hi," Carol said breathily. She beamed up at Dominic, who was at least fifteen years her senior, probably more like twenty. "Your dad sure is a lot of fun. He's going to show me how to shoot a moose."

"Oh, you'll enjoy that, I'm sure," Nicky told her. "It's easy. You just load the gun and point it and pull the trigger."

"I taught Nicky to shoot when she was twelve," Dominic told the group. "She could match any man on the place with a rifle. Even won trophies at it."

Winthrop, quietly smoking a cigarette, studied her curiously. "A girl of unusual talents."

"An unusual girl altogether," her father

148

replied. He laughed shortly. "We haven't spoken in two years, have we, Nicky? I'm in disgrace, you see. I made the unforgivable error of falling out of love with her mother. Nicky holds me responsible for Brianna's death. And for cutting her off without a dime after the funeral," he added with killing precision. "She's been living by her wits ever since, haven't you, darling? Which one of these rich Christophers have you set your cap for?"

Just like old times, Nicky thought, feeling panicky. Her father was turning everything around, taking the blame off himself and throwing it at others. Winthrop's expression told her that he believed her father, and it grew even harder.

"I'm Gerald's secretary," she said with what little pride she had left. "And I'm not chasing anyone."

"You mean you've learned to love being without those Dior gowns you fancied and having to make do with the same fur several years running?" her father persisted. He looked like some middle-aged playboy even in his hunting clothes, and Nicky wanted to scream at him. All her life he'd made her feel inferior, and now he was destroying her one chance at happiness. He was convincing a once-betrayed man that he was being betrayed all over again. How would she ever make Winthrop listen to her?

Nicky's fists clenched by her sides. Her father had always enjoyed creating scenes. He should have been an actor, she thought bitterly.

"Let me introduce you to the other guests," Winthrop interrupted, wondering even as he did it why in hell he should bother to save her any discomfort after the way she'd deceived him. She'd pay for that, he promised himself. "Ben Harris —" he nodded toward the man in leather "— and Jack, his brother." He indicated the other, thinner man, in the plaid. "They come up every year looking for a good rack to go on their walls back in Kentucky. This year Dominic decided to come with them."

"I don't suppose you knew I was here, of course," Nicky asked her father with some of his own flair of stealing the advantage.

"I haven't known where you were in two years," he replied shortly. His eyes, so like her own, searched her face. "I haven't cared," he added with a mocking smile. "There's been a noticeable financial difference since you moved out, honey. I can balance the checkbook these days."

"Stop it," she whispered, near tears of enraged helplessness. "You know that's not

150

true."

He simply turned away from her, refusing to take any notice of her embarrassment.

It wasn't the way he'd insinuated. She hadn't wanted his money — not even the trust her mother had left her. She'd refused all of it, but he was making sure both Christophers thought he'd done it himself, and that she was out for what she could get in the way of financial security. And it wasn't true.

"I hope you find someone to support you, honey, but it won't ever be me again," Dominic laughed, bending to brush a kiss across Carol's hair. "Your mother was enough."

"Don't you talk about my mother," Nicky said huskily. Her green eyes spit fire at him. "Don't you dare!"

Dominic laughed. "You always were dramatic."

As if he'd have noticed, with his eternal philandering. She almost said so, but Gerald was looking worried, and Winthrop's eyes were promising a confrontation.

"Do you have TV?" Carol asked, searching around. "It's so boring, just sitting around."

The woman was bored already? Nicky thought with surprise. Boy, was Carol in for a shock. Neither Gerald nor Winthrop watched much television. But Nicky was taken aback herself when Winthrop abruptly got up, and led Carol off to show her the TV and VCR in the living room.

"Fast worker, isn't he?" Dominic asked Gerald with a smile that wasn't quite friendly. "He'd better remember that she's my property."

"Your good manners are exceeded only by your arrogance," Nicky remarked coolly. "And if you try it on Winthrop, you'd better be wearing body armor. He doesn't like jet-setters."

Dominic glared at her. He stuck a diamond-ringed hand in his pocket and pulled out a cigarette case. "Something you've already discovered?" he asked with a pointed smile.

"Why did you do that to me?" she asked, searching the face that was so like her own. "Why did you make me out to be a cheap gold digger?"

"Tit for tat, darling," he drawled, and his own eyes kindled angrily. "You didn't think about the effect your defection would have on things at home, did you? I was blamed for everything. I don't like being humiliated. I don't think you will, either. And just for the record," he added coldly, "I didn't kill your mother, although I felt like it a time or two. She was no saint, Nicky, for all that you're trying to canonize her posthumously."

"So you've always said," she returned. "And who are you to judge anyone, you with your bought-and-paid-for playmates?"

"I'm not a plaster saint," he shot at her. "Your mother turned me out on the town as soon as she knew you were on the way, in revenge for what I'd done to her. Making her pregnant was a cardinal sin, in case you didn't know. She paid me back twenty times over. Are you shocked, Nicky? Didn't you realize that people are human?"

Nicky listened, only half hearing him. Why should her mother have hated him for that? She was suddenly aware of Gerald, an unwilling eavesdropper to the argument. The Harris brothers were sitting in the corner, talking hunting, and hadn't heard much. She shifted away from her father, and tried to smile.

"Do you have anything for me to do?" Nicky asked Gerald, her tone conciliatory and faintly hopeful. He caught on quickly.

"As a matter of fact, we've got about ten letters to get out this morning," Gerald replied. He smiled vaguely at the three men. "If you'll excuse us . . ."

"Is he your partner?" Dominic asked

Nicky, frowning.

"He's my boss," she replied coolly. "I'm his secretary."

Her father stiffened. "You're joking, of course," he said curtly. "No White has worked for a living for three generations —"

"Until now," Nicky interrupted with a mocking smile. "Some of us like the real world better than the artificial life of upper-crust luxury. You ought to try it. It has a humbling effect on a haughty spirit."

"You should know," Dominic countered coldly. "You were a haughty enough child."

"Living in a combat zone does have that effect on children." She turned and left the room.

"So he's your father," Gerald murmured when they were in the study with the door closed. "He wasn't originally supposed to be included in this group. He invited himself along with the Harris brothers at the last minute. Odd that Winthrop didn't connect you with Dominic White, since you were from Kentucky, too."

"He did," she said reluctantly, averting her eyes. "But I lied to him. I told him that White is a common name. I imagine I'm about the most unpopular person in Winthrop's acquaintance right now, especially after what my father just said about me. And

154

it's not true."

"You don't have to defend yourself to me," he replied gently. "Your father strikes me as a vindictive man."

"You don't know the half of it," she replied. "He's used to cutting people's throats. That's how he got so rich."

"Well, he can't be all bad," he said after a minute.

"He's not," she said pleasantly. "He likes his horses, and once I saw him feed a hungry dog. He just doesn't like me. He never wanted children." That was true enough, but she'd always thought that her mother wanted her. She was still puzzling over what her father had said.

Gerald didn't press further. Instead he chose a different tack. He pursed his lips, stared at her and asked, "Why didn't you tell Winthrop the truth?"

"Because I was sure he'd get the wrong idea," she sighed. "He'd think I was a bored heiress out for a good time. Ironically, that's probably exactly what he thinks now, thanks to my father and his big mouth. I must sound like the world's most experienced spendthrift and a gold digger as well."

"You don't like him, do you?"

"My father, you mean?" Her green eyes gleamed. "I do not. I'm sure he has some good points somewhere, but I've never found them."

He searched her face quietly. But he didn't say another word. He pulled up a chair and sat down behind the desk. After a minute, he began to dictate.

Nicky spent the rest of the day trying to avoid the other guests, and the snow continued to fall. Mary never said a word about the extra people to look after. She just kept cooking, imperturbable even when Carol dashed into the kitchen and asked in all innocence if there was a boutique anywhere close by because she wanted to shop for a new fur.

Nicky had to bite her tongue to keep from asking if the girl knew that in these parts, a mink set consisted of a trap and a skinning knife.

But to Nicky's irritation and her father's frank anger, Winthrop seemed to enjoy Carol's company.

"Maybe she forgot who she came with," Nicky muttered to Mary late that day as she helped the older woman set the long dining table.

"Not likely," Mary said. She glanced at Nicky. "Winthrop looks through you today. Why?"

Nicky hesitated before she put down the

last plate. "He thinks I lied to him because I didn't tell him about my background. I let him think I came from a poor family. But it's true in a way," she added, her face open and sad. "I was poor in love, at least."

"And your father?"

Nicole pursed her lips. "You tell me. What kind of man is he?" she asked, because she'd learned how perceptive the Sioux woman really was.

"He is a sad man," Mary said surprisingly. "He draws attention to himself out of loneliness and pain. He has not learned to admit fault, only to find it in others. I pity him. As you should. In your youth, you have twice his wisdom."

Mary left and went into the kitchen, leaving the younger woman thoughtful and quiet.

If Nicole thought the day had been bad, she soon found that the evening meal was an even worse ordeal. Winthrop sat at the head of the table with the hateful Carol on one side and Gerald on the other and completely ignored Nicky and her glum father. The Harris brothers ate and sipped their coffee merrily, exchanging pleasantries and hunting experiences with Nicky, but she hardly heard them. She was watching Winthrop's dark eyes light up as he spoke

157

to the nubile redhead, and hating the other woman for arousing the tender side of the man she could no longer reach.

"You wear your heart on your sleeve," Dominic said coolly. He stared over his coffee cup at his daughter. "Never let it show."

"Never cry. Never show emotion." She laughed shortly. "A page right out of your book. You're frozen clean through. I suppose I'll be just like you when I'm your age. What a lovely future to look forward to."

"It beats having your emotions lacerated twice a day," he said nonchalantly. He stared hard at the redhead. "She's barely your age," he mused. "And your host is a hell of a man, limp and bad temper and all. I won't like losing her to him. I'm not a good loser."

"Winthrop doesn't want a society girl," she replied. "He's had enough misfortune because of one."

"I remember reading about the wreck," her father said surprisingly. "Deanne something-or-other, that ski heiress. I had a fling with her myself. She was a real honey. The kind who'd stroke your fevered brow while stealing your wallet."

It hurt, knowing that her own father was that kind of man. An aging playboy with no real emotion underneath his elegant facade. "You ought to compare notes with Winthrop. I'm sure he'd be interested," she said sweetly.

"Stop sniping at me, Nicky," he said coolly, and his green eyes met hers. "All your regrets and all mine won't change the past. Neither will giving up your rightful legacy. Brianna wouldn't have wanted that. She had high hopes for you."

"Did she? I don't remember her being sober enough to discuss them in the past."

"I thought you'd become wiser with time, but you still see the past with blinders on," he remarked. "Grow up, honey. Life isn't all black and white. Your mother was neurotic. She couldn't handle responsibility. In fact, neither could I. We were two kids playing at life, and when you came along, the dream fell apart. Neither of us could cope and you got caught in the middle. I'm sorry, but I can't remake the past."

"If neither of you wanted me, why did you bother to have me?" she asked, wounded by the confession. "Or was I just an accident?"

She read the answer in his face before he could even try to disguise it. And suddenly, her whole childhood made more sense. The endless fights, the indifference of her parents to each other's lifestyles, the drinking and womanizing . . .

"So," she let out the word as a sigh. "So

159

that's why." She smiled ruefully. "Thank you. At least now I know why you both hated me so much."

"Oh, Nicky," he said, "that's not so. We never hated you."

"You never had time for me, either of you."

"That's true," he admitted. His green eyes searched hers and he smiled wearily. "We were just kids when you came along, Nicky. Both of us. Kids playing house. And then there we were with a real live baby, but we couldn't put you back on the shelf. We had to be responsible for you. That wasn't an easy task for two people who'd never known what it was to be responsible."

She stared at him as if she'd been slammed in the head with a pole. She'd never thought of her parents as people, only as parents. This new perspective was enlightening, but disturbing.

"You don't understand, do you?" her father asked quietly. "You thought because we were your parents, we had to be perfect. But it doesn't work that way. Parents make mistakes. They aren't perfect."

She shifted restlessly. "Mother drank herself to death because of your womanizing," she said accusingly.

"Your mother drank herself to death

because she was unhappy," he replied, without heat. He leaned back, and despite the trendy shirt and the gold chains he wore, he looked old and tired. "So was I. I ran after women looking for my rainbow, and she climbed into a bottle looking for hers. Neither of us ever found it." He pursed his lips and studied her. "Have you found yours, Nicky? Does anybody ever really get the brass ring in life?"

"There are better ways to try for it," she began.

"Sure there are," he agreed. "But when you've got all the money in the world, why look past your wallet?"

"I can think of some very good answers to that question," she told him. "I've watched you buy people all your life. I hate the ugliness that money can bring out in people."

"You can't bribe an honest man, honey," he said sagely. "Can you?"

"But everyone has a price. Some prices are less materialistic than others — a promotion, a holiday for a hard-working parent, a hospital bill for a sick child. Those are less obvious prices, but they still mean people can be bought."

He nodded. "So you begin to see."

"What you and mother had wasn't a marriage," she accused him, all the hurt of the past coming back.

"We didn't love each other enough," he said simply. "In the beginning, maybe we did. But we had families that lived in each other's pockets and constant interference. We were never let alone, not even when you came along. You were the last straw, Nicky. You were the knot that we couldn't untie. Divorce, in our day, was scandalous. Our families had never had a divorce."

"Better a divorce than unending war," Nicky shot back.

"My sentiments, exactly. And your mother's. If we'd divorced, she'd have married one of her old beaux and I'd have married — probably several more times," he acknowledged with a wicked grin. "And we'd both have been very happy. As it was, we sought our separate remedies and your mother's was fatal. Nobody's fault," he tacked on, watching her. "Nobody's fault at all. But you can't accept that, can you?"

"Somebody has to be at fault," she said doggedly, glaring at him.

"Why?"

The question threw her off balance. She stared at him. "What?"

"Why does somebody have to be at fault?" He fingered his chains. "Your mother and I were nice people, separately. We just weren't compatible. Who do you blame for that?"

She felt herself losing ground. He always had been like a trial lawyer, able to twist things around to suit himself. If only he didn't make so much sense. She'd blamed him for two years for her mother's untimely death, just as she'd blamed herself. But what if neither of them were responsible?

She shifted a little and finally got to her feet, looking down at him. He always seemed laid back, very relaxed. Nothing seemed to bother him.

"I'm a black sheep, Nicky," he said. "I always have been. I like women and I'm rich enough to indulge that habit, and I try to come out ahead in business. But I never hated you, honey. I never could."

She tried to smile. "No? It seemed like it when you got here."

"That was dirty pool, all right." He glanced down and then up again. "I missed you," he said curtly, as if he hated even saying the words. "I missed Brianna. Everybody left me at one time. Damn it, how do you think I felt?"

He got up and stormed out of the room without even a backward glance. Nicky stared after him with confused emotions. He'd sounded, and looked, hurt. Perhaps he had cared about her mother in his fashion. Maybe even about Nicky, too. But the wounds were still raw and she couldn't cope with this new facet of her father just yet.

She turned, oblivious to the others in the room, and went upstairs. Her father was only forty-one, she realized with a start; he wasn't even old. And there was no reason he shouldn't have women friends. It was just . . . she'd wanted him to love her mother. She'd wanted her mother to love him. She'd wanted a warm family life . . . and she'd never had it.

She changed back into her jeans and the yellow sweater, hating the gray dress. She wished she had something as slinky and svelte as Miss Kansas City downstairs, so that she could tempt the antagonism out of Winthrop's dark face. But she'd probably lost her chance with him. He hadn't come near her since her father's arrival, he hadn't spoken to her or acknowledged her. He'd even avoided looking at her.

It was amazing how deeply his turning on her had hurt. She sat down at her vanity and ran a comb through her hair, dreading the return trip downstairs. She'd never felt quite so lost and alone, not even as a child. She missed her mother suddenly and wished that they could have talked. There had been a few precious times when her mother had been sober, when she'd actually listened to her daughter's rambling.

The door opened, cutting into her thoughts, and the comb paused in midair over her short, dark hair as Winthrop walked into the room and slammed the door behind him.

He'd unbuttoned his long-sleeved chambray shirt at the throat. His dark hair caught the light and gleamed, like his unblinking dark eyes under that jutting brow. He stared down his straight nose at her and bad temper mingled with pure male arrogance in the way he watched her.

"Go ahead," she sighed, putting down the comb to sit with her hands folded in her lap. "Get it out of your system. Shall I start it for you? I betrayed you, lied to you —"

"You could have told me," he replied. His eyes narrowed on her face. "I even asked you point-blank if you were related to Dominic White and you sidestepped the question."

"Guilty as charged," she confessed. "I should have told you the truth. And if I had," she continued, turning to face him, "you'd have shot me off the ranch like a bullet."

"Trust comes hard to me," he said unexpectedly. "I won't be able to forget that you didn't level with me."

Even though she had expected it, the words hurt. She tilted her chin up and looked at him, drinking in the sight of his face, adoring it with her soft green eyes. "I'm not a bored heiress. I've lived in Chicago for two years —"

"Patiently," he agreed with a smile that would have been pleasant any other time. "Waiting for your chance. Gerald was first choice, I realize that, but I was the second-string, wasn't I?"

She blinked. "I don't follow you."

"You set your sights on Gerald, honey," he replied. "He was going to be your meal ticket. You played him for two years —"

"I what?" She got to her feet.

"I'm no fool," he ground out. "You've been hanging on him ever since you got here! I overheard what you said to him, about no other man ever being able to take you away from him. I heard it all. And you even held back last night, because you were afraid of what he might say if he saw us together."

"I did? Amazing, how much restraint I showed in the kitchen, wasn't it?" she taunted.

His jaw tautened angrily. "I'm no innocent

boy. I've had my share of adventures with women. And this morning, I got a good look at the real Nicole White. No, honey, you won't pull the wool over my eyes again. I'm on to you now. And there's no way I'm going to be your meal ticket. Neither is Gerald. I'll see to that."

She couldn't believe what she was hearing. All the growing tenderness between them, everything he'd said last night . . . After all of that, he could believe her father's lies, could he? How could he believe that she was just a gold digger?

"Gerald's in love with Sadie," she said, almost in a daze.

"Is he? Too bad. I guess you're brokenhearted. So that's why you turned to me, was it?" he laughed coldly. "And if your father hadn't arrived, I might still be deluding myself. What a lucky break. One cheap adventuress in a lifetime is damned enough."

"Oh, Winthrop," she sighed achingly. "Are you so afraid to believe what you feel, instead of what you hear? Can't you take my word for it?"

"I did," he reminded her, his tone icy. "And look where it landed me."

"My father was getting even," she said, moving closer. "He was paying me back for

167

walking out on him after Mama's funeral. It was just revenge. He's over it now, he'll tell you the truth if you ask him!"

"I know the truth." He lifted his chin as she came closer, and the expression on his hard face was not welcoming. "You've been stalking me. I knew it was no accident that you wound up at the corral that day and you deliberately came on to me at the dance last night."

"That's right," she said sarcastically as she looked up at him. Her heart was breaking and he didn't even care. "That's right, all I wanted was to get my hands on your wallet. I never cared a fig for you!"

She pressed against him and his steely hands caught her, holding her away.

"Do I make you nervous, big, bad rancher?" she teased, moving as close as his hands would allow. Her eyelashes fluttered at him, her fingers went to his chest and her nails drew lazily across the cotton fabric, making sensuous little scratchy sounds there. His heartbeat increased sharply.

"No," he denied. But he was looking down at where her hands were touching him, and something flickered in his dark eyes.

"Well, you make me nervous," she whispered. "You make me shake all over when you touch me, and that doesn't have a thing to do with how much money you've got in the bank. And I didn't lie to you about being innocent, I am."

"You and Madame Bovary . . ." he chided, but his touch had become caressing on her arms.

"And when we made love in the kitchen, I would have died for you," she breathed ardently, her lips parted, welcoming, pleading as she looked up into his eyes.

His hands tightened while he tried to fight what she made him feel. His body suddenly went taut but he couldn't help it, he wanted that soft mouth under his until it was madness.

"Damn you, Nicky."

"Winthrop." It was a moan, and he covered it with his lips.

He muttered something under his breath, but Nicky didn't hear it. She was lost in the strength of his arms, the ardent hunger of his hard mouth as it moved breathlessly on hers.

It seemed to take a long time for him to realize what was happening. Her warm body in his arms drugged him. The soft warmth of her mouth, trembling gently as he explored it, made him vulnerable. But minute by aching minute, the past came back. Deanne had once melted like this against his hard body. She'd murmured words of love, promised heaven. And then . . .

He eased his mouth away from Nicky's, steeling himself not to care about the soft accusation in her drowsy eyes as she watched him pull away.

"Please . . ." she whispered, and made a move to go to him.

"No, thanks," he said quietly. And the very tone of his voice halted her in her tracks. He was as politely indifferent as if he were refusing a drink of water when he wasn't thirsty.

She looked up at him with slow comprehension. He didn't even seem to be affected by that sweet interlude. He was just indifferent. She felt a sudden, sharp emptiness. Was this how it was going to be from now on? Was he so uninvolved that it didn't require any effort for him to draw away from her? She'd banked everything on his desire for her; she'd seen it as her one way to reach him. But it hadn't. She'd lost. He didn't trust her. And now he was showing her that he didn't even want her anymore.

"I'm not a gold digger," she said with what pride she had left. She was trembling, and he had to know it. She wrapped her arms around herself and watched him, like a hurt child. "Money doesn't matter to me. Surely you can see that?"

"I don't know you," he answered. His dark eyes narrowed as he studied her face. "And maybe it's better this way. I remember telling you once that we could hurt each other badly. I let you get to me last night, honey, but I won't make that mistake again. The last thing I want is involvement."

"But you said . . . I mean, I thought . . ." she faltered, trying to put into words what she'd felt the night before, what she'd thought he meant.

"I've been alone a long time, daffodil," he said with a mocking smile. "And I'm no saint. A man gets lonely from time to time."

In other words, she'd been a nice little interlude with no strings attached, but now it was broad daylight and he'd come to his senses. He'd just proved his indifference by showing her that he could pull away from her anytime he wanted to without regret.

"That's plain enough," she said quietly, studying his dark, impassive face. It was a long way up, despite her own height, and she felt at a disadvantage. "I guess I misread the whole situation."

"Just as long as you realize you'll never get to first base around here, except in business. Get my drift?"

She should have pasted him one, but she

was disillusioned and sick at heart. Her dreams were shattered. "I can't really blame you for the way you feel," she said dully. "I should have told you the truth in the beginning. I guess it was a hard knock."

"Nothing I couldn't handle," he replied coolly. "Don't flatter yourself too much. A few kisses doesn't make a relationship."

"Oh, I know that," she laughed coldly. "And just for the record, I was lonely, too. You see, men haven't noticed me for a long time; not since I had money, in fact," she said with a cynicism that suddenly matched his. She felt old and world-weary and battered. "Too bad I can't go home to Daddy and accept that trust my mother left me. That would up my bank balance by about three million."

She went to the door and opened it, watching him scowl as her remark registered.

"Dream on, honey," he said, but without a lot of conviction.

"You don't believe that, either, of course," she nodded. "Why don't you ask my father why my fiancé threw me over? The answer might open your eyes."

He stared at her for a long moment. "If you've got that kind of money, why work for my brother?"

"Because I got sick of a warped lifestyle where promiscuity and alcohol and pills seemed to replace love in my parents' relationship! Because I got lost somewhere and went hungry for just a little love!" Tears welled up in her eyes and she set her lips together to try to stop the trembling. "The man I thought I loved walked out on me the day he found out I'd given up all that nice money. And here I am, two years later, being accused of the very thing he was guilty of. You think I'm mercenary," she said in a husky whisper. She laughed tearfully. "How's that for irony?"

He stopped in the doorway to look down at her. His conscience and his pride were at war. "You lied to me once, damn it!"

"So you can't ever trust me again," she returned. "Okay, you've judged me and found me guilty. I don't want your pity. I don't want you at all. My father was right all along — everybody's got a price. I should go home with him and let him teach me how to buy people!"

"You're talking nonsense," he said curtly.

"I'm talking sense," she said on a laugh, although her chin was trembling. "I've been chasing rainbows. Thanks for putting me back on the right track."

"You're crying," he said half under his

breath and lifted a hand to catch a stray tear.

But she jerked away from his hand like a wounded thing, raw from his rejection, sick at heart. "Go away," she whispered furiously. "I hate you! I hate you, Winthrop! I wish I could leave here tomorrow and never have to see you again as long as I live!"

He tried to speak, but he couldn't seem to find words. In the end he turned and stormed off down the hall, smoldering. He was the wronged party, so why in hell did he feel guilty? He didn't even want to think about how he might have messed up things if she was telling the truth. Surely she wasn't. She'd lied to him once, hadn't she? He closed his mind tight. He just wouldn't think about it. She was another Deanne. He was well rid of her.

She watched him go with a sore heart. Well, if he wouldn't believe the truth when it was staring him in the face, who cared? She closed the door and gave up any idea of going downstairs again. She took off her clothes and cried herself to sleep.

CHAPTER SEVEN

Somehow, Nicky got through the night. Winthrop had excused himself and gone out to help his men keep a check on the cattle. The snow had made the mountain roads impassable except with a four-wheel drive. The hunters didn't seem to mind. In fact, they were apparently used to mountain weather and since they were planning a week-long outing on the ranch, they settled in with easy acceptance.

Carol, however, became a pill. Nothing pleased her. Her room was too cold, the bed was lumpy, there were no shopping centers and she couldn't even get a manicure. Furthermore, she missed her parents, whom she visited every few days. She wanted to go home.

Nicky's father spent the better part of the second day, in between cleaning his hunting rifle and getting himself kitted out with the proper attire, calming down his playmate. It seemed he had a knack for communicating with Carol, because he finally got through to her that it would be impossible to get out until a chinook blew in. That could be any day, he'd added with careful insight.

Mary had already told Nicky that the snow could go on for days or even weeks, but Nicky wasn't sharing that tidbit with the excitable redhead. After Dominic's comforting statement, anyway, Carol went off into the living room and watched a popular science-fiction thriller until even Winthrop started to grow tired of the film.

At dawn on the third day, the hunters piled into Winthrop's Jeep and headed down the valley. Gerald and Nicky worked alone in the study, leaving Carol to her science-fiction habit.

"I can't tell you how sick I am of light sabers," Nicky remarked after the sound became louder in the next room.

"Sure you can," Gerald invited, leaning back in his chair. "Go ahead. Then I'll tell you how sick I am of laser cannons. And then we'll make silly faces in the mirror and see about renting straitjackets in a matched set."

She giggled. "Let's pray for a chinook."

"I'm for that. The Sioux used to have a prayer for it, come to think of it. We'll ask

Mary."

She looked at her steno pad. "Winthrop said something to her at breakfast with sign language. Mary's been teaching me a little bit of signing, so I tried to watch carefully."

"I watched for years and never learned a thing," he confessed. "What did he say, do you know?"

She smiled ruefully. "Either he wanted bicarbonate of soda or he was melancholy."

He frowned. "What?"

"When you want to express melancholy or gloom, you make the sign for *heart* and then the sign for *sick*. It's really a fascinating insight into another language," she added. "For instance, if you want to say that you're disgusted, you sign *heart* and then *tired.* The sign for enemy is *friend* and *not.* Drunk," she grinned, "is expressed by making the signs for *whiskey, to drink, much* and *mad.* See?"

He shook his head. "Fascinating. Smart girl."

"Intelligence is this," she said, touching her right index and middle fingers to her forehead.

"How about smart aleck?" he taunted.

"I'm not that good, yet," she sighed. But she was learning. Already, Mary had taught her enough that she could translate what

Winthrop had "said" to her on the porch the morning he'd brought her home from the Todds'. He'd said that he was jealous of Gerald, and that he wanted her very much. How different things might have been if she'd known that at the time. But Winthrop had become a coolly considerate host and nothing more. All the lovely soft feeling that had been growing so gently between them was gone forever.

"I'm worried about Sadie and Mrs. Todd," Gerald said abruptly, tapping a pencil on the blotter. "I tried to phone them an hour or so ago, and the lines are down. Sadie had to put their Jeep in the shop a couple of days ago, so I know they don't have any transportation. I drove by there before the snow started, just to say hello."

"Could you get Winthrop to run up and check on them?" she asked.

"Winthrop is in a snit lately, haven't you noticed?" he asked miserably, his gaze apologetic as he added, "Your father did a job on your character. Although, to give the man credit, he tried to tell Winthrop it was mostly just bad temper and vengeance. But Winthrop didn't listen. He walks off every time your name is mentioned."

"We had an argument and didn't exactly part friends," she told him, without going into details. She didn't add that Winthrop's attitude had broken her heart. "You wouldn't want to go back to Chicago anytime soon?" she added hopefully.

"Poor Nicky," he said, smiling at her knowingly. "I'm sorry it turned out like this. In the beginning, Winthrop was so different when you were around. He smiled and laughed and seemed to enjoy life for the first time since the accident. I'm sorry it fell apart."

"So am I," she confessed, feeling her eyes sting with unshed tears. "I guess he's soured on me because I didn't tell him who my father was. He thinks I lied to him. And perhaps, in a sense, I did. But I didn't mean to be devious. I was only trying to forget the past. My childhood was pretty rough, and my mother's death shook me up. There are so many scars. I guess that's why I understand Winthrop so well. I have scars, too, and time isn't all that healing when your emotions have been ravaged."

"I guess so." He got up and went to the window. "I wondered why Winthrop was flirting with Carol. I supposed he was trying to make you jealous."

"On the contrary," she laughed, "he was showing me that I don't matter. And believe me, he's succeeded. I wouldn't go near him now with a whip and a chair."

"I can understand how you feel," he said, turning. "But you have to understand how it's been for my brother, Nicky. It was several months after the accident before he was even able to walk without a cane, and they'd threatened at first to take off the leg entirely. Winthrop said they'd take it off after he was dead, and he meant it, but he doesn't realize even now how close it came to that. It took one of the best orthopedic surgeons in the country to save it — and he performed an operation that used techniques he invented as he went along. One of the bones in his lower leg was shattered; the surgeon completely rebuilt it, like putting a jigsaw puzzle together."

"He said there were complications," she probed.

"His impatience," he said, confirming her suspicions. "They told him exactly what he could and couldn't do, and he ignored them and tried to ride a horse the day after he came out of the hospital. He tore the cartilage and had to go back into surgery to have it resewn. Consequently it hasn't healed as well as it could have. But the doctors said he could get rid of that limp if he'd work half as hard at his exercises as he's worked at fighting them tooth and nail over the manner of his recovery. Winthrop," he added dryly, "is impatient."

As if she hadn't already noticed that, she mused sadly. "I suppose at the time he didn't much care what happened to him."

"It was the closest I've ever seen him come to the edge," Gerald agreed. "He took chances and pushed himself even harder than he used to in his wild days. Finally I asked him if the stupid woman was worth his life. And that seemed to snap him out of it. But he's not the same man he was."

"What was he like then?" she asked, because she wanted to know everything there was to know about him.

"Full of fun," he said. "Reckless, with a devil-may-care attitude, but in a suave kind of way. He liked music and parties and ski-ing — in the water or in the snow. He was forever on the go. The ranch was important to him, but not in the way that it is now. He left Mike in charge and went out to beat the world. Now," he said softly, "he just sits up here in the mountains and broods. Less since you've been here, I have to admit, but he still has that streak of melancholy."

"Maybe he found out that money and glitter don't wear well," she said. "I learned it young."

"Perhaps he did." He studied her quietly

for a long moment. "It hurts you that he believes your father, doesn't it?"

"More than I can tell you."

"Give him time, Nicky. Trust comes hard to a man who's been betrayed. But if the feeling is there, inevitably it's going to break through the ice."

"Think so?" She smiled. "I wonder."

They went back to work, but she brooded about what Gerald had said. Would Winthrop eventually come to his senses? Or had it been just a mild physical attraction and he wanted nothing more to do with her? She didn't know.

Later that afternoon, Gerald began to pace, and rubbed his stomach as if it were troubling him.

"Need an antacid?" Nicky asked.

"What?" He glanced at his stomach. "Oh. It's just acting up. I forgot my medicine. I guess I'd better take it. No, it isn't that," he said suddenly, turning. "I'm worried about Sadie."

"Then let's go see her. Isn't there a four-wheel drive around here somewhere that we can use?"

He grinned. "Sure. Are you game? It could be dangerous."

"I'd like some fresh air myself." She glanced toward the living room door, where the sound of laser blasts was echoing loudly. "And I need a reprieve from that movie that I loved until we got snowed in with her."

"My sentiments, exactly. I'll tell Mary where we're going. Dress warmly."

Warmly meant putting on her jeans, two pair of socks, boots, a long-sleeved shirt, a sweater, and her heavy coat, gloves and a stocking cap. Even that was hardly enough against the thick snow and biting wind. The mountains were cold in November, she learned quickly. And the snow was flying at them in an unending sheet of white, provoked by a wild wind. Nicky had misgivings about this trip, but she had more about being cooped up inside with Carol.

Gerald had the old Jeep idling when Nicky climbed in beside him. She glanced around her with a curious smile. "Will it get us there?" she asked hesitantly.

"I hope so," he confided. "It hasn't been used for a while, but Mike has one and Winthrop has the other new one, so we're stuck with this. I think it will be all right."

The vehicle sputtered and lurched as he put it in gear, and the chains on the heavy tires made a nice clanking sound as he shot down the mountain road. Thank God it was a wide one, but by the time they turned off onto the dirt road that led up to the Todd place, Nicky was regretting her decision to go with him. Gerald wasn't the driver Winthrop was, and as the heavy snow continued to fly at them, Gerald swung too wide around a curve and the Jeep suddenly left the road.

Gerald moaned something. The Jeep lurched crazily sideways and slid down onto a lodgepole pine and hung there, shuddering. Nicky pitched against his shoulder, and got a sudden and terrifying view of a sheer drop out his window.

"Oh, for heaven's sake!" she squeaked.

He caught his breath, staring beside him. "Damn," he breathed. "I couldn't see the roadbed and I ran right off. Nicky, we'll have to get out of here. This is a dead pine, and if it gives way . . ." He glanced at her with pure terror in his dark eyes.

"Then we'll get out," she said, more calmly than she felt. "How?" she added.

"Well . . ." He studied the Jeep's position for a minute. "I think it might be easier if we tried to get out on your side. The tree will balance us. You go first. I'll help."

Climbing out of the Jeep looked impossible, but there was no choice; plunging down that deep ravine would be as sure as death. She thought of Winthrop and wondered if he'd miss her if she pitched down there. Morbid thoughts, and she shook them off. No, sir, she wasn't about to give him the satisfaction of dying.

With Gerald's help, she managed to lever herself up to the passenger door and gingerly open it. The Jeep pitched a little, and she caught her breath and shuddered, certain that the end was near, but the vehicle remained fairly secure against the pine. She prayed as she caught hold of the opening and began to drag herself up and over. She got grease from the dirty undercarriage all over herself, but in the end, she managed to tumble out. Then she reached up to help Gerald, who managed the task with more deftness than she had.

They cleared the Jeep and collapsed onto the thick, soft snow, almost buried in it while they caught their breath. Behind them, the Jeep lay on its side against the tall pine, unmoving, despite the fierce wind.

"At least it hasn't gone over," Gerald sighed. He held his stomach and groaned. "Damn. I wish I'd stopped long enough to take that medicine."

She stared at him, snow sticking to her face. She felt bitterly cold. "Can you make it?" she asked, frightened.

"I think so," he sighed. "My ulcer isn't sure, but I am," he said with a wan smile.

"So am I." She smiled back. "Well, shall we start out?"

"We're closer to the ranch than the Todd's place," he said when they were standing in the road. But the snow was coming harder and thicker, and it was blinding, stinging their eyes. "We can follow the road back . . ."

We hope, she added silently, because the blizzard wasn't letting up. If anything, it was getting worse. The brilliance of the snow was as blinding as the flakes whipped up by the biting cold wind.

She leaned into that wind, pulled the cap down and her collar up to cover as much of her face as possible, and started walking. Beside her, Gerald kept up the pace. But when they'd gone a few hundred yards, the going got harder and harder. Incredibly, she started to feel hot in all the freezing cold and snow. She wanted to throw off her coat and walk in her sweater, but Gerald shook his head sharply when she started to do it. He mouthed something that looked like "frostbite," but she wasn't sure.

She concentrated on putting one foot in front of the other, watching her boot sink into the deep snow. It came over the boot top and down into her warm socks, wetting them, chilling them. She'd left her gloves in the Jeep, like an idiot, so she had to keep her hands in her pockets, but they were freezing cold, too.

They rounded a bend, and found the road suddenly buried under a huge drift of snow. Nicole stopped, her eyes on the blanket of white around them, but there was no alternative route. They had to get through that drift or die.

Gerald moved close to her, panting. "Oh, God," he muttered, clenching his hand over his stomach. "It's hurting, Nicky. How in hell are we going to dig through that?"

She looked at it dubiously. She didn't have gloves and Gerald was in no condition to do it alone. There were no tools. A ranch hat like Winthrop's Stetson would have helped or even a shoe, but if she took off her boot, her foot would freeze. She stared at the huge mound of snow with helpless frustration.

"Oh, damn," she wailed, hating the hot sting of tears in her eyes. She wasn't beaten. Oh, God, she couldn't be beaten! She had to do something, but what?

"I'm so tired," Gerald sighed. He sank down with his back to the snowdrift. "So tired . . . stomach hurts . . ."

"You can't go to sleep," she burst out. "It's fatal! Gerald, we have to go on."

"How? The snow's too deep. We can't get through, Nicky." He closed his eyes, leaning back against the bank that angled against the snowdrift. "Nice . . ."

Nicky shook him, but he was too weary to try anymore. She looked around at the white forest, its tall trees rising over them like shrouds while the wind blew and the snow fell and the world was as hushed as a cathedral.

She sank down beside Gerald and sat there, looking around at the deadly white beauty of it. A hundred years before, men must have seen such sights and been killed by them, she thought. The Lewis and Clark expedition probably had its share of snowstorms, and they'd survived. But they were strong, well-equipped woodsmen. Nicky was a city woman with no woodcraft skills. She didn't even know how to build a fire, if she could have made her hands do the work.

Her green eyes went up to the sky. Well, it wasn't such a very bad place to die, she mused as drowsiness swept over her. She was near Winthrop, even though he didn't care anymore. Maybe he'd bury her here, and she'd be near him forever . . .

She closed her eyes. Somewhere she heard an organ. It was making beautiful music in the distance, and there was singing. It was an old hymn of some kind, exquisite in the stillness . . .

"Amazing Grace."

Her grandfather used to sing it when he worked with the horses. "Amazing Grace, how sweet the sound . . ." she began to hum.

Voices . . . coming close. The organ stopped, but a cat was purring. Something touched her. Shook her. That voice — it was deep and urgent and somehow familiar — but she didn't understand what it was asking. She was warm and safe and she protested when someone tried to move her. She fought, but she was subdued. Then she was rising, floating. White clouds. Snow. Cold. The organ drifted in and out. She tried to open her eyes, but it was just too much work. She slept.

Her head ached. She sneezed and the sound echoed around her. Was she dead?

She opened her eyes slowly. A ceiling. Very white. A canopy, pink, overhead. She turned her head and there was Winthrop. He was unshaven, his hair needed combing. He was sprawled beside the bed in a chair half his size, his booted feet splayed, his mouth open. He was snoring.

She stared at him for a long moment, memorizing him. He looked good, even without a shave. His shirt was open, and his hair-roughened chest looked like leather. She wanted to touch it, smooth her hands over its masculine contours, feel his heart beating under that rough skin. His hands were clasped over his lean waist, darkly beautiful masculine hands, their strength evident even in rest. She remembered their delicate touch on her soft flesh, and trembled a little with pleasure.

"Winthrop." His name sounded rusty. She frowned, because it had hurt her throat to call him. Her hand went to it. Her fingers were cold, but they didn't hurt. Had she escaped frostbite? She held out her hands, palms down, and looked at them.

"You were damned lucky," Winthrop said, opening his eyelids without moving a muscle. He glared at her out of eyes as black as night. "You didn't even get frostbite, although you'll have a hell of a cold."

"Gerald?" she rasped.

"He's fine, thank God. What possessed you two greenhorns to scale the Rockies in a blizzard?"

"He was worried about Sadie," she defended.

"Sadie had the good sense to stay inside," he said coldly. "I sent Mike up to take supplies to her and her mother. They're fine. More than I can say for you and Sir Galahad."

"We can't all be brilliant mountain men," she said sweetly.

"Do you want something to drink?" he asked.

"Not until I can have it analyzed for poison," she threw back at him.

"I'll send Mary with it," he replied. "I might not be able to resist the temptation, at that."

She watched him get up and tears gathered behind her eyes. Such an ordeal, only to find him still unforgiving and hateful at the end of it. He might have said he was glad she was alive or smile at her, or something.

"Sorry to put you to the bother," she muttered.

He bent over her, his eyes dangerous. "Don't bait me," he threatened softly. "I've had a hell of a night watching you fade in and out. You little fool, people have died in snowdrifts out here!"

"Sorry, but I do seem to be alive. I hope you aren't too disappointed . . . oh!"

The exclamation was in response to the sudden, unexpected descent of his mouth, square over hers.

"Disappointed —" he bit off, and kissed harder. His hand at her throat tilted her face at a more inviting angle and he caught his breath as his lips became gentle and began to play with hers. His breath was as ragged as her own now, but he didn't even care. She could have died. Knowing it made him wild.

Her hands went to his hard cheeks, trembling and cold as they pressed there, holding him to her mouth. Her brows knitted in exquisite anguish. Dreams came true like this, she thought achingly. Dreams. She'd lived on them for so long.

"Oh," she whispered softly, a tiny whimper of sound that echoed in his mind.

His mouth opened against hers, lifting, teasing, his breath mingling wildly with hers while his hands caught hers and pulled them down to the bed beside her head, his fingers interlocking with hers.

"I could ravish you," he ground out huskily, and the eyes that glanced at her were blazing.

"I thought . . . you hated me," she breathed unsteadily.

"I did. I do. I hate what I feel when I touch you." He bent again, tormenting her mouth with his lips, brushing, lifting, teasing until she began to writhe on the sheets. "Yes, that's exciting, isn't it?" he whispered roughly, watching her face. "I'm going to make you wild, Nicky, and then I'm going to walk off and leave you with it. . . ."

She arched softly, her eyes wide and quiet, her body trembling. "No, you won't," she whispered. "Because you'll be just as wild as I will."

His jaw tautened as he looked down at her, his pride aching, his body aching. She was killing him. His eyes went to her bodice, where her breasts were outlined under the gossamer-thin white cotton of her gown. The arousal she couldn't help was blatant.

His fingers, linked with hers, contrasted roughly. His eyes adored her breasts, caressed them. "That," he whispered slowly, "is beautiful."

"Everything is beautiful with you," she said, her heart in her eyes as she looked up at him, too much in love with him to even be embarrassed at his bold stare.

"Nicky!" He groaned her name as he bent, his mouth so tender, so exquisitely gentle with hers that tears ran hotly down her cheeks. He was the world, and everything in it. She loved him so.

Even as she thought the words, she whispered them under his warm mouth, breathed the truth against him, echoed her feelings like a prayer.

"No." He drew back suddenly, sharply.

His fingers pressed hard against her lips while he sat over her, trying to breathe, with eyes as black as the night outside the window. "No. Don't say it."

"But I do love you," she said, her face like a child's, full of pleading and hope.

His thumb rubbed against her lips roughly in a reluctant caress. "I don't want that," he said quietly. "I'm sorry. But I . . . can't, Nicky."

"I can't help it," she whispered softly. "I'm sorry, too, but I do. I do, I do!"

His thumb pressed harder and he caught his breath. "Listen, I've been alone a long time. I've gotten used to my own company. I don't want anyone with me. I don't want ties, commitment. For God's sake, Nicky, I'm not a marrying man!"

Her face flamed when she realized where the conversation was leading. She stared at him, horror-struck. She hadn't meant that, but he'd assumed she was begging him to marry her.

"I . . . I didn't mean . . ." she faltered.

"I can't saddle myself with a wife," he said flatly. "And you're too frail for this country, even if I went crazy and invited you to live with me. You're too used to the city. This is a man's country, Nicky, not a woman's. You'd never survive it."

She bit her lower lip. "Are you sure?"

"Yes." He took her hand in his and smoothed over its softness, wondering at the delicious sensation that washed over him as he savored it. "Just as I'm sure that I don't want a woman here," he added deliberately, holding her gaze.

She searched his dark eyes quietly. "All right. I'm sorry if I've embarrassed you."

"I think you're more embarrassed than I am," he mused, smiling gently at her red cheeks. He frowned a little as he studied her. "Are you sure this isn't reaction? You've had a rough time of it lately."

She took the out he was offering her, grateful for a little salvaged pride. "Probably it is. Being rescued, and all," she explained. "You don't hate me anymore, do you?" she added weakly, the expression in her eyes so eloquent that he felt himself choking to death on pride.

"No, I don't hate you," he said shortly. "I never did. I hated being lied to, that's all." And she had lied, he recalled. Numbly, he laid her hand down on the covers, wondering why he felt so empty. It had warmed him when she'd whispered that she loved him, God knew why. Love wasn't something he coveted these days. His eyes drifted up to hers, but she was concealing them under

195

her lids. Could she love him?

He bent toward her, watching her face lift for him, her mouth part. Yes, she wanted his mouth, that was sweetly evident. He looked into her eyes while he kissed her, seeing the pupils dilate, the lids close drowsily. That excited him more, and he drew back before he got in over his head. He scowled down at her curiously. She disturbed him all too much. He didn't need this. She'd already betrayed him once, he wasn't giving her a second shot at him. It might be an act, even this talk of loving. Just an act. He couldn't trust her.

"I'll see about some orange juice," he said with a faint smile. "Want some soup?"

"I guess I could eat something, if it won't put Mary to too much trouble," she added quietly.

"I can't remember the last time any woman guest considered Mary," he mused, his gaze quietly possessive. "Get some rest. I'll be back after a while."

She watched him get up, trying to hide her feelings. But he limped suddenly and she sat up, her breath catching. "Winthrop, you're hurt!" she burst out.

The caring note in her voice cut him to the quick. He didn't want it, or what he was feeling for her. He glared at her. "I don't need a nurse," he bit off. "Get yourself well. I can take care of myself. I've had years of practice."

He went out and slammed the door, leaving her stunned and hurt. She wished she knew what she'd done to make him so angry. She felt like she'd made an utter fool of herself by telling him she loved him. Tears stung her eyes as she lay back. Well, maybe he'd believe she'd lied, or, as he'd said, that it was reaction. He'd made it all too obvious that her love was the last thing on earth he wanted. So she'd just have to learn to hide it from him.

CHAPTER EIGHT

Soon after Winthrop left the room, Nicky had an unexpected visitor. Her father, neatly dressed in a gray suit, came in and took the chair Winthrop had vacated.

"Feeling any better?" he asked, and seemed to be genuinely concerned. Nicky could remember being sick as a child and having neither of her parents come near her.

"I'll be all right," she said. "I just feel a little tired."

"I guess so," he said with a smile. "Your nose is red."

"It feels red, too." She returned the smile. "Did anybody shoot anything?"

"I got a deer," he said. "Six-point buck. Nobody else had any luck." He pursed his lips. "I offered Carol a jacket made from the skin and she stormed off in a snit. I shot Bambi, you see."

Nicole laughed in spite of herself. "You cold-blooded killer, you."

"I love venison," he sighed. "Mary's fixing us a big stew out of the hindquarter, but you won't get any until lunch tomorrow. She says it has to simmer a long time to get done right."

"She's a good cook."

He leaned back in the chair to study her. "What possessed you and your dim-witted boss to go driving in a snowstorm?" he asked pleasantly.

"He was worried about Sadie Todd," she explained. "And I just wanted to get some fresh air."

"In a snowstorm?" he asked.

"Well, we were kind of getting tired of watching science-fiction movies . . ."

"That's no reason to commit suicide. Snow is deadly, as you damned near found out. If Winthrop hadn't decided to call it quits early, the two of you would have frozen to death."

"I guess Winthrop was pretty angry."

"Angry." He pursed his lips. "That's an interesting choice of words. Mild, considering his reaction when he found you. I thought I had a good command of four-letter words, but he taught me some new ones. He carried you over that drift all by himself, weak leg and all. I guess he's hurting like hell, from the way he limps, but he was determined."

She felt her heart leap with the pleasure that knowledge gave her. She toyed with the sheet. "He's quite a man."

"I think so," he agreed. "I told him the truth, by the way. I think you've paid enough for the past."

"Thanks. But it won't do much good. Winthrop isn't a marrying man," she added when he didn't seem to understand. "And I'm not a liberated woman."

Dominic sighed heavily. "Well, different people, different attitudes." His green eyes twinkled. "I'm very liberated, myself. But I'm kind of glad you aren't. And do you think I'm ever going to get any grandkids?" he added thoughtfully.

She flushed, averting her eyes. "Not anytime soon. I'm barely twenty-two."

"Kids are nice. I wish I'd enjoyed you more, while I had the chance." He frowned. "Say, would you like to go to a carnival or something? I could buy you cotton candy and ride the rides with you. Or we could go fishing. . . ."

"This sounds serious," she said with mock fear. "Are you suffering from an attack of fatheritis?"

"Feels like it." He grinned. "We could at least speak. Maybe we could exchange

Christmas cards. Then, as time goes by, you might come to Kentucky to see me."

"Or you might come to Chicago to see me." She sighed. "You and Carol," she amended.

"Carol won't last," he shrugged. "She's temporary. They all are. You see . . . in some crazy way, I loved your mother, even if we couldn't quite get our act together. She's pretty irreplaceable." His eyes fell. "God, it hurt when she died. I couldn't even tell you how it hurt."

"I don't think I would have listened if you'd told me then." She sat up straighter. "I think I understand a little better now. And maybe we could exchange Christmas cards."

He grinned at that dry remark. "Maybe we could." He got up. "Well, I'd better go rescue Mary. Carol is trying to teach her how to walk like a model."

"Carol models?"

"Doesn't it show? She's got style, all right. And Mary was just eating it up." He scowled. "She mentioned something about the Rockettes. . . ."

"That's kind of a family joke," Nicole said, enlightening him. "Thanks for coming up to see me."

"You look a little peaked to me," he said.

"Mary was fixing chicken soup in between parading around with a book on her head. I guess she's going to bring you some."

"No, she isn't," Winthrop said from the doorway, limping heavily toward them with a tray on which were perched a soup bowl and a teacup and saucer. "She's too busy trying to do a pivot without falling into the venison stew."

"Sorry about that," Dominic murmured sheepishly. "I did tell Carol to stay out of the kitchen."

"No harm done. Mary seems to be having the time of her life." With a hard glare, Winthrop bypassed Dominic and put the tray down on the bedside table. "Well, don't just lie there, prop yourself up. You can't eat flat on your back."

"I was just trying to do that," she shot back, "and you don't have to snap at me!"

"I'll check on you again, Nicky," Dominic said as he started toward the door.

"Okay."

He closed the door and Nicky tried to take the soup from Winthrop's steely hands without letting him see how much hers were trembling. But the bowl seemed pretty unsteady even before she touched it.

He looked down into her eyes and they exchanged a glance that set her heart running away.

"Here, this won't do," he said under his breath.

He sat down beside her on the bed and began to ladle the soup gently into her mouth. She watched him, fascinated at his unexpected tenderness. The way he pampered her, the way he looked at her — even the gentle smile that touched his hard mouth as she accepted the soup like a child — tugged at her heart.

"Feeling better?" he asked.

"Much, thank you." She swallowed some soup. "Winthrop, my throat hurts," she whispered.

"Yes, I imagine so. I've got something for that, and for your cold. Nonprescription, but they're what our doctor always prescribes for head colds. I'll take care of you, daffodil."

"Somebody needs to take care of you," she said softly, studying his hard face. "Your leg must hurt terribly."

"It usually does after a day as hard as this one," he said carelessly. "I've got something to take for it."

"Well, thank you for rescuing us, anyway."

"Gerald sounds worse than you do," he told her. "You're both greenhorns."

"You were out in it, too," she reminded

him.

"That's so," he said agreeably. "But I'm a woodsman, honey. I know how to survive a snowstorm. You and my citified brother are lucky to be alive."

"Yes, I realize that." She took the last bit of soup and sat quietly while he mopped her up with a napkin. She knew she must look terrible. Her hair hadn't been combed, her face was pale and her throat felt scratchy. But Winthrop was looking down at her with pure pleasure . . . almost possession.

"You need sleep," he said.

"I've been asleep on and off since you brought me home," she said. "I don't want to sleep."

"It will help you heal." He got up, put down the bowl and offered her a cup of steaming tea to swallow down the capsules he'd put in her hand. She hesitated but he looked determined, so she swallowed them, finished the tea and lay back against the pillows.

"I hope you don't catch my cold," she said.

"I don't usually get them," he replied. He smiled slowly. "Even from kissing sick little girls."

Her face colored and she lowered her eyes

to his chest. That was even worse. He had a sexy chest, and she wanted very much to draw her hands over it.

"You have expressive eyes, Nicole," he murmured, watching her intently. "You want me, don't you?"

The color in her cheeks deepened. She glared at him. "Well, I do realize that it isn't mutual. You don't have to throw it in my face. It isn't something I can help."

His eyebrow arched. "Was I doing that? I didn't mean to. I'm pretty used to speaking my mind."

"Well so am I." She stared at the coverlet. "What I said . . . earlier," she faltered, glancing at him and then away. "I was over-wrought and tired, and I guess I kind of got carried away."

"You mistook a chill for true love?"

She glared at him. Damn that mocking smile. "I got carried away."

"You're one of a kind, Nicky," he mused. "As for getting carried away, if you weren't so frail, I'd throw you back against those pillows and lie down against you. And in a very few minutes, we'd both know what you feel for me."

He was doing it again. She felt completely out of her element when his voice dropped into that sensuous drawl and his eyes began to make love to her body. She felt her breasts tautening and drew the sheet slowly over her bodice so that he wouldn't see what he was doing to her.

But he did see her response. His eyes seemed to darken at the proof of how easily he could arouse her. She couldn't know that it made him feel ten feet tall.

"Don't worry," he said as he picked up the tray, still watching her. "I've got sound survival instincts. I meant what I said about commitment."

"You'll grow old all alone," she said quietly, her eyes steady on his hard, dark face. "You won't have anyone to look after you or care about you. Eventually, you'll grow a thicker shell than you have now, and no one will be able to touch you. Is that really what you want?"

For just an instant, his expression was open. "No," he replied. "But I don't want my heart torn out of my body a second time, either. I like my life as it is."

"Unhampered," she said.

"Exactly." He left her with that parting shot. He was still limping badly, and he was scowling when he left the room.

Nicky must have slept then. She wasn't aware of the quiet, watchful man sitting beside the bed. He looked at her as if he couldn't help himself, staring at the steady rise and fall of her firm young breasts under the sheet. She looked innocent in sleep. Everybody did, he reminded himself.

But there was something different about this woman. She was special. Much too special. He was going to have to get a grip on himself before he pitched headfirst into that sweetly baited trap. He'd fought it too long to give in now.

He closed his eyes finally, with a long sigh, and tried to get comfortable in the chair. His knee was giving him hell. Probably he'd torn a muscle. But he hadn't wanted anyone else to touch Nicky. She belonged to him. She was his responsibility.

The sound of the windup alarm clock was unnaturally loud. It woke Nicky in the early hours just before dawn. She opened her eyes and glanced at the tall man sprawled again in the chair, grimacing as he breathed. His leg was probably hurting, and here he sat, when he could have been comfortable in bed.

Nicky got up, just staring at him. Even unshaven and unkempt, he was a sexy man. His shirttail had been pulled from his jeans, and his shirt was half unbuttoned down a chest thick with hair and dark from exposure to the sun. He might not love her, but he was oddly protective of her these days. That was some small comfort.

She touched his hard, warm cheek with her fingertips, tracing its high cheekbones.

"Winthrop?" she whispered.

He made a sound and his head turned, but his eyes didn't open.

"Winthrop, come to bed," she whispered.

He never did wake up completely. He let her tug him out of the chair and he sprawled onto the bed with a mumbled protest. Nicky was glad that he'd already taken his boots off, as she wouldn't have relished trying to remove them. She eased his legs onto the bed, careful not to jar the bad one. Then, with a mischievous grin, she crawled back under the covers and snuggled close.

His arm came around her instinctively, drawing her cheek to the soft cotton of his shirt. His fingers caressed her hair gently, and she thought that she'd never been quite so close to heaven. She lay quietly beside him in the dim light of the lamp and tried to imagine how it would be if they were married, if she had the right to lie in his arms every night like this, while the wind howled angrily outside the darkened window and snow fell.

It was so sweet that she lost all fear of the future and simply went to sleep, Winthrop's chest rising and falling steadily against her.

A drum was beating somewhere. She heard it in the back of her mind, its steady rhythm comforting. It was nearby. Growing louder. Louder. It stopped suddenly and then increased. Something moved against her. Her head fell back onto a pillow and she mumbled when she felt the mattress lower then return to its normal position.

The sound of footsteps grew dim. A door opened and closed. What a crazy dream, she thought, and drifted back to sleep again.

The light streaming in the window woke her. This time she opened her eyes, and found Mary standing at the curtains.

"How you feel?" the Sioux woman asked.

"Fi . . ." Her voice sounded hoarse. She tried again. "Fine. I think."

"You look pale. I bring oatmeal. Best thing for scratchy throat and cold. Also buttered toast and coffee with lots of cream. Sound good?"

"Oh, yes," Nicky sighed. "I'm so hungry!"

Mary paused beside the bed and bent down to touch Nicky's forehead. "No fever. Good. You live yet." She pursed her lips at the clear indentation of a head in the pillow beside Nicky's. "You have pajama party last night?"

Nicky grinned. "He was sprawled in the

chair and groaning in his sleep. I figured his leg was giving him the devil. So I got up and led him over here and tucked him in. He never knew."

Mary's normally placid face came alive. "He never knew?"

"That's right," Nicky told her, smiling broadly. "He was gone when I woke up, but I'll bet he doesn't remember how he got in the bed."

"Well, well. New weapon, hmm." Mary grinned, too, showing even white teeth. "Poor man. Shame on you. You should not take advantage of the helpless."

"He wasn't very helpless yesterday, was he?" Nicky asked with pride. "He carried me through a snowbank."

"That leg is not as bad as he thinks it is," Mary returned. "If he exercised it more and favored it less, it would heal properly. It is his hiding place, Nicky. He cannot accept being a whole man again because that would make him vulnerable to his emotions."

"Not so anyone would notice," Nicky sighed ruefully. "He can be pretty formidable."

"He is still only a man." Mary tucked Nicole back into bed. "Need medicine for your throat?"

"A lozenge would be wonderful. It's scratchy." She paused to sneeze and grab for a tissue. "And I think I have a cold."

"It would seem so. I will bring your breakfast. And I will bring you venison stew for lunch. That should help clear your head."

"It may take more than venison stew to do that," Nicky replied.

"I make it with Tabasco sauce." Mary leaned over her. "Trust me." And she grinned again before she went out.

To Nicky's dismay, Winthrop didn't come back all day. She expected him every time the door opened. Mary brought breakfast and then Gerald came, red-nosed and sniffling, followed by her father and even Carol, who gave her a pretty scarf to cheer her up. But no Winthrop, not even when the venison stew was served.

When Mary came back after lunch to pick up the dishes, she cocked her head at Nicky's forlorn expression.

"Something troubles you?" she asked.

"Of course not." Nicky finished her cup of hot black coffee and set the cup on the tray Mary was holding. "I don't care if he ignores me. I'll just lie here and die."

"He cannot get up just yet," Mary said after a minute.

Nicky was immediately contrite and worried. "It's his leg, isn't it?"

Mary nodded. "The strain, you see. I think he may have pulled a tendon. I have made a poultice for it, which will take away the pain and make it heal. But in the meantime, he is an invalid. Mr. Mike has taken the hunting party out for him, and Miss Carol is watching . . . would you care to guess?"

"I thought I heard laser cannons," Nicole replied grimly. "Does he have something for pain?" she persisted, her green eyes troubled.

"He will not take it," Mary grumbled. "Even now, he is trying to work with a board across his lap on which to write."

"It sounds as though he might need a little nursing," Nicky suggested.

"You need it more. Lie down."

"I could talk to him. It's only a cold and a reaction," she said and then added when the other woman looked doubtful, "Oh, please, Mary. How can I lie here knowing that he's in pain?"

Mary shrugged. "Good point. All right. But put on your robe and leave door open." Her dark eyes held Nicky's with subtle warning. "He is still a man."

"I love him," Nicky said simply.

212

"Yes, I know. That will make it harder for you. He is a man who does not trust love." The expression on her face was serious. "He will fight being vulnerable. Now more than ever."

"I wouldn't hurt him," she said.

"You will have to prove that to him. And it will not be easy. But I would think less of you if you did not try," Mary added. And she smiled as she went out.

Nicky put on her long white chenille robe and went along to Winthrop's room, a little nervous about how she'd be received.

Her nervousness was justified as it turned out, because he was moody and restless and more irritable than she'd ever seen him.

He glared at her from his bed, where he lay taut-faced with only a sheet drawn haphazardly over his lean hips for cover. His dark hair was disheveled, his face unshaven. His long, powerfully muscled legs were bare, like his tanned chest, and all of him was covered with a very masculine feathering of black hair. He looked like an outlaw in his sprawled dishabille, and Nicky wondered if any woman could see him like that and not be affected. Her heart began to run away from her the minute she knocked on the door and was invited to open it.

"What do you want?" he asked curtly, and

she noticed the scattered paperwork that had apparently been cast to one side with irritation.

"I thought you might need something," she said, hesitating.

"If I did, Mary could get it."

"Mary's got her hands full with your hunting party."

"They've gone out again. Carol's watching movies. Gerald's on the phone. So all Mary has to do is look after me. In any event," he said with a mocking smile, "that's what she gets paid to do."

"And here I am about to cause a labor dispute by offering to do it for free," she sighed. Her throat still felt a little raw, but at least her nose had stopped running. She moved closer to the bed, eyeing him warily. "How about some fruit juice?"

His dark eyes narrowed. "How about telling me how in hell I wound up in bed with you last night?"

Her eyebrows arched. "You were in bed with me?" she asked with pretended horror. "How scandalous!"

His lips made a thin line. "Don't be cute," he ground out. "And it wasn't scandalous. Nothing happened!"

She lifted her chin. "A likely story," she said.

He sat up, disrupting the sheet, but her eyes stayed on his face so that she didn't see what it revealed. "Nothing happened," he enunciated. "I don't ravish women in their sleep."

"Ah, but you don't know what I might have done to you," she said, lifting her eyebrows mockingly.

The glare got worse. "Cute. Real cute."

"Anyway, you rejected me," she reminded him. "You cut and ran before I woke up. But not," she added with a slow smile, "in time to fool Mary, who saw the imprint of your head on the other pillow and asked how it got there."

His eyes widened. "What did you tell her?"

"Oh, nothing at all," she assured him. "I told her I didn't have the slightest idea how you'd gotten in my bed."

"Oh, my God." He put his face in his hands.

"It's all right, she understands perfectly that these things happen. She didn't say a word; she just grinned."

"Oh, my God," he repeated.

"And she promised she wouldn't tell anyone except family and close friends and any acquaintances that happen past the mailbox."

"Oh, my God!"

"Now, now, you don't have to get upset, this is the twentieth century, after all —"

"This is rural Montana," he said, half shouting. His eyes blazed at her. "You little fool! Your reputation will be in shreds!"

"People in Chicago don't notice things like that," she reminded him. "And Gerald and I are going back next week, you know. Your reputation will have hardly a blemish. In fact, it might even make you more desirable to some of the local belles if it gets around that you're the same devil-may-care rake you used to be."

He narrowed one eye. "How do you know what I used to be like?"

"I asked Gerald, of course. He said you used to score with every woman you dated —"

"Nicky!"

"Well, not in exactly those words, of course," she amended at his shocked expression.

"Have you lost your sweet mind?" he demanded. "What were you trying to do?"

"Get you comfortable and warm," she said with a smile. "You were groaning and I knew your leg was hurting you. Since you seemed determined to sit up with me, I thought you should be comfortable. So I led you into bed, and you went with me just like a lamb."

"Which wasn't what I felt like when I woke up," he replied curtly. "Your gown was up around your hips and half off your shoulder, and men have it rough early in the morning anyway. Oh, honey, you had a close call you didn't even know about!"

"I did?" Her eyes were wide, trusting and innocent. He sighed impatiently.

"Never mind. What did you really tell Mary?"

"The truth. She grinned and mumbled something about a new weapon."

"It will backfire." He bit his lip suddenly and grimaced. His hand went to his knee, where she noticed a poultice tied with white gauze.

"Will that help?" she asked.

"Mary says so. She usually knows. Even the local doctors have a measure of respect for her way with herbs. In the old days, the Indians had to have a healthy knowledge of it, since they didn't have a neighborhood clinic."

"Mary's told me a lot about Montana and the way it used to be," she said. "It's a fascinating country. Big and sprawling and special."

"That's why I stay here," he said. He leaned back against the pillows, studying her face. "I have no desire to go back to the life I used to lead."

"Well, that's one thing we can both agree on," she said quietly. "Neither do I."

His chiseled lips pursed thoughtfully. "Are you really worth three million?"

She nodded. "If I sign the necessary papers. But I don't want three million dollars. If I refuse that trust, do you know what the money will be used for?"

"No."

He seemed honestly curious, so she told him. "It will fund a research program to find new ways of treating cancer in children."

"Three million would go a long way," he said.

"Yes, wouldn't it?" She smiled. "And since I've gotten used to working for the Christopher Corporation, and nobody's fired me yet, I expect I can support myself without that trust."

He stretched lazily, watching her eyes drop to his chest with the movement and follow the sensuous tautening of muscle under thick hair. He liked the way it felt to let her look at him like this.

"You're a surprising girl, Nicole," he said, his voice dropping an octave, deep and sexy.

"Am I? I thought I was a gold digging

adventuress."

"That sounds bitter," he mused.

She shifted from one foot to the other and stared down at the thick beige carpet. "It felt bitter, too. You never believed a word my father said, really, but it gave you the excuse you needed to draw back before things got complicated." She looked up, catching the surprise in his dark eyes even as it registered that she'd hit on the truth.

"I told you at the beginning that I didn't want commitment," he reminded her sulkily.

"I don't remember asking for any," she replied.

"You said you loved me." His dark eyes slid down her body. "Several times."

"You'd just saved my life." She steeled herself not to let him see how vulnerable she was. She'd thrown herself at him for the last time. He didn't want to make a life with her, and there was only one other thing he might offer. She couldn't accept that kind of relationship, so what was left?

His face didn't reveal a single emotion. "And it was only gratitude?"

"Gratitude, and a natural response to a very experienced man. Which you are," she said, watching his eyes narrow. "I must have been a real pushover."

"You're twisting it." His voice was deep, but a little more curt now. "What I saw in your eyes wasn't completely physical."

"I'm young, as you keep reminding me," she shot back.

"Yes." His gaze swept over her face, memorizing lines and curves and expressions. "Eleven years my junior. Almost another generation, especially in sensual ways."

"You don't have to remind me about how experienced you are."

"In my day, I was," he agreed. He propped himself against the pillows, righting the sheet with a careless hand. "But in recent years, I've given up jet-setting around the world. I've changed my values, Nicole."

"Through choice?" she asked gently. "Or just because you were unsure of being accepted with your battle scars?"

"Honey, you believe in cutting to the bone, don't you?" he asked with a half-angry laugh.

"You aren't the kind of man to be spoon-fed things, are you?" she returned gently.

"No." He drew up his left leg and studied her quietly. "Why did you think I'd order you off the place if I knew your real name?"

"You'd already said you hated rich people, and Gerald said you had no use whatsoever for jet-setters. I guessed that if you knew I was in that class, it would make you hate me," she said simply.

"You might have given me the benefit of the doubt."

She managed a smile. "I didn't have enough self-confidence for that. As it was, you were only tolerating me."

"I thought you and Gerald had something going," he said. He studied the coverlet. "I love Gerald. I couldn't take away something he wanted as badly as he seemed to want you."

"And all along, he was in love with Sadie. I've never had ulterior motives," she added, wanting to make him understand. "I don't want a rich man, Winthrop. I have a job I enjoy, I can make my own way in life. I was never looking for a . . . a meal ticket."

"I didn't know that. All I had left were my instincts, and they'd already let me down once. I haven't trusted a woman since this happened." He touched his knee.

"Were you ever in love before her?" she asked hesitantly, because it was suddenly important that she know that.

He met her searching gaze. "Love is an illusion. I don't believe in it. I never did. I wanted Deanne until she was an obsession with me. I got drunk on her. When she walked out, I thought I was going to bleed to death, and for two years I felt like a zombie. Is that love? I don't know. It's the most intense thing I'd ever felt, so maybe it was. But I'm over her now and I have no inclination whatsoever to go through it again."

He'd probably never spoken so candidly about his feelings before, and she was flattered that he'd trusted her even that far. She sat down slowly on the bed beside him, her soft weight moving the mattress.

"Love shouldn't be all physical," she told him, her voice as gentle as the fingertips that went hesitantly to his firm mouth and touched it. "It should be a sharing between two people. A bonding of thoughts and hopes and dreams. A linking of intangible things. Companionship. Friendship. Openness and honesty."

"You lied to me," he said curtly. His fingers caught her wrist.

"What do you care?" she asked. "You don't believe in love, and you don't really want it anyway. You're safe from ever being hurt again. Nobody can reach you. If you stay up here another ten years, you'll be a walking dead man!"

"At your age, what do you know about love?" he demanded. "You said you loved me, but we both know all you feel is pity. I've been hurt and I'm scarred, so you see me as a charity case!"

Her eyebrows went up. "You?"

The one word was more expressive than any argument she could have made. He glared at her and let go of her wrist. "You feel sorry for me," he continued doggedly.

"I feel sorry for anybody who gets close to you all right," she mumbled. "You aren't my idea of the perfect lover."

"How would you know, when you've never had one?"

"You said my innocence was all an act —"

"Oh, for God's sake, I was mad as hell, I'd have said anything! I didn't mean it. I know lack of experience when it stares me in the face. You blushed that night in the kitchen when I looked at you."

"I wish you'd stop bringing that up. I was . . . overwrought," she concluded helplessly.

"You got too damned close," he said suddenly, every last bit of caution gone. His eyes glittered dangerously. "You got under my skin. What did you expect me to do — lie back and enjoy it? I won't be owned by some little city girl with a rich daddy!"

"Now just hold on one minute," she said slowly. "What do you mean 'with a rich daddy'?"

"Your father mentioned that if I wanted to marry you, he'd give us a racehorse for a wedding present, and an interest in the farm to boot."

She was horrified. Absolutely horrified. In his usual bulldozing way, her father was trying to help. This scheme sounded like his idea of building a fire under the man he thought Nicky wanted.

Somehow she got to her feet, her heart slamming in her throat. "How nice of him," she said huskily.

"He needs looking after," he replied. "He shouldn't be let out alone. And you're not much better. Neither of you do things the right way."

"Which is?" she taunted.

"Straightforward. Don't you know how to get what you want in life?"

"Your way would probably be to reach out and grab it," she muttered.

"You're catching on, sugarplum."

Before she could react, he had her by the wrist again. He levered her down onto the bed, on her back, and loomed over her with a purely arrogant look in his dark eyes.

"I don't want to be another one of your conquests," she told him, struggling.

"Sure you do. If you keep thrashing around like that, you're going to dislodge my sheet and the mystery of life will be over!"

She stopped immediately, glaring at him with wide green eyes as she tried to catch her breath. Smiling down at her, all unshaven and with his hair down over his forehead, he looked sensuous and a little dangerous.

"You don't want commitment, remember?" she reminded him bitterly.

"I don't have to propose marriage to kiss you," he returned, bending.

"I have a cold — I'm contagious!" she squeaked.

"I have a sore leg, and that's not catching. But desire is," he whispered against her lips. "Shall I show you how easy it is to catch?"

"It isn't fair," she wailed.

"Probably not. But it's sweet, all the same." He nuzzled her face with his, in soft, gentle caresses that wore her down all too easily. "You smell of gardenias, Nicky. You smell sweet all over. Here," he breathed, taking her hand in his to press it against his hard, warm chest. "Touch me."

Her hand faltered shyly, but he guided it over the hard muscles, letting her feel the silky hair that covered him, the ripple of muscle under rough skin. "You feel furry," she whispered.

"And you feel like satin." He traced her cheek with his fingers as he kissed her very lightly, and his hand slowly lowered to the buttons of her bodice under the robe.

"No," she protested.

"Go ahead, fight for your honor," he chided. "And I'll wear you down anyway. It's only going to be a token resistance. You want to be touched as much as I want to touch you. So just give in, Nicky, and enjoy it."

"You conceited ape!"

"Enjoy it," he whispered. His fingers moved to the edge of her breast, tracing around it with maddening expertise, making her moan and stiffen suddenly in an explosion of unexpected pleasure.

"Winthrop!" she gasped.

"It isn't new," he whispered, drawing his mouth slowly over hers. "We did this in the kitchen that night . . . you let me touch you then, too. You let me kiss you."

"You shouldn't," she whispered shakily.

"You belong to me," he said simply as he began to unfasten buttons. "I have every right in the world."

"You don't," she tried to protest, but his hand was inside the gown now, his lean, cool fingers against virgin flesh, teasing, tracing, until she arched up and trembled.

"Mine," he breathed against her mouth. Her movements were exciting him, her little cries caught in his lips, making him hungry. "All of you. Here and here . . . sweet young body, ripe for my hands. I could make a meal of you, Nicky."

He had her gown around her waist, and she couldn't even protest. Her eyes closed, tears falling down her cheeks while he looked, touched, delicately tasted her pretty, firm breasts. She let him, and his whirling mind registered her complete abandonment to his ardor. She wasn't resisting him anymore — verbally or physically. He could do anything now and she'd let him.

And that realization was what slowed him down. He lifted his head quietly, looking at the helpless reaction of her body to his lovemaking. She was beautiful, he thought, and he stared at her with something akin to reverence in his dark, tender gaze.

His fingers traced around an erect nipple, gently loving. "I've never seen anything so perfect, Nicky," he whispered. "It's like touching satin."

Her eyes opened. She was embarrassed, and her face felt hot as she met his gaze. "I'm afraid," she whispered.

"There's no reason to be frightened. I'm not going to ravish you." He drew the backs of his fingers against her, loving the way she tensed with pleasure. "But I could, couldn't I? You want me pretty badly right now."

"Obsessively," she confessed. Her voice shook a little. "Do you enjoy humiliating me?"

"Is that what you think I'm doing? Think again." He lifted his hand, and she saw its faint tremble. "That isn't faked, Nicky," he added solemnly. "I go just as high as you do when we make love. It's mutual, this chemistry. It has been from the very beginning."

"I won't have an affair with you," she said quietly.

"I wouldn't let you," he returned. He nuzzled her nose with his. "On the other hand, I don't want marriage."

"I'll have to leave," she whispered, feeling her heart break.

"Inevitably," he agreed. He looked down at her as his fingers drew tenderly over her bare breasts and she trembled. "It knocks the very breath out of me to touch you this way," he breathed.

"You aren't the only one," she said shakily.

He bent and put his mouth gently on the soft curve, and then he drew back, while it was still just a whisper of sensation. "You'd better sit up and pull up your gown, honey.

Someone's coming up the steps very loudly."

His words registered, but she felt as if she was caught in a dream. In the end, he helped her up, buttoned her gown and belted her robe with exaggerated indulgence. He'd only just finished when Mary ambled into the room with two mugs of steaming black coffee.

"Still here?" She clicked her tongue at Nicky. "You should be in bed. You will never mend this way."

"We were talking," Winthrop said. "Don't run her off just yet. I'm not through."

"Yes, you are," Mary said with unexpected stubbornness. "Must get her well, first, and you back on that leg. Then you can talk. Up!"

Nicky managed a rueful smile at Winthrop, feeling disappointed and a little shy. His expression, on the other hand, gave nothing away. He didn't protest, so she went with Mary, too subdued to even notice the twinkle in the older woman's eyes.

But Nicky didn't go back to Winthrop's room again, and he didn't ask for her. It was a kind of world-weary truce, but without any fraternizing. She didn't even see him, but Mary said that he was almost on his feet again. That was good news.

Meanwhile, Mike brought Sadie and Mrs. Todd down the mountain for the duration, so at least Nicky had someone to talk to. That is, she had Mrs. Todd to visit with, not Sadie, who was taking a delicious pleasure in nursing her Gerald back to health.

The little group got along very well. That was unexpected and enlightening, because Nicky had thought they wouldn't fare that well. Even Carol found things to talk to Mrs. Todd about. And Dominic White discovered that his lady love had a compassionate side to counterbalance her mercenary tendencies. He didn't seem to want to cut at Nicky anymore, although he did keep mentioning fairs and cotton candy. . . .

Nicky was back taking dictation when Gerald felt up to it, in between wondering why Winthrop hadn't come near her and how she was going to bear to leave him when she and Gerald had to go home to Chicago. Even living in the same house separated from Winthrop was agony. How was it going to feel when she was hundreds of miles away, separated for life?

CHAPTER NINE

It was Saturday, and the hunters were packing to go home. A chinook had blown in Friday to take away the snow, unlocking the grip the storm had on the ranch, leaving the roads passable if slushy.

"Well, it's just been great," Carol sighed as she left. "I can't think when I've enjoyed anything as much. Especially your movies," she added, smiling demurely at Winthrop in the hall.

"You'll have to get Dominic to bring you again," he returned with a smile.

"I might be persuaded," Dominic said. He put an arm around Carol. "This one might be worth keeping."

"Well, she's certainly pretty enough," Nicky volunteered. "And I like her, if that carries any weight."

Carol's eyes brightened. Impulsively, she hugged Nicky. "We won't tell anyone that I'm only five years older than you are. We'll

231

just let people gape when you call me Mom, okay?" she laughed.

"Okay," Nicky said gently. She winked at the redhead.

"By the way," Dominic hesitated, luggage in hand, "I, uh, put my foot in it again, Nicky."

She knew what he was going to say, about trying to buy Winthrop. He was a rascal, but he was still her father. She liked him sometimes, warts and all.

She hugged him briefly. "I've fouled things up all by myself, thanks. You just added your two cents' worth. I like you anyway."

Dominic looked uncomfortably emotional for a minute before he pulled himself together. "Come see an old man once in a while," he managed finally.

"I don't know any old men, but I guess I could come see you. If I get to help Eddie with the horses," she added. "It's been a while since I've ridden."

"We can remedy that. Don't wait too long. See you, Nicky."

"See you, Dad."

They went out, followed by the Harris brothers who were mumbling their own thanks and goodbyes. Nicky found herself alone with Winthrop, who towered over her in jeans and that huge sheepskin jacket he liked to wear with his creamy Stetson.

"You seem to have arrived at a truce with your father," he mused.

"I misunderstood a lot of things. Grief plays havoc with the brain," she said quietly. "I loved my mother very much."

"So did he, unless I miss my guess." He touched her short hair, the simple gesture sending thrills down her spine. "Was she like you, to look at?"

"Oh, no. She was beautiful," she recalled gently. "Long black hair and pale blue eyes — Irish. She even had the lilting speech. She was a lady, in every sense of the word. I adored her."

"And what does that make you — the ugly duckling?" he chided. He tilted her chin up, searching her suddenly flushed face. "Nice eyes. Big and soft. Pretty little mouth. High cheekbones. Soft skin. You'll do, sugarplum, even without long hair. But let it grow anyway. I like long hair."

He turned her loose then and started out the door, still limping a little.

"Your knee . . . is it better?" she asked hesitantly.

He half turned toward her, his dark eyes alive and quiet. "It's no worse, at least. Why? Were you thinking of offering me a massage?"

"I don't go around playing with men's legs."

"Oh, you're one of those kind of women, are you?" he taunted. "Marriage or nothing?"

"I don't want to marry you. I'm sorry if that breaks your heart."

He smiled slowly, the sight of it almost knocking the breath out of her. Heavens, he was handsome! Bigger than the whole outdoors, sexy, sensuous . . .

"Tease," he accused.

"You're the one making references to playing with men's legs. Which I don't do."

He grinned at her high color. "I know a lot of things you didn't do until I came along," he mused, and his eyes went straight to her yellow sweater.

"Aren't your guests going to miss the plane?" she asked in a high-pitched parody of her normal voice.

"That's their problem, not mine."

"You're driving them, aren't you?"

The roar of the Jeep interrupted her.

"No," he answered as it sped away. "Mike's driving them. Gerald wants you in the office, by the way. He's got a hundred letters to get out yesterday."

"Thanks a lot," she muttered darkly.

"Better toe the line, honey, or you could

get fired. Since you're throwing away money hand over fist lately, you do need the work now, don't you?" he asked, playfully looking down his arrogant nose at her.

It had only just occurred to her that he was teasing. It was new, like that look on his dark face, that twinkle in his eyes. Her heart skipped a few beats and she turned her head, a little unsure of this new Winthrop.

"Yes, I guess I do," she admitted. But the words didn't match what her soft, searching eyes were telling him. Not at all.

He tilted her chin up with a lean, strong hand and looked down at her. "I'm going out to check on my purebred herd," he murmured. "I'd take you with me, but you're a distraction, Kentucky girl."

Her pulse jumped again. "I thought . . . you said . . . you didn't want me around," she managed breathlessly.

"Did I say that?" he asked, lifting his eyebrows. "My goodness, it must have been the painkillers."

"Listen here, Winthrop —"

"Say it like that again," he whispered at her lips, taunting them from a fraction of an inch away, so close that she could almost taste him.

"What?"

"Whisper my name like that again," he

repeated, and his nose brushed lazily against the tip of hers.

"Win . . . Winthrop," she obliged.

"Mmm," he murmured. His lips nuzzled hers, tempting them, urging her closer to him in the dim light of the hall. "Come up here. . . ."

He actually lifted her off the floor with two steely hands at her waist. "That's better," he whispered. "Now open that pretty mouth and kiss me properly."

He had the most incredible way of getting to her. She was lost and witless, drugged on his nearness. She gave him her mouth, parted her lips, and moaned when he deepened the kiss hungrily and his arms swallowed her up against him.

Time got lost somewhere in the middle of that long, sweet kiss. A dog barked, and pans banged in the kitchen. A door opened and closed. Winthrop finally lifted his head, his breath coming hard and quick on her faintly bruised lips.

"Do you like it that way?" he whispered roughly. "Or do you want me to be gentle with you?"

She buried her face under his chin, trembling with reaction. "I like it . . . any way at all, with you," she whispered, clinging to him.

"Same here." He let her slide down his powerful body to the floor, savoring the feel of her against him. Her eyes were wide and soft and drowsy, and he couldn't help bending to brush her mouth once more with his. "Don't overdo it. You're not quite fit yet."

"Look who's talking."

"And no sass." He tapped her on the cheek. "See you."

He was gone, then, and she watched him until he was out of sight.

In between long talks with Sadie, Gerald managed to give a little dictation. Mrs. Todd had decided at long last to go and visit her sister in Florida, and it didn't really come as a surprise when Gerald announced a little hesitantly that he'd asked Sadie to marry him.

"It's about time," Nicky said, beaming. "Congratulations!"

"I can hardly believe it after all this time," Sadie sighed, leaning her head against Gerald's shoulder. "But I've never been happier."

"Neither have I. And I'm sure your mother's going to love Florida. The climate will be good for her. We can visit her every other week if you like."

"Well, maybe once a month anyway," Sadie compromised, her eyes bright with love and happiness.

Nicky had to look away. There wouldn't be any such happiness for her. She'd go back to Chicago and take up her job, and try to forget Winthrop. That wasn't much of a future. She wondered how she was going to manage without him. He might enjoy teasing her and kissing her, but he'd said too often that marriage wasn't for him.

"You look glum, Nicky. What's wrong?" Gerald asked.

She forced herself to smile. "Nothing at all. I'll get my pad and take down some of that correspondence you're so anxious to get rid of."

"Good girl." He smiled down at Sadie. "I think life is going to be a lot easier to cope with from now on."

For him, at least, Nicky agreed. Not for her.

She couldn't quite handle sitting at the supper table without the buffer of guests to protect her from Winthrop's dark, searching gaze. So she offered to have hers upstairs with Mrs. Todd. Mary gave her a hard look, but she fixed two trays and helped Nicky carry them upstairs.

"It is not like you to run away," Mary said stoically at the door to the guest room Sadie and Mrs. Todd were sharing.

"I'm very good at it, actually," Nicky replied. "Especially when I'm outgunned."

"The biggest fish are the hardest to land."

Nicky shrugged. "Sometimes they're the boniest, too."

Mary grinned. "Good bones, though." She opened the door. "Nicky is having supper with you," she told Mrs. Todd. "Thought you might enjoy some company."

"Why, Nicky, how thoughtful," Mrs. Todd said with a smile. "I'll enjoy that."

"Mary even fixed you a pudding," Nicky said, nodding toward the creamy vanilla treat.

"My favorite. How kind, Mary."

"No trouble," the older woman said. "I like them, too. Hearty appetite."

Mary left them, and Nicky arranged Mrs. Todd's tray and silverware before she sat down to eat her own food. It tasted like cardboard, but she forced herself not to pick at it. She'd have to get used to not seeing Winthrop across the table from her. Now was a good time to start.

"My sister is looking forward to having me stay with her," Mrs. Todd said. "She's been alone for five years now, since her husband died. She lives in one of those retirement communities, and she says there are lots of things to see and do. Best of all," she sighed, "the weather is warm and sunny. This chill goes right through me. I haven't been comfortable with the cold weather, but I didn't have the heart to tell Sadie. She was so happy, especially when Gerald came here on his holiday."

"He really came to see Sadie, I think," Nicky laughed. "And I'm glad it all worked out so nicely."

"So am I. Sadie will take care of him, and he of her." Mrs. Todd's gaze searched Nicky's face curiously. "Why are you hiding up here?"

Nicky jumped. "Hiding?"

"Hiding. You can't tell me it's my company you want. Are you and Winthrop trading blows again?"

Nicky shifted restlessly, crossing her jean-clad legs. "We just agree to disagree, that's all."

"He's a stubborn man. You'll have to be patient if you want him."

"I don't want him!"

"Don't be silly, of course you do," Mrs. Todd said nonchalantly. She finished the last of her pudding. "When it comes time, he won't let you leave. Mark my words, he knows a good thing when he sees it."

"Think so?" Nicky wanted to believe the old woman's words, but she knew Winthrop

too well. He didn't want a long-term relationship. In fact, he'd probably be happy to
wave her goodbye. The thought depressed
her even more.

The last thing she expected was to find
Winthrop at the door when it opened suddenly. She'd thought it was Mary and
hadn't looked up until she heard his voice.

"There you are," he said pleasantly. "I
wondered where you'd gotten to. How're
you doing, Mrs. Todd?"

"Very well, Winthrop, thanks to you," the
older woman beamed. "It's been like old
times visiting here."

"I'm glad you're enjoying it. I thought I'd
walk Nicky down to the barn and let her
look at my colt. She helped deliver him, you
know."

"I didn't! Nicky, that's quite a feat for a
city girl."

"But she isn't," Winthrop said proudly,
watching her. "She's a country girl.
Kentucky-born and reared. Her people were
horse fanciers."

"How interesting."

"How is the colt?" Nicky asked, keeping
her voice steady when her heart was racing
wildly in her chest.

"Growing like a weed. Come on and I'll
show you. Good night, Mrs. Todd. Mary

will be up soon to check on you."

"Thank you, Winthrop. Good night, Nicky, and thanks for keeping me company."

"It was my pleasure," Nicky assured her, bending to kiss the wrinkled cheek. "Night."

She followed Winthrop out the door with faint hesitation. He seemed friendly enough, but she sensed something beneath the outward calm. Something disturbing. Exciting.

"Isn't it late to be looking at horses?" she asked as they walked down the staircase.

He glanced down at her. "Why? Are you afraid to be alone with me after dark?" he asked.

She hated that arrogant look. "Of course not!"

"Then why ask the question?"

"I thought you might have better things to do."

"I could do some bookwork, I guess." He glanced at her. "Or watch the VCR —"

"I'd just *love* to see the colt!" she interrupted.

He chuckled softly. "I thought you would."

He led her down the side hall and helped her into her coat and stocking cap. "It's still cold, although the snow has stopped."

She couldn't imagine why he wanted her

company, but she was touched beyond reason that he did. It felt so good to be with him, alone with him under the wide sky, crunching through the snow toward the barn.

"Did Dad look at the colt while he was here?" she asked.

"He sure did. He thinks I've got a young champion on my hands. He said that if I wanted him to, he'd train him for me."

"That's not a rash offer," she said. "He's good with horses, and he's never backed a loser yet."

"So I hear." He took her arm and turned her at the barn door. "Turning down three million dollars is crazy. You could accept the trust and still give a million to research."

"I don't want to be rich," she said simply. "I tried it, and I didn't like it. My values got fouled up. I like them the way they are."

He sighed. "I can understand that. It just seems a waste. You could do a lot with that kind of money."

"You can only wear so many diamonds at a time, and fur makes me sneeze," she said with a straight face.

"You'll be working for the rest of your life, damn it. What if Gerald ever fires you? What will happen to you?"

The prospect really seemed to bother him.

She searched his dark eyes, shadowed by the wide brim of his hat. "I might get married someday," she said. "I like children. I'd like to have a family."

He touched her arm lightly, smoothing her coat sleeve. "Yes. I'd like that, too, one day. Kids are nice."

"How many do you plan to adopt?" she asked.

His eyebrows arched. "Adopt?"

"You said marriage wasn't in your vocabulary," she reminded him. "So if you want children, you'll have to adopt them."

He moved restlessly. "A wife would be an encumbrance."

"So would children."

"It's not the same thing."

"It is."

He glared at her. "I won't marry you, honey, if that's what you're hinting at."

She glared back. "Who asked you? I don't want a walking icicle."

"I'm anything but an icicle in bed," he told her.

"Talk is cheap!"

"Not half as cheap as that statement," he returned. He scowled down at her. "How in God's name did we get on this subject?"

"You said you wanted children —"

"Well, I don't. Not anymore." He started

walking again. He glared at the barn door as he opened it. "Women! They twist everything around to suit themselves."

"So do men."

He stood aside to let her enter the barn. "Marriage was invented by women to legalize sex."

"Don't look at me," she said airily. "I don't want to marry anyone. I'm just twenty-two. I have years and years of living to do before I tie myself to a man's housework."

"Time passes quick. Before you know it you'll be my age."

"God forbid," she glared up at him. "I'm not ready for the Home."

"Stop that," he grumbled. "I'm not old."

"Neither is the Statue of Liberty," she said with a sweet smile. "Where's the colt?"

"Over there."

She followed his irritated gesture and leaned over the gate, watching the little chestnut colt nuzzle at his mother's belly.

"Aw," she cooed. "Isn't he cute?"

"I'm not old," he repeated, still nettled by her offhand remark.

She looked up at him carelessly. "All right. You're not old. Isn't he cute?"

"Thirty-four is a man's prime."

"If you say so."

"It is, damn it!"

"Was I arguing?" she asked innocently.

He pushed back his hat with an irritable sigh. "Gerald says you and he are going back Monday to get the office shipshape so he and Sadie can get married Friday and have an extended honeymoon."

"That's nice," she said absently. She hadn't known, but it was good to have it out in the open. Two more days to be with Winthrop. It would be heaven and hell.

"You won't lose your pay. He's going to let you handle his office while he's gone."

"That's nice, too."

"Don't you know any other words?" He glowered down at her. "Look here, Nicole, we won't see each other again."

"Yes, I know." She looked up at him quietly. "That should please you. It must be hell, having a lovesick woman making calves' eyes at you all the time."

He shifted restlessly. "I've gotten used to having you around," he said reluctantly, but he wouldn't look at her.

Like an old shoe, she thought miserably. She watched the colt in silence for a few moments, then said, "I imagine you'll get used to not having me around just as easily."

"I guess so."

She peeked up at him. His face was hard and cold, but his eyes were glittering faintly as he looked down at her.

"I'll always limp," he said unexpectedly. "Gerald says I can work the kinks out, but the doctors don't agree. There's always going to be a degree of impairment."

"That's too bad," she said.

"Is that all you can say?" he growled.

Her eyebrows arched. "What would you like? Shall I sit down on the ground and start crying?"

"I'm a cripple!"

"Sure." She stared back at the colt. "You and the Marine Corps."

"Nicky . . ."

"If you want to limp, go ahead. I don't care."

"You aren't listening."

"Of course I'm listening. You're telling me what a bad risk you are, and I'm agreeing with you. You've been right all along, Winthrop. I need a younger man who doesn't limp, who wants marriage and children. You're absolutely right, so now I'm going to go back to Chicago to find one." She looked at the growing anger in his hard face. "That should satisfy you."

"Would you like to know what would satisfy me right now?" he asked under his breath.

"Not really. I'm tired and I'd like to go to bed."

"At last, we agree on something." He moved toward her.

"Oh, no, you don't. I'm saving myself for my future husband."

"Thank you."

"It won't be you," she told him doggedly. "I'm not crazy enough to think that. You aren't a marrying man, remember? You don't want commitment."

"I don't know what I want anymore," he muttered.

"Well, I do," she said. "I want to go home."

"To a lonely apartment in Chicago?"

"It won't be lonely long," she assured him. "I'm going to start my very own lonely hearts chapter."

"Over my dead body."

"Nobody would want to meet over your old dead body."

"Nicky . . ."

She got as far as the barn door and opened it to freedom. "You only want my body," she burst out. "And that's not enough!"

"Will you listen to me?!"

"No!"

She turned and ran for the house, easily outdistancing him. She passed Gerald and

Sadie on the steps, shot up the staircase into her room and locked the door. So much for trying to reason with Winthrop. All he wanted to do was back her into a corner and seduce her. Well, he wasn't getting another chance to do that! She'd just avoid him until she could leave. Better to walk away with a broken heart than a broken spirit as well. She loved him, but she couldn't settle for a one-night stand. Not even with the only man she'd ever wanted.

She tossed and turned all night, thinking about the ironies of her life. Even if nothing else had come out of this trip, at least she'd made peace with her father. But she wished that Winthrop could have returned just a little of the feeling she had for him. Her heart was going to break in two when she walked out that door Monday morning. And Winthrop wouldn't even miss her. On that thought, she cried herself to sleep.

Chapter Ten

It was as if Nicky's impulsive action had brought a wall down between herself and Winthrop. He wasn't around the next morning when Gerald and Sadie and Nicky got into the Lincoln to go to church in Butte. He wasn't around when they got back, either, and Gerald remarked on it, because Winthrop almost always went to church.

The day wore on, and Nicky got her things packed since they were leaving early the next morning. The corporation jet was scheduled to pick them up about eight.

Gerald spent all his free time with Sadie, finalizing their wedding plans. A special plane was taking Mrs. Todd to Florida that afternoon, so that she could make the flight in luxurious comfort. Gerald had arranged everything, and Mrs. Todd was enthusing about her future son-in-law to anyone who had time to listen.

Since there was a chance that Winthrop

might show up, Nicky stayed behind when Gerald and Sadie drove Mrs. Todd to the airport. But Winthrop was still missing.

"Gone hunting, he said," Mary told her with a curious glance. "Funny thing, to see him hunt on Sunday when he curses if others do same."

"He's avoiding me," Nicky murmured.

"Thought as much. What did you do?"

"He was telling me all the reasons I ought not to get involved with him and I agreed, that's all," Nicky sighed.

Mary grinned from ear to ear. "Just like man, to state truth and then get mad when others agree."

"I suppose he'll never speak to me again." Nicky was remembering their talk. Perhaps he'd been trying to say something and she hadn't given him the chance. Either way, she'd never know now. She was going home and he wouldn't follow. Most likely, he'd be glad to be rid of her.

"Winthrop is deep," Mary said unexpectedly. "Hard man to predict." She glanced at Nicky. "But be sure that he thinks before he acts. Weighs the odds. He is surefooted."

"I used to think I was, too," Nicky said. "But I'm not anymore."

"Give it time."

"Now that," she replied, "I have plenty of.

251

What's for supper?"

"Something different," Mary told her secretively. "Old family recipe. You'll like it."

"But what is it?"

Mary leaned forward. "Moussaka."

"You're putting me on," Nicky laughed.

"Had Greek uncle. Taught me to make it, eggplant and all. Nice change of pace."

"I'll bet!"

"Here." She handed over the utensils. "Set the table. No doubt Gerald and Sadie will be late. They have much to discuss."

"They'll make a happy couple."

"Yes."

Since there was no more reply than that, Nicky went about her business and began to set the table in the dining room. And all the while she wondered where Winthrop had gone and why he hadn't come home. She had so little time left here. It was going to be agonizing to go off and leave him, and here he was wasting precious minutes they might have spent together. But why should he care, she reminded herself. He didn't trust her. He might want her, but he didn't love her. He'd said himself that love was an illusion. Besides that, he didn't ever want to marry. So why bother about him?

She finished the place settings and put

napkins all around. At least her nice boss was going to come out ahead, she thought. Gerald would marry Sadie and have a perfectly wonderful life while Nicky grew old taking dictation. It didn't bear thinking about.

Maybe she could do what she'd threatened Winthrop with — get married and have children. Sure. Nothing easier. First, she had to find a man. And who could measure up to old stone face?

Even as she was asking herself the question, the kitchen door opened suddenly and Winthrop came in with something furry by the tail.

Mary stared, but Nicky went forward. "Oh," she exclaimed. "A wounded squirrel! Wait, I'll rush and get a bandage!"

"Oh, for God's sake," Winthrop ground out. He slid the squirrel onto the sink for Mary to deal with and glared at Nicky as he eased out of his sheepskin jacket and hat, dumping them untidily on the floor.

"There ought to be a law against shooting unarmed squirrels," Nicky muttered for something to say.

Winthrop went to the sink to wash his hands, ignoring her.

"Nice squirrel," Mary defended him. "Plump. Make good stew."

"I'll bet he was somebody's daddy," Nicky murmured.

"You're breaking my heart," Winthrop said nonchalantly. He dried his hands on a towel and looked straight at her. "Where's Gerald?"

Her heart was beating double time, but she wasn't about to let him know it. "He and Sadie drove Mrs. Todd to the airport. She left for Florida today."

"I know. I said goodbye before I went out. What's for dinner?" he asked Mary.

"Moussaka."

"That stuff with eggplant?" He made a face. "Whatever happened to beef and potatoes?"

"Need change of pace."

"No, I don't," he argued. "I like having the same thing every day. It gives me a sense of security."

"Then why go out and kill an innocent squirrel when you really wanted a steak?" Nicky asked.

"He wasn't innocent," he replied. "I have it on good authority that he was a rounder with unspeakable taste in women squirrels."

"Well, in that case, let's all eat him," Nicky agreed.

Winthrop actually grinned at her. She had to spoil it all by blushing.

"Sit down. I will bring the dishes," Mary told them.

Winthrop motioned for Nicky to go ahead, and even pulled out her chair for her.

"I'm impressing you with my manners," he informed her.

"Are you really?" She smiled vacantly. "When do you begin?"

"Watch it, Kentucky girl." He sat back in his chair and studied her intently while Mary brought in the main course, followed by rolls, vegetables and fruit.

"We leave tomorrow," she said when they all three were seated and enjoying Mary's exotic dish.

"Yes." He didn't seem disturbed. But when he finished his meal, he lit a cigarette. That was the first time Nicky remembered seeing him with one since her early days at the ranch.

"Bad smell," Mary scowled at him. "Why you do that? Thought you quit."

"I quit several times a month," he reminded her. "I'll start quitting again tomorrow."

Mary shrugged as she got up to fetch the coffee pot for refills. "Your lungs, not mine."

"Thank you so much," he said with a mocking smile.

Mary hit him on her way to the kitchen.

"You sure are cheerful tonight," Nicky remarked. "It wouldn't be because I'm getting out of your hair tomorrow?"

"The thought did cross my mind."

"I'll bet it did."

She sipped her coffee and he stared at her for so long that her heart began to run wild and her breathing became quick and labored. She gripped the cup tighter so that he wouldn't see how badly her hands were trembling.

"You aren't limping," she said suddenly, shocking herself with the flat statement. But he hadn't been. He'd been walking straight and steady.

"I've been practicing," he replied easily. He tapped the ashes into an ashtray. "Nice of you to notice."

"Are you going to cut Mary off by auditioning for the Rockettes yourself?" she asked demurely.

"I'd never pass muster," he replied. "My legs are too hairy."

"Ah, well, another career shot to hell by lack of a straight razor."

"Cute." He chuckled softly.

"Thank you, my mother always said I was."

"How did she die?" he asked unexpectedly, and stared at her until she was forced to answer.

"She fell into the swimming pool and drowned during a party," Nicky told him, and the dark memory was reflected in her eyes. "Nobody even noticed, can you imagine? She fell in front of two dozen people and drowned right there. And nobody noticed."

Something in her expression caught his eye. "And where were you when it happened?"

Her face drew in. "Haven't you guessed?" she asked in a faint whisper and forced a smile. "I was one of the two dozen people who didn't notice. . . ."

He got up without haste, crushing out the cigarette in the ashtray and pulled her up into his arms. "Stupid," he accused, drawing her close to him. "Holding it in like that, never telling anyone."

"I didn't see her," she wept. "Winthrop, I didn't see her. I was dancing with Chase and I never even looked. Not until someone screamed. . . ."

"Your father?"

"He wasn't around. I guess we both had our share of guilt over it, wondering if we could have saved her if we hadn't been so caught up in the glitter." Her hand came up to wipe away a tear. "She was so unhappy.

And so alone."

"We're all alone," he replied quietly. "Some more than others."

She looked up at him, searching his dark eyes. "Do you remember your mother?"

He smiled. "Very well. She and my father were deeply in love. It never faded, all the long years." He touched her face lightly. "I was looking for something similar. I found Deanne instead."

"All women are not like Deanne," she said doggedly.

His thumb rubbed lazily across her lips. "Maybe. Maybe not."

"Cynic," she burst out, exasperated. "You're scared to death to find out."

His eyebrows arched. "I like not having my heart used for target practice. Which reminds me — your father said you were something of a markswoman."

"I used to be," she corrected. His thumb caressing her mouth was disturbing. "I used to ride, too. But I'm out of practice."

"You might come back with Gerald for the wedding," he said abruptly. "I could give you a refresher course."

Her heartbeat increased. But even as she heard him say the words, she knew that the minute she left the ranch, he'd forget her. She'd be out of his thoughts. His offer was just a sugar pill — something to keep her happy until she left. He didn't mean it.

"That would be nice," she said, without any real conviction.

"Nicky . . ."

Whatever he was about to say was lost, because Mary came back in with the coffee pot and didn't lift an eyebrow at the two of them practically standing in each other's arms.

"More coffee?" she offered, and the spell was broken.

Winthrop watched Nicole for the rest of the meal, and then Gerald and Sadie came back, and the conversation centered on the wedding. Bedtime came and there wasn't a single opportunity for any more discussion. Nicky went to bed halfheartedly, more disappointed than she could ever remember being. She loved Winthrop, but he was making it patently obvious that he didn't return that feeling. But, then, what had she expected?

The next morning, before she had time to plan what she was going to say, she and Gerald were in the Jeep with Mike and being driven to the airport. Winthrop was long gone, apparently out hunting again. Nicky didn't even get to say goodbye to him before she flew back toward Chicago.

CHAPTER ELEVEN

Back at work, Nicky found herself haunted by a particularly vivid ghost. Winthrop drifted around in her thoughts constantly so that she couldn't eat or sleep or rest. She didn't understand why he couldn't have managed the time to say goodbye to her. Of course, there was always the possibility that he was simply indifferent.

She was a nervous wreck by the time Thursday rolled around. Gerald was equally anxious, all thumbs as he waited for the driver to take him to the airport. And tomorrow was the wedding at the ranch.

"Why aren't you packed and ready?" Gerald asked suddenly, as if it had only occurred to him that Nicky wasn't coming.

"I'm not going," she said quietly.

"But why not?" he asked, and smiled. "Winthrop invited you, didn't he?"

"I suppose he felt obliged to," Nicky confessed. She sighed heavily. "You see, I

. . . well, I kind of . . . I told him I loved him," she concluded, and went scarlet. She buried her face in her hands while Gerald gaped at her. "Of all the stupid things I ever did, that was by far the stupidest. He told me right up front that he didn't want commitment. I should have listened."

"Oh, Nicky," he murmured. He patted her shoulder awkwardly. "Nicky, I'm so sorry. With all due respect, you could have found a more approachable man. Winthrop has too many scars and he's lived completely alone for so long. . . . I'm just really sorry. If I'd thought anything like this would happen, I'd never have forced you into going to Montana with me."

"It's not your fault," she reminded him. "I didn't have to go." She forced a smile. "But I can't quite manage the wedding. I hope you understand. Having to be around him, and having him know how I feel . . . I just couldn't bear the embarrassment."

"I'll make some kind of excuse for you. Don't worry." He studied her worriedly. "You'll be all right?"

"Sure I will. I thought I might go and spend the weekend with my father. Christmas is coming up in three weeks."

"So it is." He patted her shoulder again. "Can you cope while I'm on honeymoon?"

"You bet, boss," she said brightly.

"Okay. Well . . ." The driver appeared in the door and announced that he was ready when Gerald was.

"Kiss Sadie for me," Nicky said.

"I'll do that with pleasure. You'll have to come over for supper one night when we get back in town."

"That would be nice."

"I'll see you soon, Nicky."

"Yes, sir." She smiled, and waved goodbye to him.

She wanted to go to the wedding. It would have been heaven to stand and look at Winthrop just once more. But she'd do better to get him out of her mind, and going back to the ranch would only open old wounds. She'd had enough torment. And he'd never led her on. He'd told her exactly how he felt, so if her heart was broken she could only blame herself.

She settled back into the office routine the next day, fielding questions and phone calls and correspondence with a flair that would have pleased her absent boss.

She wasn't prepared for the phone to ring and an angry, irritated Winthrop to be on the other end of the line.

"Where in hell are you?" he demanded coldly.

She stared at the phone as if it had grown teeth. "I'm . . . here. Working," she faltered.

"You were invited to the wedding," he reminded her.

"Yes, I know."

"Then why aren't you here?"

She stared at her feet. "I didn't want to come," she said in a ghostly tone.

"I don't bite," he grumbled. "And I hadn't intended to drag you off into the underbrush."

"I know that," she moaned. She bit her lower lip. "I made a fool of myself," she said after a minute, almost choking on the words. "I . . . couldn't face you."

There was a pregnant pause. "Made a fool of yourself? How?"

She twisted the cord around her fingers. "I threw myself at you like a lovesick teenager."

"Was I complaining?" he asked unexpectedly.

"I know how you feel about women."

"Do you?" he asked in bemusement. "I'd planned to take you hunting with me."

Her heart leaped. "Had you?"

"Your father tells me you can handle a .30-.30 with the best of them," he added. "I thought we'd hunt deer."

"I would have liked that."

"It's not too late," he reminded her. "Gerald could send the plane for you."

She closed her eyes and prayed for strength. "I don't think it's a good idea, Winthrop."

"Why not, for God's sake?"

"Because I can't live on dreams," she burst out. "And the sooner I face it, the better off I'll be. I know you mean well, but it . . . it tears the heart out of me, that's all. I won't come."

She hung up quickly, before he could talk her into going to Montana. He was offering her comfort, but he didn't realize the torment it would cause her. Loving him, being near him, and knowing he didn't care for her would have been the last straw.

All the rest of the day she expected him to call back. But he didn't. And she went to Kentucky and spent the weekend with a surprised and very different father. They talked, she and Carol went shopping, and when the time came to go back to Chicago, she was frankly reluctant to go.

"This has been fun," her father remarked, grinning. "We'll have to have a big Christmas this year. I'll get a tree and everything."

"And we'll have a party," Carol added, clinging to his arm with real affection. "Nicky needs to meet some men her own

264

age. I know at least one with a good character I could invite." She glanced at Nicky ruefully. "Notice I didn't say with money — just with character."

"Yes, and I appreciate that," Nicky grinned back. She liked Carol. The more she saw of the redhead, the more depth she found in the other woman.

"Come home for Christmas," her father coaxed. "We'll have a big time."

It would at least keep her mind off Winthrop. "All right," she agreed, smiling. "I'll plan on it. See you in a couple of weeks, then."

"I'll send a plane up to get you," he grinned.

She went back to her apartment feeling vaguely happy. But the bubble burst at work the next morning. Becky was waiting in her office with a cold message from Winthrop.

"The iceman calleth," Becky said, whistling through her teeth. "And was he in a snit! He said to tell you that you can —" She cleared her throat. "Well, that you can sit up here in the city and freeze for all he cares, and that if he never sees you again, it will be too soon." She cocked her head at Nicky. "Does he drink? Because he sounded as if he had a *snootful!*"

That didn't sound like Winthrop. "Are you

sure it was Winthrop?" she asked.

"Boy, am I sure." Becky shook her head. "He even spelled it for me." She smiled with mischief in her eyes. "He got it right on the third try, anyway."

"Oh, my."

"Oh, my, isn't what the switchboard operator had to say. She's thinking of filing charges against him for his use of language." She turned to go back to her own office, still shaking her head. "Poor old guy. What did you do to him, Nicky?"

Nicky wasn't sure. But if he was that angry, she must have gotten under his skin a little. She sat back and waited for new developments.

But when a week went by with no more word from him, she fell into a black depression. Gerald came back to work a new man. The honeymoon in the Bahamas had been ecstatic, and he could hardly keep his feet on the floor while Nicky brought him up to date on what was happening in the office.

"Yes, I can handle all that," he sighed. He watched her closely. "I hear Winthrop called you."

She flushed. "Sort of."

"I hear he was drunk at the time," he added.

"How did you hear that?"

"Mary," he said. "She was snickering so hard that I could barely understand her. She said he went off into the mountains and dared anybody to bother him."

"Will he be all right?" she asked with concern she couldn't help.

"Winthrop?" he asked as if she'd taken leave of her senses.

"Well, he isn't Superman."

"Don't tell him that. He's just taken out another lease on the cape," he murmured.

"If he wants to go off in the mountains in a snit just because I wouldn't come to the wedding, that's his problem," she said shortly. "Anyway, he didn't really want me there."

"That isn't what Mary said."

"What do you want to do about this letter?" she asked, attempting to change the subject.

He started to speak, then changed his mind and settled for work. They fell back into a pleasant routine, and Winthrop wasn't mentioned again. Nicky was sure that he was only angry because she hadn't fallen all over herself getting back to Montana. She didn't dare hope it was because he'd started to care for her.

He didn't call. He didn't write. Christmas Eve came and Nicky gave up hoping that she'd hear from him. She wished her boss a merry Christmas, sent her love to Sadie and went to Lexington for the holidays.

Her father met her at the airport in his Lincoln, with Carol beside him, and took time to have the driver run them through town so that she could see the beautiful Christmas decorations.

"It's just like old times," Nicky sighed. "I always did love the way they decorate the city."

"Me, too. You ought to see the decorations we have at the house," her father said with a twinkle in his eyes.

"And your present," Carol added, also twinkling. "It was really hard to wrap, so I gave up trying and just stuck a bow on it."

Nicole had presents for both of them in her luggage: a pipe for her father and for Carol a bottle of her favorite perfume. But she frowned, wondering what they could have gotten her that made them both look so smug.

She didn't have long to wait. They piled out at the steps and she walked toward the enormous brick house with feverish curiosity. It was decorated with boughs of holly and red velvet ribbon, and she took a minute to tell Carol how pretty it looked.

"Thanks," Carol laughed. "I did it all

myself. With a little help from your dad," she acknowledged with a wink in his direction.

"Your present's in the living room," her father added as he helped Carol out of her mink coat. "We'll go see about some hot cider while you open it."

"Aren't you coming?" she asked.

Her father helped her out of her tweed coat, nodding at the pretty green silk dress that matched her eyes. "You look very nice. No, we're not coming. Not just yet. Go on, now. And Merry Christmas, sweetheart."

He kissed her cheek and then went away, whispering to Carol, who glanced over her shoulder at Nicky and giggled.

Boy, it sure was some strange Christmas, she told herself as she opened the living room door. And then she stopped dead. Because her present wasn't under the huge lighted Christmas tree. It was sitting on the sofa, looking toward her furiously, with a glass of whiskey in one lean hand.

"Merry Christmas," Winthrop said curtly.

Her mouth flew open. He had a bow stuck on the pocket of his gray vested suit, and he looked hung over and pale and a little disheveled. But he was so handsome that her heart skipped wildly, and she looked into his dark eyes with soft dreams in her own.

"You've got a bow on your pocket," she said in a voice that sounded too high-pitched to be her own.

"Of course I've got a bow on my pocket. I'm your damned Christmas present. Didn't you listen to your father?" He got up, setting the glass down with enough force to shake the table, and started toward her, limping just a little. He didn't look like a present, he looked murderous. "I can't eat," he said accusingly. "I can't sleep, I can't work. I spent a week up in the mountains trying to get you out of my head, and all I got was drunk. I'm hung over, bleary-eyed and half mad with wanting you."

"Oh, I'm so glad, Winthrop," she whispered. Her heart went wild. "Because I'm half mad with wanting you, too . . . Oh!"

The tiny cry was lost under his devouring mouth. He had her up in his arms, barely pausing to kick the door shut before he carried her back to the sofa and stretched her out on its velvety length under the formidable weight of his body.

She protested the intimacy of his hold, but he shook his head and took her mouth under his again, glorying in its breathless response.

"No more fighting," he breathed into her

parting lips. "There's no need. You're mine, now. That gives me the right to take any liberties I please with you, and this is only the beginning. You're going to marry me, lady. I've got all the necessary papers. All we need is a blood test, and that's scheduled an hour from now. We're going to have a Christmas wedding."

Tears stung her eyes. She looked up at him through a drowsy haze, her body intimately pressed to his, her eyes wide and soft and loving. "You don't want to get married," she whispered.

"Yes, I do," he corrected her. He looked stern and solemn and very adult. But the look in his eyes was so tender that it knocked the breath out of her. "I just didn't know it until I let you walk out the door. And then I couldn't get you to come back. I thought I didn't care." He bent, brushing her mouth with exquisite gentleness. "But I can't quite make it without you, Nicky," he added huskily. "I've never been so alone. Come home where you belong. I'm too old, and too cynical, and not quite the man I used to be, but I . . ." He took a slow breath. "I love you, little one."

Tears ran down her face. She didn't imagine he'd ever said that in his life, and she felt the faint shudder that ran through his body when she arched hers to search blindly for his mouth.

"I love you, too," she breathed. "Deathlessly. Hopelessly. With all my heart!"

"Yes, I know, you say it quite often," he murmured, nuzzling her nose with his. "After a while, I began to enjoy hearing it. You got under my skin from the very first time I saw you, so busy at your desk. I convinced Gerald that he needed to bring you out with him," he confessed lazily, shocking her. "I didn't realize why, of course, until I had you in my arms. Then it all fell into place, and I did my best to run. But I was caught, even then. God, I've been miserable without you!"

He kissed her hungrily and she felt his hands at her hips, lifting her up into an embrace that made her shudder and gasp and go scarlet.

"This is part of loving," he whispered into her mouth. "Part of marriage. It's beautiful. Don't be afraid of it."

"I'm . . . not." She looked straight into his dark eyes and imagined how beautiful it would be joining with him in loving union, softness to hardness, tender rhythm on cool sheets in the darkness. And she gasped again. "Oh, my," she whispered shakily.

"Oh, my, indeed," he whispered. "Yes,

sweet, just that way. Intimate and ardent . . . your body and mine. For all the long, achingly sweet nights of our lives. I'll be your fulfillment, and you'll be mine. And there'll never be another secret between us."

She cradled his head in her hands and pulled it gently toward her. "I'll give you children."

He smiled softly. "Yes." His head bent. "Merry Christmas, sugarplum."

She smiled back as she gave him her mouth. "You delicious Christmas present, you . . ."

Outside the door, two people with a bottle of champagne and four glasses were congratulating themselves on their little surprise.

"Should we knock?" Carol asked.

Dominic White pursed his lips. "Sounds a little premature." He grinned at the muffled laughter behind the door. He lifted an eyebrow. "Suppose we sample the champagne? Just to make sure it's not corked?"

"A brilliant idea," Carol agreed, linking her hand through his arm.

"I have another. How do you feel about a double wedding?"

Carol reached up and kissed his cheek. "Ecstatic," she sighed. "Can we get a blood test and a license in time?"

"Honey, I ain't a millionaire for nothin'," he drawled.

"As long as you know I'm only marrying you for your money," she reminded him with a mischievous smile.

"Mercenary hussy," he accused. And he grinned. They went into the office and closed the door. And after a minute, laughter was coming from that room, as well. Outside, the first flakes of snow began to fall. A white Christmas was well under way.

■ ■ ■ ■

IF WINTER COMES

■ ■ ■ ■

CHAPTER ONE

It was an election morning in the newsroom, and Carla Maxwell felt the excitement running through her slender body like a stab of lightning. The city hall beat which she shared with Bill Peck was a dream of a job. Something was always happening — like this special election to fill a vacant seat created by a commissioner's resignation. There were only five men on the city commission, and this was the Public Works seat. Besides that, the two men running for it were, respectively, a good friend and a deadly foe of the present mayor, Bryan Moreland.

"How does it look?" Carla called to Peck, who was impatiently running a hand through his gray-streaked blond hair as he hung onto a telephone receiver waiting for the results from the city's largest precinct.

"Neck and neck, to use a trite expression." He grinned at her. He had a nice face, she thought. Lean and smooth and kind. Not at all the usual expressionless mask worn by most veteran newsmen.

She smiled back, and her dark green eyes caught the light and seemed to glow under the fluorescent lights.

"What precinct are you waiting for?" Beverly Miller, the Society Editor, asked, pausing by Peck's desk.

"Ward four," he told her. "It looks like . . . hello? Yes, go ahead." He scribbled feverishly on his pad, thanked his caller and hung up. He shook his head. "Tom Green took the fourth by a small avalanche," he said, leaning back in his chair. "Now there's a surprise for you. A political novice winning a city election in a three-man field with no runoff."

"I'll bet Moreland's tickled to death," Carla said dryly. "Green's been at his throat ever since he took office almost four years ago."

"He may not run again now," Beverly laughed. "He hasn't announced."

"He will," Peck said confidently. "Moreland's one hell of a fighter."

"That's the truth," Beverly said, perching her ample figure on the edge of Peck's desk. She smiled at Carla. "You haven't been here long enough to know much of Moreland's background, but he started out as one of the best trial lawyers in the city. He had a national reputation long before he ran for mayor and won. And despite agitators like Green, he commands enough public respect to keep the office if he wants it. He's done more for urban renewal, downtown improvement and city services than any mayor in the past two decades."

"Then why do we keep hearing rumors of graft?" Carla asked Peck when Beverly was called away to her phone.

"What rumors?" Peck asked, even as he began feeding his copy into the electronic typewriter.

"I've had two anonymous phone calls this week," she told him, pushing a strand of dark hair back under the braided coil pinned on top her head. "Big Jim gave me the green light to do some investigating."

"Where do you plan to start?" he asked indulgently.

"At the city treasury. One particular department was singled out by my anonymous friend," she added. "I was told that if I checked the books, I'd find some very interesting entries."

"Tell me what you're looking for, and I'll check into it for you," he volunteered.

She cocked her head at him. "Thanks —" she smiled "— but no thanks. Just because

I'm fresh out of college, don't think I need a shepherd. My father owned a weekly paper in south Georgia."

"No wonder you feel so comfortable here," he chuckled. "But remember that a weekly and a daily are worlds apart."

"Don't be arrogant," she chided. "If you tried to hire on at a weekly, you'd very likely find that your experience wouldn't be enough."

"Oh?"

"You have one beat," she reminded him. "City Hall. You don't cover fashion shows or go to education board meetings, or cover the county morgue. Those are other beats. But," she added, "on a weekly you're responsible for news, period. The smaller the weekly, the smaller the staff, the more responsibility you have. I worked for Dad during the summers. I was my own editor, my own proofreader, my own photographer, and I had to get all the news all the time. Plus that, I had to help set the copy if Trudy got sick, I had to do layout and paste-up and write ads, and set headlines, and sell ads . . ."

"I surrender!" Peck laughed. "I'll just stick to this incredibly easy job I've got, thanks."

"After seventeen years, I'm not surprised."

He raised a pale eyebrow at her, but he

didn't make another comment.

Later, as they were on their way out of the building, Peck groaned while he scanned the front page of the last edition.

"God help us, that's not what he said!" he burst out.

"Not what who said?" She pushed through the door onto the busy sidewalk and waited for him.

"Moreland. The paper says he stated that the city would pick up the tab for new offices at city hall. . . ." Peck ran a rough hand through his hair. "I told that damned copy editor twice that Moreland said he *wouldn't* agree to redecorate city hall! Oh, God, he'll eat us alive tonight."

Tonight was when one of the presidential advisers was speaking at a local civic organization's annual meeting, to which she and Peck were invited. It would be followed by a reception at a local state legislator's home, and Moreland would certainly be there.

"I'll wear a blond wig and a mustache," she assured him. "And you can borrow one of my dresses."

His pale eyes skimmed over her tall, slender body appreciatively, before he considered his own compact, but husky physique. "I'd need a bigger size, but thanks for the thought."

"Maybe he won't blame us," she said comfortingly.

"We work for the paper," he reminded her. "And the fact that a story I called in got fouled up won't cut any ice. Don't sweat it, honey, it's my fault not yours. Moreland doesn't eat babies."

"I'm twenty-three, you know," she said with a smile. "I was late getting into college."

"Moreland's older than I am," he persisted. "He's got to be pushing forty, if he isn't already there."

"I know, I've seen the gray hairs."

"Most of those he got from the accident," he murmured as they got to the parking lot. "Tragic thing, and so senseless. Didn't even scratch the other driver. I guess the other guy was too drunk to notice any injuries, even if he had them."

"That was before my time," she said. She paused at the door of her yellow Volkswagen. "Was it since he was elected?"

"Two years ago." He nodded. "There were rumors of a split between him and his wife, but no confirmation."

"Any kids?"

"A daughter, eight years old."

She nodded. "She must be a comfort to

him."

"Honey, she was in the car," he told her. "He was the only survivor."

She swallowed hard. "He doesn't look as if bullets would scratch him. I guess after that, they wouldn't."

"That's what I hear." He opened the door of his car. "Need a ride to the meeting?"

She shook her head. "Thanks, anyway. I thought I might toss my clothes in the trunk and stop by a laundromat after the reception."

He froze with his hand on the door handle. "Wash clothes at a laundromat at midnight in an evening gown?"

"I'm going to wear a dress, not an evening gown, and the laundromat belongs to my aunt and uncle. They'll be there."

He let out a deep breath. "Don't scare me like that. It's not good for a man of my advanced years."

"What a shame, and I was going to buy you a racing set for Christmas, too."

"Christmas is three months away."

"Is that all?" she exclaimed. "Well, maybe I'd better forgo the meeting and go Christmas shopping instead."

"And leave me to face Moreland alone?" He looked deserted, tragic.

"I can't protect you. He towers over me,

you know," she added, remembering the sheer physical impact of the man at the last city commission meeting.

"He's never jumped on you," he reminded her. He smiled boyishly. "In fact, at that last budget meeting we covered, he seemed to spend a lot of time looking at you."

Her eyebrows went up. "At me? I wonder what I did?"

He shook his head. "Carla, you're without hope. Men do look at attractive women."

"Not men like Moreland," she protested.

"Men like Moreland," he insisted. "He may be the mayor, honey, but he's still very much a man."

"He could have almost any socialite in the city."

"But he rarely dates," he said. "I've seen him with a woman twice at a couple of social functions. He's not what you'd call a womanizer, unless he's keeping a very low profile."

"Maybe he misses his wife," she said softly.

"Angelica wasn't the kind of woman any sane man misses," he recalled with a smile. "She reminded me of a feisty dog — all snap and bristle. I think it was an arranged marriage rather than a love match. They were descended from two of the city's founding families, you know. Moreland could get along very well without working at all. He does it for a hobby, I think, although he takes it seriously. He loves this city, and he's sure worked for it."

"I still wouldn't like to have him mad at me," she admitted with a smile. "It would be like having a bulldozer run over you."

"Ask me when the party's over," he moaned, "and I'll let you know."

"Wear your track shoes," she called as she got into her car and drove away.

Carla and Peck sat together with his date, a ravishing blonde who couldn't seem to take her eyes off him. She felt vaguely alone at functions like this gigantic dinner. It was comforting to be near someone she knew, even if she did feel like a third wheel. Reporting had overcome some of her basic shyness, but not a lot. She still cringed at gatherings.

Even now, chic in an emerald green velour dress that was perfect with her pale green eyes and dark hair — which she wore, uncharacteristically, loose tonight — she felt self-conscious, especially when she caught Bryan Moreland's dark eyes looking at her from the head table. It was unnerving, that pointed stare of his, and she had a feeling that there was animosity in it. Perhaps he was blaming her as well as Peck for the story in the paper. She was Peck's protégée, after all, his shadow on the city hall beat while she was getting her bearings in the new environment of big-city journalism.

"His Honor's glaring at me," she told Peck over her coffee cup.

"Ignore him," he told her. "He glares at all reporters. See old Graham over at the next table — the *Sun* reporter?" he asked, gesturing toward a young, sandy-haired man with a photographer sitting next to him. "He axed the mayor's new landfill proposal without giving the city's side of the question. Moreland cornered him at a civic-club banquet and burned his ears off. In short," he concluded with a smile, "he would like to see you and me and Graham on the menu tonight — preferably served with barbeque sauce and apples in our mouths."

She shuddered. "How distasteful."

He nodded. "I'd sure give him indigestion, wouldn't I, lovely?" he asked the blonde, who smiled back.

"Never mind," Carla told her companionably, "we'll flatter him by pretending we don't think he's a tough old bird."

"Don't listen, Blanche," Peck told the blonde.

The blonde winked at Carla. "Okay, sugar, I won't."

When they finished the lavish meal, the tall young presidential adviser, Joel Blackwell, took the podium and Peck and Carla produced pads and pens. It had been Peck's idea to let Carla cover meetings such as this, to give her a feel for it, but he took his own notes as well, as a backup, and wrote his own copy to compare with hers. She was proving to be an apt pupil, too. He was grudging with his praise, but she was beginning to earn her share of it.

Most of the speech was routine propaganda for the administration: pinpointing the President's interest in his fan mail and highlighting some less known aspects of his personal life. When he finished, he threw the floor open for questions, and foremost on the audience's mind was foreign relations. Domestic problems had a brief voice, followed by some questions on what a presidential adviser's duties consisted of. Carla took notes feverishly, blissfully unaware of Peck's indulgent smile as he jotted down a brief note here and there.

Finally, it was over, and the guests were gathering jackets and purses for a quick exit. Carla threw her lacy shawl around her shoulders and stood up.

"Well, I'll see you at the cocktail party," she told Peck and his girl friend. "I wish it were informal. My feet hurt!"

He gave her tight sandals with their high, spiked heels a distasteful glance. "No wonder." He caught Blanche by the arm, and drew her along through the crowd. "In the office, she kicks off her shoes and walks around barefoot on the carpet," he whispered conspiratorially.

"Can I help it if I'm a country girl at heart?" Carla laughed. "I'm still adjusting to big-city life."

"You'll get used to it," Peck promised her.

She sighed, smothering in perfume and cologne and the crush of people. "Oh, I hope so," she said under her breath.

CHAPTER TWO

The cocktail party was far more of an ordeal for Carla than the dinner had been. She stood by the long bar that featured every kind of intoxicating beverage known to man, plus ice and shakers and glasses, trying to look sophisticated and nonchalant. Around her, expensively dressed women wearing jewels Carla couldn't afford time payments on were discussing new plays and art exhibits, dripping diamonds and prestige. A tiny smile touched Carla's full mouth. How horrible, she thought wickedly, to be that rich and have to worry about having your diamonds stolen. Or to have a swimming pool and all the bother of getting leaves cleaned out of it every fall.

The mind boggles, she told herself as she idly glanced around the room. Ironically, the first person she recognized was the mayor.

Bryan Moreland was unmistakable, even

with his broad back turned. Carla studied him from across the room, her dancing eyes curious. She'd seen the big man often enough on television, not to mention in the flesh, but every time she was around him he seemed to be bigger and broader and darker than he looked before.

His hair was dark, threaded with gray, and thick and straight. His complexion was very tanned, as if he spent a lot of time in the sun rather than in an office, and her eyes were drawn to the hand holding his cigarette — a darkly masculine hand with long fingers and a black onyx ring on the little finger. His suits looked as if they had to be tailormade for him, because he was well over six feet tall. He had an athlete's build, and he moved like a cat, all rippling muscle and grace as he turned abruptly and strode toward the bar.

Carla started at the suddenness of the move. She almost stepped away, but she wasn't quick enough. He saw her, and since her face was one he knew, he headed straight for her.

His dark eyes narrowed as he stopped just a couple of feet away and glowered down at her, pinning her. She felt apprehension shiver through her frozen body before he spoke, and her hand tightened on the glass of cola she was drinking instead of liquor.

"That was one hell of a mistake in your morning edition," he said without preamble, his voice deep and slow and cutting. "My phone rang off the hook all day and I had to get on the damned evening news to get the noose off my neck."

"I'm sorry," she began automatically, "but it wasn't my . . ."

"The next time, check your facts with me before you run back and print some pack of lies!" he growled, his deep voice reverberating like thunder. "What the hell do you people do with news down there, make it up as you go along?"

She licked her lips nervously. She wasn't usually intimidated this easily. Being attacked went with the job, and most of the time she handled it well, diplomatically. But it wasn't easy to be diplomatic with a steamroller, and that was what Moreland brought to mind.

"It was the . . ." she began again.

"Why don't you go back to journalism school and learn how to verify information?" he growled. "My God, children are taking over the world!" His eyes narrowed dangerously. "I'll expect not only a retraction, but an apology."

"Mr. Moreland, I'm really sorry. . . ." she

whispered unsteadily, feeling about two inches high.

He poured himself a drink — Scotch, she noticed — with incredibly steady hands, his face like granite, and she wondered idly if anything ever rattled him. He would have made a fantastic racing driver or doctor, she thought suddenly, with those steady hands and nerves.

"I didn't go to Ed Hart this time," he said, tossing the publisher's name at her. He speared her with those demon eyes. "But if it ever happens again, I'll have your job."

He walked away without another word, and she wanted to stand there and cry. The party had been ruined for her. Being blamed for a mistake was fine, if it was hers. But to get stuck with somebody else's, and not be given a chance to defend herself, now, that hurt.

She took a long sip of her drink and set it back on the bar, moving slowly, quietly, toward the ladies' room. Tears were welling in her eyes, and she didn't want the humiliation of shedding them in public.

She darted into the empty bathroom, locked the door, and leaned back against the wall, her eyes unseeing on the spacious, fully carpeted room with its lush champagne and gold decor. Tears ran silently down her cheeks. Why Moreland could affect her like that, she didn't know. But he seemed to have some inexplicable power to reduce her to the level of a wounded child.

She wiped at the tears with an impatient hand. This was ridiculous, she told herself. She couldn't afford to let people or things get to her like this. Hard knocks went with the job, and it was either get used to a little rough treatment or spend the rest of her life in tears. She'd have to toughen up. Her father had told her that at the beginning, the day she announced that she'd entered journalism school at the university.

She found a washcloth and tried to erase the telltale marks from her flushed young face. When she finished, her eyes were still red-rimmed, but all traces of tears were gone. She straightened her dress and ran a comb through her long, gently waving hair. Her pale green eyes surveyed the result coolly. It wasn't a pretty face, but her eyes were big and arresting, and her face had a softly vulnerable look about it.

She turned, adjusting the V-neckline of her dress with cold, nervous hands. She'd rather have been shot than go through that door, but there was no way around it. Running away solved nothing. She'd learned that much, at least, in twenty-three years.

293

As she went back into the spacious living room, ironically, the first person she saw was Bryan Moreland. He stared over a shorter man's head at her, and his narrow dark eyes caught hers at once. She raised her chin proudly and gave him her best south Georgia glare.

Amazingly, as she watched, a slow, faint smile turned up his chiseled lips as if that silent show of rebellion amused him.

Carla turned, purse in hand, and made her way through the crowd to Bill Peck and Blanche.

Peck's eyes narrowed thoughtfully on her face. "He got you," he said immediately.

"Uncanny insight, Mr. Peck," she replied with a wan smile. "I didn't get the chance to plead my case. He must be absolute hell in a courtroom."

"You'd think so if you'd ever seen him in one," the older reporter agreed. "I've seen prospective witnesses cringe when they saw him coming. Was it rough?"

She shrugged, pretending a calm she didn't feel. "A little skin's missing," she said with a laugh.

"Sorry," he said. "That was my hiding you took."

"The rewrite man's," she corrected. "Don't worry about it. It goes with the job, remember? That's what everybody tells me."

"Amen."

"Well, I've gritted my teeth and made my appearance," she added. "I've got my notes in my grubby little hand, and I'm getting out of here before His Honor takes another bite out of me. See you in the morning."

"Don't brood on it," he cautioned.

"I won't." She smiled at the blonde. "Good night."

"Good night." Blanche smiled back. "Don't sweat it, honey, we all get our lumps occasionally, deserved or not."

"Sure," she said.

She wound her way through the crowd to Senator White and thanked him for the invitation, then she turned and moved quickly to the door. Just as her hand touched the doorknob, a large, warm hand covered it, effectively stopping her, and before she turned, she recognized the black onyx ring on the tanned, masculine hand.

"Peck told me what happened when you darted out of the room," Bryan Moreland said quietly, and she had to look up a long way to his face, despite her two-inch heels and her formidable five feet, seven inches of height. So that was why Bill had looked so unconcerned.

"Did he?" she asked wanly, meeting the

darkness in his eyes with uneasiness.

"I like to place blame where it's due," he said in his deep, lazy voice. "Why didn't you tell me you weren't responsible for that story?"

Her eyes flickered down to his burgundy tie. "You didn't give me much of a chance, Mr. Moreland," she said.

"Mister?" His heavy eyebrows went up. "God, do I look that old?"

"No, sir."

He sighed heavily. "Not going to forget it, are you?" he taunted.

She raised her eyes to his with a faint grin. "Not going to apologize, are you?" she returned.

Something kindled in his dark eyes, making them velvet soft, sensuous. A hint of a smile turned up a corner of his wide, firm mouth. She found herself blushing and hated the way she felt: young and gauche and very much outmatched.

"I haven't had much practice at it," he admitted.

"Always right, huh?" she asked.

"Cheeky little thing, aren't you?" he challenged.

"Nosey," she countered, and he chuckled deeply.

"Well, good night," she said, reaching

again for the doorknob.

"Do you have a way home?" he asked unexpectedly.

All of a sudden, she wished with all her heart that she didn't. She somehow felt warm and soft inside, and she wanted to know more about the big man.

"Yes," she replied reluctantly.

"Good night, then." He turned and left her at the door with her sudden, nagging disappointment.

She got down to the street where her car was parked just in time to be confronted with two tall, menacing boys. There were streetlights around the senator's palatial home, but it was a little-traveled street, and there wasn't a soul in sight. Carla started toward her car with sheer bravado, mentally cursing herself for coming out here alone.

"Ain't she pretty," one of the boys called with a long whistle, his voice slurred as if he'd been drinking.

"A looker, all right," the other commented, and they moved quickly toward her.

She fumbled in her purse for her car key, frantically digging through makeup and pens and pads with fingers that trembled.

"Nice," the older of the boys said, smiling at her from an unshaven face. "Where you going, baby? Me and John feel like a little company."

She straightened jerkily, fighting to remember her brief class in karate, the right moves at the right time.

"I don't want company," she said quietly. "And if you don't go away and leave me alone, I'm going to scream, very loud, so that those people in the house come out here."

"I'm scared," the one called John laughed drunkenly. "God, I'm scared! You think the old senator's going to come down here and save you?"

"He might not," Bryan Moreland said from the shadows, "but I'll be glad to oblige."

"I ain't scared of you, either," the older boy said, moving forward to throw a midriff punch toward the big man.

Moreland hardly seemed to move, but the next minute, the boy was crumpled on the pavement. The big man looked at the one called John. "You've got two choices. One is pick up this litter from the street and carry it home. You don't want to know what the second one is."

John stared at him for a moment, as if measuring his youth and slenderness against the older man's experience and pure athletic strength. He bent and helped his winded companion to his feet and they moved on down the sidewalk as quickly as they could.

Carla slumped against the small Beetle, her eyes closed as her heart shook her with its wild pounding. "That was close," she murmured breathlessly, opening her eyes to find Moreland very close. "Thank you."

"My pleasure. Are you all right?"

She nodded. "Sheer stupidity. I forgot how deserted it is out here."

"You'll remember next time, won't you?"

"Oh, yes," she said with a smile. "You're very good with your fists. I didn't even see you move."

"I boxed for a while when I was younger," he said.

"I didn't know boxing was around on the Ark," she commented seriously.

He chuckled. "That's a hell of a way to say thank you."

"You're the one harping on your ancientness, not me," she told him. "I just do my job and catch hell from bad-tempered public officials."

"I'm not always bad-tempered."

"Really?" she said unconvincingly.

"Have dinner with me tomorrow, and I'll prove it."

She stared at him as if she'd just been hit between the eyes with a block of ice.

"What?"

"Have dinner with me. I'll take you disco dancing."

"You're the mayor!" she burst out.

"Well, my God, it didn't de-sex me," he replied.

She blushed. "I didn't mean it that way. It's just . . ."

"You can't maintain your objectivity, is that it? Honey, I don't mix politics and pleasure," he said quietly, "and right now I don't give a damn about your objectivity."

She felt the same way. Something strange and exciting was happening to her. Something she felt that he shared. It was almost frightening.

"I . . . I was going to do a series of articles on city officials," she said, seizing on a chance to do some quiet investigating about the information in her anonymous phone calls. "I could start with you . . . if you wouldn't mind," she added.

He pulled a package of cigarettes out of his pocket and offered her one, lifting an eyebrow when she refused. He lit one and repocketed his lighter, smoking quietly while he studied her from his superior height.

"How deep into my life do you want to delve?" he asked finally, and she knew he was thinking about the accident.

"Into your *political* life," she corrected. "I think privacy is a divine right as far as anyone's personal life is concerned. I wouldn't like mine in print."

"Oh?" His dark eyes sketched her oval face in the light from the street lamp overhead. "You aren't old enough to have skeletons in your closet."

"I'm twenty-three," she said.

"I'm thirty-nine," he replied. His eyes narrowed. "Sixteen years, little one."

"Fifteen," she murmured breathlessly. "I'll be twenty-four this month."

He caught her eyes and held them for a long time, with the sounds of the night and the city fading into oblivion around them. Her heart swelled, nearly bursting with new, exciting emotions.

"I'll let you do a story," he said finally, "if I get to okay it before it goes into print."

"All right," she replied softly.

"We might as well start early. Are you free in the morning?"

Things were moving so fast she hardly had time to catch her breath, but it was a chance she couldn't pass up. So, ignoring the county commission meeting she was supposed to go to with Bill Peck, she nodded.

"Be in my office at nine a.m. and we'll get

started."

"I'll be there." She unlocked her car and got in. "Thanks again for saving me."

"My pleasure," he replied. "Good night."

"Good night." She started the small car and put it in gear. Bryan Moreland was still standing on the sidewalk smoking his cigarette when she rounded the corner.

CHAPTER THREE

The excitement was still with her the next morning, when she grabbed her thirty-five millimeter camera and her pad, quickly checking her desk calendar before she started out the door in her usual mad rush. She was neatly dressed in a tweed jacket with a burgundy plaid wool skirt and matching vest, and her small feet were encased in brown suede boots. Bill Peck took in her appearance with a critical eye, and grinned.

"Who are you dressed up for?" he asked pleasantly.

She blushed, hating the color that rushed into her cheeks. "I'm going to interview the mayor," she confessed.

"Oh?" He threw her a questioning glance.

"Well, I do need to do some snooping on the tip I got," she defended, "and I can't help but turn up something if I comb through all the city departments."

"You'll be an old woman by then," he

commented. "It's a big city."

"There are only five commissioners over all those departments," she reminded him, "plus a handful of lesser commission posts, like planning and —"

"I know, I know," he said with mock weariness, "don't forget that I had to cover all those groups before you came along to save me."

"Am I saving you?" she asked.

He only shook his head, perching himself on the corner of her desk while around him telephones were ringing off the hook. "I thought the mayor took several bites out of you last night," he remarked.

"Only a small one, thanks to you," she said dryly.

He shrugged. "I don't like anyone else taking my lumps."

"Sure." She smiled. "Anyway, he saved me from a pretty scary gang of toughs last night — two anyway," she amended, shivering at the memory. "For a man his age, he packs a pretty hefty punch."

His eyes bulged. "The mayor popped a tough, and you didn't get the story? My God, haven't I taught you anything?"

She glared at him. "That comes under the heading of my personal business," she told him tightly, "not news."

"But, Carla . . . he's the mayor, baby, anything he does is news! Think of it like this — Mayor saves reporter in distress!"

"No. Period," she added tightly when he pursued it.

He sighed angrily. "You'll never make a reporter unless you harden up a little."

"If I have to harden up that much, maybe I'll hire on as a hit person for the mob," she said coldly, picking up her camera as she turned to go.

"Wait, Carla," he said quietly and rose to tower over her. "Don't be like that. I was only kidding."

"It didn't sound like it," she replied, casting an accusing glance up at him.

He shrugged, his pale hair catching the light to gleam gold. "I've been at this a long time. I forget sometimes how it is when you're a beginner. Okay, I'll buy that you're trying to get in with His Nibs, and this wouldn't help you break the ice. But," he added darkly, "that's the only reason I'm not doing anything about it. It's news. And news comes before personal privilege. Don't forget it again."

She started to fire back at him, but his face was like stone, and she knew it wouldn't do the slightest bit of good. She turned and walked out without another word.

She stuck her head in the city editor's office, grinning as he looked up from the pile of paper on his desk over the rim of his glasses.

"I'm going to interview the mayor and stop by the financial section to do a little checking, okay?"

"On what we talked about earlier?" Jim Edwards asked with a nod. "Okay. Don't forget that interview with the new city clerk — and get a pix. And see if you can get anything out of Moreland about negotiations on the sanitation strike."

"I ought to ask Green for that," she said with a wry smile.

"When he doesn't even take office until the first?" he laughed.

"He's officially Public Works Commissioner right now," she reminded him, "regardless of when the next commission meeting is."

"Touché. He's not a bad man, you know," he added quietly. "Just dedicated."

"I know. Anything else you want me to check on while I'm there?"

He consulted his sheet. "Not that I know of. If anything comes up, I'll track you down."

She knew that already. Edwards had a knack for tracking down his reporters that was nothing short of legendary.

"I'll check back in before I go home," she said.

He nodded, already buried in his copy again.

She only had to wait ten minutes before Bryan Moreland's middle-aged secretary motioned her into his office. He was sitting behind a massive oak desk, his dark eyes stormy, his jaw clenched, when she walked in and sat down, eyeing him cautiously. His big hand was still on the telephone receiver, as if he'd only just finished a telephone call that didn't agree with him.

"Would you rather I come back later?" she asked gently. "Say, in two or three years?"

He took a deep breath, leaned back in the leather-padded executive chair with his hands behind his leonine head, and studied her down his straight nose. "I don't like reporters," he said without preamble.

She grinned. "Neither do I. See, already we've got something in common!"

His hard face relaxed a little. "That was Graham — Dan Graham of the *Sun,* on my neck again for the federal grant for the landfill experiment." He sighed angrily. "If only I could plead justifiable mayhem. . . ."

"Graham thrives on bruises and contusions," she laughed.

"So I hear."

She pulled out her pad and pen, and he watched her curiously.

"I thought modern reporters used tape recorders," he taunted.

"I don't have a lot of luck with machinery," she admitted, peeking up at him. "My car stays in the shop, my hair dryer blows fuses, and I think the garbage disposal ate my cat."

His massive chest shook with deep, soft laughter as he studied her flushed young face with a curious intensity. "What kind of cat was it?" he asked.

"A duke's mixture."

His chiseled mouth curved faintly. "No doubt, if the garbage disposal got him."

"Speaking of garbage," she said quickly, latching onto the subject, "I'd like to know about that new trash-into-power concept."

"It's all still in the planning stages right now," he told her, "but the idea is to take raw garbage and use it to produce power. We're running out of land. And it takes one hell of a lot of land to accommodate the refuse from a population the size of this city's. People don't want to live near sanitary landfills, and they're organized. Obviously, the only answer for the future is recycling."

She scribbled furiously. "And the grant?"

"The planning commissioner knows more about it than I do," he admitted, "but we lined up a matching federal grant and some regional funds to go with it. Give Ed a call; he'll fill you in."

She raised her eyes from her pad. "Mr. King isn't my greatest fan," she told him. "I called him last week to ask about the land the planning commission was purchasing for the new airport, and I couldn't even get any figures out of him."

He shrugged. "Ed's like me; he doesn't trust newsmen. We've learned to be wary," he explained.

She nodded, but her mind was still on King. "Do you, by any chance, have the figures on the cost of the land?"

His dark eyes narrowed with amusement. "Don't try to pump me. If you want information on figures, you ask Ed. That's his business at the moment."

She sighed. "Fair enough. Anyway, back to the landfill. Doesn't the incinerator tie in to that energy production idea?"

"Honey, you'll need to talk to Tom Green," he told her, "as soon as he's comfortably in office. I'm not that familiar with specific technical aspects of the project. This is one hell of a big city. I'm more concerned with administration and budget than I am with various ongoing projects — outside of my downtown revitalization proposals — and right now I've got all I can do to cope with striking Street Department workers. And the damned horse club wants to hold a parade!"

She smothered a grin. "You could make the horses wear diapers."

"Care to apply for the job?" he asked.

She shook her head. "I didn't realize how sweeping your responsibilities were. Of course, we do have a strong-mayor system here, but I'm a long way from home, and I tend to forget the size of this city. I suppose that tells you more about my background than a resume."

"It tells me that you're used to a town of under five thousand, where the mayor can tell you everything that's going on. Right?" he asked.

"Right. My father owns a weekly newspaper in the southern section of Georgia."

"Well, this city has almost two million people," he elaborated, "and no city manager. I handle all the administration, greet crown princes, cope with strikes and riots, hire and fire department heads, give the Public Safety commissioner hell twice a day and grant interviews I don't have time for."

She felt vaguely uncomfortable. "Sorry. I'll hurry. Can you tell me . . ."

The intercom buzzed. "Excuse me," Moreland said politely, and leaned to answer it. "Yes?"

"Bill Harrison on line one," came the reply.

He picked up the receiver. "Hello, Bill, what can I do for you?" he asked pleasantly.

He looked thoughtful, his darkly tanned fingers toying with a fountain pen while he listened to whoever was on the other end — apparently a friend, she surmised. Decision flashed in his dark eyes and he laid the pen down abruptly.

"Tell Carl I'll meet with him and his boys in my office tonight at seven. And try not to leak it to the press, okay?" He cast a speaking glance in Carla's general direction and winked at her lazily. "Thanks, Bill. Talk to you later."

She remembered his invitation to dinner suddenly, and felt a vague prick of disappointment when she realized that the meeting would put an end to that. Although why it should bother her . . .

"A meeting with the labor leaders?" she probed with a smile.

"Tell your friend Peck he's got a personal invitation. It's going to get a little rough for you, kitten."

"You mean," she said, prickling, "there are actually words I haven't heard?"

His arrogant head lifted. "Woman's libber?" he challenged.

She lifted her own head. "Reporter," she replied. "Sex doesn't have anything to do with it."

A slow, sensuous smile curved his mouth, and his eyes studied her with a bold thoroughness that made her look away in embarrassment. "Doesn't it?" he asked.

She cleared her throat. "Uh, where were we?" she hedged.

The intercom buzzed again. "Phone, Mr. Moreland," his secretary said apologetically. "It's the governor's office calling about that appropriations request you plan to make for inner-city revitalization."

Moreland picked up the phone. "Hello, Moreland here," he said, leaning forward to study his calendar while he listened and nodded. "Yes, that's right. Oh, roughly a couple of million. Hell, Ben, you know that's a conservative estimate! Look, I convinced the Nelson companies to invest in cleaning up the fifteen-hundred block on a nonprofit basis. They deal in building products. When the slums are cleared out, we'll have to have new housing, right? So the building companies that make this kind of investment ultimately profit from increased sales, do you see the light? All I have to do is convince a few other firms, and I'll have practically all the local funding I need to match an urban redevelopment grant. If you'll do your part, and help me get my paltry two million . . ."

Carla hid a smile at the disgusted look on Moreland's dark face. He didn't like opposition — that was evident.

"I know you're having budget problems," Moreland said with magnificent patience. "So am I. But look at it this way, Ben, slums eat up over half my city services. While they're doing that, they pay only around one-twentieth of the real-estate taxes. We have a yearly deficit of twenty-five thousand dollars per acre of slums, Ben. That's a hell of a figure, considering the concentration of them in the downtown area."

He picked up the pen again and twirled it while he nodded. "Yes, I know that. But have you considered how it affects the crime rate here? Slums account for half of all the arrests our policemen make, at least fifty-five percent of all juvenile delinquency. If we can clean up the areas and provide decent housing — give the kids something to do and get them off the streets — God only knows what we could accomplish."

Whatever he was hearing didn't suit him. The pen snapped in his powerful fingers. "Oh, good God, you mean giving a pencil pusher a two percent increase is worth more than cleaning up my slums? Where the hell is your sense of priorities?"

The answer must have been a good one, because he calmed down. Wearily, he tossed the two halves of the fountain pen onto the desk. "All right, Ben, I'll see what else I can work out before the budget goes into committee. Yes. Thanks anyway."

He hung up and studied Carla's young face. "Do you like fresh croissants with real butter?"

"Oh, yes!" she said without thinking.

"Let's go." He got up and opened the door for her, waiting while she fumbled to get her camera, purse and accessories together.

"I'm out, if anyone else calls," Moreland told his secretary.

"Yes, Mr. Moreland," she said with a secretive smile.

He led Carla to the elevator and put her in, pushing the first-floor button.

"Where are we going?" she asked breathlessly.

"Away from the telephone," he replied,

leaning back against the wall of the elevator to study her. "I feel obligated to answer it as long as I'm sitting at my desk. But I haven't had my breakfast, and I feel like a decent cup of coffee and a roll. Even a mayor has to eat," he added wryly, "although some of my supporters question my right to do that, and sleep, and go home."

"Why don't you eat breakfast?" she asked suddenly.

"Because I don't usually have time to cook," he replied matter-of-factly. "I have a daily woman who comes in to do the cleaning, but mostly I eat out. I don't like women snooping around my kitchen trying to ingratiate themselves, so I don't keep a full larder."

"Oh," she said noncommittally and let it drop.

He took her to an intimate little coffee house with white linen tablecloths and fresh roses in tiny bud vases and where waltz music danced around them. He sat her down at a small table in the corner and gave the waitress their order.

As she darted away, he pulled a cigarette from his engraved gold case.

"I wish you wouldn't," she said.

He lifted a heavy eyebrow. "I don't gamble, drink to excess, or support organized crime. But I do have this one vice, and you'll notice that the room is quite well ventilated. I don't intend giving up a lifelong habit for the sake of one interview."

She had the grace to blush. Her eyes moved from the tablecloth to the street outside, where autumn leaves blazed in a tiny maple tree embedded in concrete, a small colorful reminder of the season. The wind was tumbling fallen leaves and she watched them with a sense of emptiness. She felt as though she'd been alone for a long time.

"What else did you want to ask me?" he cut into her thoughts.

"Oh!" She dug her pad and pen out of her purse, moving them aside briefly as the waitress brought china cups filled with freshly brewed imported coffee, fresh croissants and a saucer of creamy butter. "I wanted to ask about your administration. What was the city's financial situation when you took office, what is it now, what improvements have you made, what goals do you have for the rest of your term in office — that sort of thing."

He stared at her through a soft cloud of gray smoke. "Honey, I hope you're not doing anything for the next two weeks, because that's how long it's going to take me to answer those questions."

She smiled wryly, her pale green eyes catching his. "Couldn't you manage to do a brief summary in an hour or so?" she teased.

"Not and do it justice." He leaned back in the chair, letting his forgotten cigarette fire curls of gray smoke up toward the ceiling while he took silent inventory of her facial features. "How old did you say you were?" he asked.

"Twenty-three," she muttered absently, fascinated by his dark, quiet eyes.

"And fresh out of journalism school?" he probed.

"I got a late start," she explained, crossing her booted legs. "My mother was in poor health. She died." Her eyes went sad at the admission. Two words to describe that long, painful process that ended in death. Words were inadequate.

"A long illness?" he asked, reading her expression as if he could read her mind.

She nodded. "An incurable disease of the central nervous system. There was nothing anyone could do. My father very nearly went under. He had a breakdown, and I had to run the paper until he got back on his feet."

"Quite an experience for you."

"Oh, yes, I learned a lot," she recalled with

a dry smile.

"Like what?"

She looked at him sheepishly. "Never misspell a name on the society page."

"What else?"

"Read the copy before you write the headlines. Don't leave out names in school honor rolls. Never put anything down, because you'll never see it again. And especially never go to a County Commission meeting when they're discussing a new site for the sanitary landfill."

Both eyebrows went up, and he smiled faintly. "Lynch mobs?"

"Lynch mobs. I saw in one meeting where sixty people surrounded the sole county commissioner and threatened to shoot him if he put it in their community," she recalled. "I don't suppose you have that kind of problem?"

"No," he admitted, "just dull things like street employee strikes, garbage piling up on sidewalks and into the streets."

"Why not start a campaign to get everyone in the city to mail their garbage to relatives out of state?" she suggested.

"Honey, you start it, and I'll personally endorse it," he promised. "Eat your roll before it gets cold."

"Yes, sir," she replied politely.

He glared at her. "I'm not that old."

She peeked at him over the rim of her coffee cup. "Now I know why you brought me here."

He glowered at her. "Why?"

"Real napkins," she explained, "and real cups and saucers. No wasted paper products to fill your garbage trucks!"

He shook his head. "How did you wind up in the city, little country mouse?"

"Dad sold the newspaper and took off on a grand tour of the Orient," she sighed. "I didn't want to go with him, so I caught a plane and came up here to ask one of his former employees for a job."

"And got it, I suppose," he replied, as he took a bite out of his buttered roll.

"Actually, I didn't," she told him between bites of her own roll. "It was the editor of the Sun, and he didn't have an opening. He sent me to the *Phoenix-Herald,* and I guess they just felt sorry for me. After I told them about my ten starving children and the lecherous landlord . . ."

"Ten children?" he prompted.

Remembering the tragic death of his daughter, she felt a strangling embarrassment lodge in her throat, and a wild flush stole into her cheeks.

"Don't walk on eggs with me, Carla," he

said, using her given name for the first time. "There's nothing to be embarrassed about."

She took a sip of her coffee. "Can you read my mind?" she asked in a small voice.

"Look at me."

She raised her eyes to his and felt them captured, held for ransom by a gaze with the power to stop her heart in mid-beat.

"You have a very expressive face, little one," he said gently. "Readable. Vulnerable."

"I'm as tough as used boots," she murmured.

"Don't bet on it." He finished his coffee. "You realize that damned labor meeting's polished off my dinner invitation?"

"That's all right," she murmured courteously.

"Is it, really?" he asked in a deep, slow voice that sent wild shivers down her straight spine.

She met his searching gaze squarely. "No," she managed shakily, "it isn't."

"Tomorrow?" he asked.

She nodded, and the rush of excitement that made wild lights dance in her eyes was something she hadn't felt since her early teens, her first date.

"I'll call you, in case something comes up." He frowned. "There isn't a boyfriend?"

Her heart went wild; her mouth parted,

trembling slightly, drawing his intent gaze before it darted back up to catch the hint of fear in her pale eyes.

"No," she whispered.

Something relaxed in his leonine face, and he smiled at her, an action that made his eyes soft and tender.

"Come on, country mouse. We'll talk on the way back, but I've got a budget meeting at eleven and a luncheon at twelve, followed by a visiting oil magnate at two. In other words," he said as he rose, "I've got to go bridge my credibility gap."

"Thanks for the coffee," she said, moving slowly beside him to the counter.

He glanced down at her. "Your party piece?" he asked softly. "I'm not trying to wheedle any favorable copy out of you, little one. But don't make the mistake of thinking this is just a moment out of time. This is a beginning, Carla."

The way he said it, and the slow, sweet appraisal his eyes made of her emphasized the underlying comment. She started to speak when she felt his big, warm hand catch hers and press it warmly. And the music danced within her.

CHAPTER FOUR

She was busily working on the story about the city's new clerk when Bill Peck ambled in and threw himself down in the chair behind his desk.

"God, I'm tired," he groaned. "A delegation of home owners came to the commission meeting to protest a proposed zoning ordinance. It was the hottest meeting I've covered in months."

"Did the ordinance pass?" Carla asked absently as she studied her notes.

"No way. Mass protest does have its advantages," he laughed. "How're you coming on your great exposé?"

She hated the mocking note in his voice and gave him a freezing stare. "I don't make fun of your stories," she said accusingly.

He sighed. "Okay, I won't make fun of it. But you're going to have hell pinning anything on the city hall crowd."

"You know!" she burst out.

"I know what you got the tip on, that's all," he replied. "Your mysterious caller got to me last night. But don't make the mistake of taking that kind of tip for gospel. Fired employees tell tales, and I just happened to recognize that one's voice. He's Daniel Brown, a police sergeant who was fired recently for taking payoffs."

"Allegedly taking payoffs," she corrected. "I think he's innocent."

"God, what a babe in the woods you are," he scoffed. "Little girl, don't trust people too far. The city's just full of wolves waiting to pounce on little lambs. I wouldn't put much credibility in Brown's story, either, if I were you."

She didn't mention that she'd already taken her information to the paper's editor and chief counsel and that she had approval from the top to check out that tip. Bill had been a tremendous help to her, boosting her low confidence, building her insight, teaching and encouraging. But he tended to be just the least bit lax in his efforts, and Carla was full of vim and enthusiasm for her job. So she only smiled and agreed with him.

"I hear you had breakfast with the mayor," he said.

"Gosh, news travels fast!" she gasped.

"Did you hear that I pushed him under the table and raped him?"

"No, did you?"

She sighed. "Unfortunately the tables are extremely small. But it was a very informative breakfast. For instance," she said, leaning on her typewriter to peer at him solemnly, "did you know that slums account for over fifty percent of city services while they only pay about five to six percent of real-estate taxes?"

He sighed, slumping down in his chair. "Oh, no, not again," he groaned. "I've heard Moreland's slum removal song until I can sing all twenty choruses!"

"Now, Bill . . ."

"I don't want to hear it," he pleaded.

"But, it's so fascinating," she said, and went over to sit on his desk. "Now just let me lay some statistics on you. For example . . ." and she spent the next fifteen minutes describing the downtown revitalization project, only stopping when the city editor stuck his head around the door and reminded her that the deadline was twenty minutes away.

Moreland picked her up at six-thirty for their dinner date, immaculate in his dark evening clothes and a white ruffled shirt that, on him, looked anything but effeminate. He looked sensuous and more than a little dangerous.

Carla smoothed her burgundy velvet dress down over her hips as he closed the door behind him. "I . . . I hope I'm not underdressed," she murmured.

"You're fine," he said, and his bold eyes added extra approval to the comment.

"I'll get my shawl," she said, turning to retrieve the lacy black creation from her big armchair.

With apparent interest, Moreland was studying a fantasy landscape done by a friend of hers. He turned, eyeing the tastefully decorated apartment with its floral furniture and dark brown carpet. "Earth colors," he murmured.

She smiled. "I like the outdoors."

"So do I. I have a farm out in the metro area," he replied, and she thought how that explained his dark tan. "I'll take you out for the day one weekend."

"Do you have cattle?" she asked him on the way down to the street in the elevator.

"Only a hundred head or so," he replied. "Purebred, mostly, a few crossbreeds. I do it for amusement. My grandfather ranched out west."

"It must take an awfully big horse," she

murmured absently, measuring his big, husky frame with her eyes.

A corner of his mouth lifted. "It does. Can you ride?"

"It's been a long time," she admitted, "but I think I could still hold on."

"I've got a gentle little mare you'd like."

"Dogs?" she asked as they walked out onto the sidewalk under the lofty streetlights and neon lights.

"One. A shepherd. The caretaker and his wife look after him for me when I'm here."

"You don't live there?" she asked, amazed.

"I have an apartment a few blocks from my office," he replied. "Some nights I don't finish until midnight. It's an hour's drive to the farm, but that seems like swimming an ocean after a rough day."

She followed him to a low-slung Jaguar XKE and gaped as he unlocked the passenger side. It was black and sleek and looked as if it could race the wind.

He caught the astonishment on her face and smiled faintly.

"What did you expect? A sedate domestic vintage with an automatic transmission? I'm not that old, honey," he said amusedly.

"I wasn't thinking that," she said, dropping down into the plush leather bucket seat. It even smelled expensive. "It isn't conservative."

"Neither am I," he said softly. He closed the door for her and went around the hood to get in behind the wheel. For such a big man, he managed to slide in gracefully.

The statement was easy to believe when she got on the dance floor with him in the very exclusive disco restaurant and went wild trying to keep up with the intricate steps that he managed effortlessly.

"I thought you knew how to do this," he teased when the music stopped momentarily.

She only laughed. "So did I. I'm not in your league!"

"I cheated," he replied. "I took lessons."

She was ashamed to admit that she had, too. Always graceful on the dance floor, he made her look as if she had two left feet.

But the music was invigorating, and he made dancing fun, so she danced until her legs throbbed with weariness.

Later, he took her to a quiet little bar down the street where they sat sipping drinks over a table where a single candle in a red lamp danced.

"Tired?" he asked.

She nodded with a smile. "Deliciously. It was fun."

He lit a cigarette and smoked quietly. "How did you get into reporting?" he asked.

She watched him leaning back against the booth, and her eyes were drawn involuntarily to his unbuttoned jacket, where the silky shirt was pulled tight across his massive chest. A shadowing of hair was just visible through the thin fabric.

"My father told me not to," she replied in all honesty, keeping her wandering eyes on her glass.

"He didn't want you to follow in his footsteps?"

"He was afraid to let me," she said. Her slender hands fingered the frosty glass. "Dad liked a fight. He wasn't afraid to take on anyone. Crooked politicians, policemen on the take, inept lawmen . . . anybody. He was threatened a lot, he had tires slashed and windows broken, and once he even got shot at. He's been lucky. He was afraid I might not be."

"Are you afraid?" he asked in a quiet voice.

She didn't dare look up. "A little, sometimes," she admitted. "Controversy is always frightening."

"Why bother with it?"

She smiled. "It's news."

"Do you bleed ink?" he asked conversationally.

"I've never cut myself," she replied saucily.

"Any brothers or sisters?" he probed.

She shook her head and shot him a grin. "They were afraid to try again: they might have had another one like me."

His bold, slow eyes studied her intently from the waist up. "From where I'm sitting, that would have been pretty nice."

She took a long sip of her drink and tried not to blush. He made her feel like a naïve fifteen-year-old.

"What about you?" she asked. "Do you have a family?" Her face blushed as she remembered. "Oh, my . . . !"

"Don't," he said quietly. "I told you not to walk on eggshells with me. Someone told you about it?"

She nodded miserably.

"The wounds are still there, but not nearly as fresh as they were," he told her. "Sometimes talking about it helps. I loved my daughter very much. I hate to remember how she died, but that doesn't mean I want to forget that she lived. You understand?"

"Yes," she said. "I think I do. Did she look like you? Was she dark?"

A corner of his mouth curved up. "No. She was fair, like her mother. All arms and legs and laughter. Not a sad child at all. She had promise."

Her fingers reached out and touched his, where they rested on the white linen tablecloth. "You miss her."

"Yes," he said simply. He studied her fingers and turned his hand abruptly to catch them in a warm, slow clasp. "Your hands are cool."

"Yours are warm," she replied, feeling the effects of that sensuous clasp all the way to her toes.

His thumb caressed her palm. "We'd better go," he said abruptly, dropping his hand. "It's late, and I've been stuck with a visiting politician first thing in the morning. She wants to see my ghetto."

"I'd kind of like to see your ghetto, too," she remarked.

He smiled at her. "Be in my office at nine-thirty."

"Really?"

"What's your city editor going to say? This is the second interview in as many days," he said with a wicked smile.

"He'll probably think I'm trying to seduce you," she replied smartly.

He studied her in a sudden, tense silence, and she regretted the impulsive teasing as his eyes dropped pointedly to her mouth.

"I don't think you'd know how," he said.

She got to her feet, red faced. "You might be surprised."

He moved in front of her, forcing her to look up into dark, steady eyes. "You wear your innocence like a banner," he said in a soft, deep voice that reached only her ears.

She tried to answer him, but the words caught in her throat. He seemed to read every thought in her whirling mind.

"I'll get the check," he said, and turned away.

The strained silence was still between them when he pulled up in front of her apartment building and cut the engine.

"Thank you for a lovely evening," she said as she reached for the door handle.

"I'm coming up with you," he said abruptly.

He got out and opened her door for her, eyeing her speechless stare with dawning amusement.

"Don't panic," he teased. "I'm only going to see you safely to your door. I know this city a hell of a lot better than you do, and I just got the revised homicide statistics yesterday."

She turned and went up the steps with him on her heels. "Bill Peck was furious at me for not doing a story about the night you rescued me from those punks."

"Any other reporter would have," he reminded her.

She went into the elevator with her green eyes flashing. "There is such a thing as personal privilege."

"Not in the eyes of the media," he said, joining her. He pressed the sixth-floor button and leaned back. Only the two of them had boarded the conveyance, and she felt very young as he watched her.

"You're nervous," he commented.

She ran her tongue over her dry lips. "Am I?"

One heavy eyebrow went up over dancing dark eyes. "I almost never rape women in deserted elevators."

Her face went poinsettia red. "I wasn't . . ."

"Yes, you were," he mocked. "I'm aware of the dangers even if you aren't, little girl. I didn't plan to pounce on you at your front door."

She studied his face, trying to figure out the enigmatic statement, but it was like reading stone. "Mr. Moreland . . ."

"My name is Bryan," he corrected, standing aside to let her off the elevator as it stopped on her floor.

"Yes, I know," she murmured, "but it sounds so presumptuous . . ."

"I won't be ninety for fifty more years," he reminded her.

She laughed in spite of herself. They were at her door now; she turned, looking up at him, and some vague longing nagged in the back of her mind as her eyes swept over his hard, chiseled mouth. She couldn't help wondering if its touch would be rough or tender, and she was suddenly, dangerously, curious. . . .

"Don't forget," he was saying. "Nine-thirty, my office."

"Can I bring a photog?" she asked huskily.

"Bring the whole editorial staff, if you like," he replied amiably. "It's my favorite story, and I love to tell it."

"Thanks again for tonight."

"My pleasure, country mouse," he said with a quiet smile. "Good night."

"Good night," she replied nervously.

His dark eyes dropped to her mouth, then slanted up to catch the mingled curiosity and apprehension in her shy gaze. He smiled mockingly just before he turned and walked away.

She lay awake half the night wondering why he hadn't kissed her. It would have been the normal end to an evening. It was customary. But he'd only smiled, and left her, not even bothering to brush a kiss against her forehead.

Was something wrong with her? Wasn't she pretty enough, attractive enough to appeal to him? Or did he already have a girlfriend? The question tortured her. He had women, she realized. He was certainly no monk. But why had he asked her out in the first place, and what did he really think of her? Had it all been a ploy to get her interested in his urban renewal program?

Bryan Moreland was one puzzle she couldn't seem to put together, and he got more complicated by the day.

Bill Peck gave her an odd look the next morning when she explained why she couldn't attend a City Planning Commission session with him.

"We've done three pieces on that damned downtown revitalization theme of his already," he said dourly. "Don't you think he's had enough free publicity?"

"I'm working on a story, in case you've forgotten," she replied, irritated.

"A story? Or the mayor?" he returned.

She gathered her purse and camera and went toward Edwards's office in a smouldering fury.

"I'm gone," she told him.

"Wait a sec. Come in and close the door," he called.

She shut out the sounds of typewriters and ringing telephones. "What's up?"

He motioned her to a chair. "Suppose you tell me that," he replied.

Her brows came together. "I don't understand."

"Moreland took you out. Then, this bogus story this morning — Carla, you're not getting involved with him, are you?" he asked kindly.

"Why . . . no," she lied. "But, he isn't even involved . . ."

"Your informant called me this morning."

"Is he after a job?" she asked with a flare of anger. "First Bill, now you . . . is he going to call everyone on the staff?"

"He knows you're seeing Moreland," he replied calmly, leaning back in his chair, "and he thinks the mayor may be involved in this."

She felt something inside her freeze. A cold, merciless, nameless something that had been in bud.

"He isn't," she said.

"How could you possibly know? Be reasonable. You haven't even been able to get to the records."

She clutched her purse in her lap, her eyes staring at the skirt of her simple beige dress as she fought for control.

"All we know for sure," she replied, "is that land was purchased by the city for a new airport. The evaluation was twenty-five thousand dollars an acre — a steal even though it was in a sparsely populated section. But the city paid a half million for it." She sighed. "It's not unusual for a realtor to mark up his asking price when he knows he has a buyer like the city. But Daniel Brown said that the land owner only received two hundred fifty thousand dollars and that records will bear him out. The problem," she added ruefully, "is that when I asked for the records of the transaction, that icy-voiced little financial wizard promptly called the city attorney and they refused to let me see the records on the grounds that it hadn't been formally approved by the city council."

"That's a lie," Edwards said.

She nodded. "I know, and I told the city attorney so. But we did a piece on his department last month that he didn't like, and he can quote the obscure law to you verbatim if you call and ask him."

"God deliver me from disgruntled lawyers!" he groaned.

"It doesn't matter," she said. "I'm going to ask the mayor for permission to look at them." She smiled. "I think he'll agree."

He eyed her. "Unscrupulous little minx."

"Me?" she blushed.

"You. Get out of here. And if you don't have any luck with Moreland, I'll get our legal staff on it."

"No problem."

She walked out the door in a daze. Was she trying to get close to Moreland to get information? It might have been that way at the beginning. But not anymore. She remembered what Edwards had said about Moreland being involved in what could be the biggest city scandal since the City Council chairman was arrested picking up a streetwalker. It couldn't be true. Not Bryan Moreland. Perhaps Edwards had misunderstood Brown. She smiled. She'd have a talk with the ex-cop tomorrow. It was about time she got the whole story firsthand.

Moreland was waiting for her in his office with a woman she recognized as the new mayor of a city in a neighboring state: Grace Thomas.

"Grace, this is Carla Maxwell," he told the older woman, "with the *Phoenix-Herald*. She's going to do a follow-up on the revitalization."

"Nice to meet you," Grace said with a pleasant smile. She was years older than Carla, a contemporary of Moreland's most likely, despite her dark brown hair that didn't show a trace of gray. "I'm very interested in the renewal idea. It might be feasible in my own city."

"If you're both ready, let's get moving," Moreland said as he helped Grace on with her plush wool coat. "I've got a budget meeting in two hours, and that doesn't leave us much time."

Carla watched the way the older woman's eyes slid sideways to Moreland as he held her coat, and she wanted to drop her heavy camera on the woman's foot. It was ridiculous to feel this surge of jealousy toward the visiting mayor. After all, she wasn't even pretty, and she was wearing a wedding ring! But that didn't stop her from wanting to push Moreland away from her.

Inexplicably, Moreland looked up at that moment and caught the expression on her face, and something darkened his eyes.

She averted her gaze quickly while Mrs. Thomas went right on talking about her city council woes without even noticing the undercurrents around her.

Walking through the streets with Moreland and City Planning Commission Chairman Ed King and the two other commission members, Carla was impressed with plans to renovate the run-down area. While Mrs. Thomas pumped King, Moreland dropped back beside Carla.

"Interesting, isn't it?" he asked quietly, indicating the windowless old houses with their sagging porches and littered yards. Some were deserted, but children played aimlessly in the yards around others, and deserted store buildings were interspersed with the homes.

"Tragic," she replied. "It reminds me of shacks I've seen back home. Poverty has many addresses."

"Yes," he replied.

"Is this area where you're concentrating?" she asked as she paused to photograph a house with blackened, paneless windows where a little girl stood, ragged and barefoot, clinging to a post.

"Yes. I got a manufacturing chain to bear almost half the cost of construction; their headquarters office is located near here. When we get this project going, you won't recognize the neighborhood."

"How about the people?" she asked, gazing up at him. "You can change their environment, but can you change them? Poverty doesn't go away because the setting is changed. How about employment?"

He smiled. "One step at a time, honey. I've got experts working on that aspect of it."

She glanced ahead, where Mrs. Thomas had cornered Ed King and his two planners. "Why won't your legal department let me look at the airport land purchase records?" she asked suddenly, catching his eyes.

Both heavy brows went up, and he paused before he replied, "Honey, that's between you and Ed King. I've told you before, I'm not going to interfere."

"But . . ."

He turned away. "We'd better catch up."

She followed along, puzzled and a little disappointed at the answer he'd given her. And try as she might, a nagging suspicion began to work on her mind.

"Mr. King tells me that the slums account for half of all your arrests," Mrs. Thomas was saying as they walked.

"That's right," Moreland agreed. "And fifty percent of all disease, as well as thirty-five percent of all fires. With proper housing, we could save almost a million dollars a year in fire losses and communicable disease."

Carla found herself beside Ed King, and the mayor's voice faded in her ears as she put the question to the planning commissioner. "May I ask you a question, Mr. King?" she asked abruptly.

He glanced at her, eyes sharp through his heavy glasses. His bald head gleamed in the cold sunlight. "If it concerns the airport land purchase, I'm sure the city attorney told you that the information is privileged until the council formally approves the purchase."

"Excuse me," she countered coolly, "but the council approved the purchase two meetings ago," she snapped her notebook closed, "and construction on the terminal is already underway."

"You choose to misunderstand me," he said with a cold smile. "the council hasn't approved the paperwork. A formality, of course, but legally binding. Check the city charter."

"I have," she told him, her green eyes narrowed. "If everything is up and aboveboard, Mr. Chairman, why all the secrecy?"

He purpled. "As usual, you reporters want to make something of nothing! I've told you, it's a formality, the figures will be released."

"When?" she shot back.

"Carla!" Moreland stopped speaking in the middle of a sentence to thunder her name. She jumped, turning to face him. "That's enough, by God," he growled. "This isn't an interrogation."

The clipped, measured tones made her flinch. "I apologize," she said tightly. "I didn't mean . . ."

"If you'll excuse me, Bryan," King said curtly, "I think I'll pass on the rest of the tour. You know my position."

"Sure," Moreland said. "We'll talk later."

"A pleasure to meet you, Mrs. Thomas," King told the visiting mayor with a smile. He ignored Carla as he walked away, taking his planners with him.

"Well," Mrs. Thomas said with a mirthless laugh, "I suppose that little scene ended my chances of a discussion with your planners."

Carla flushed to the roots of her hair. She pressed her camera close to her side. "I . . . I have an interview with the public works commissioner at eleven," she said unsteadily. "I'd better get going. Thanks for the tour."

She almost ran for her car, deaf to Moreland's deep voice calling her name.

She was shaking all over by the time she got to Tom Green's office. He was a public accountant, and she had a feeling he'd made a good commissioner, if for no better reason than his outspokenness.

At least, she thought wearily as she waited in his outer office, he wouldn't be angry. She could still see Bryan Moreland's dark, accusing eyes. Why, oh, why did she have to open her big mouth? It was all part of the job, but the argument had left a bad taste in her mouth, along with Moreland's obvious disapproval.

"Miss Maxwell?" the secretary repeated. "You can go in now."

She put on her best smiling face and went into Tom Green's carpeted office.

He rose, tall and gray haired, towering over her as he shook her hand. "I have to agree that the media gets prettier every day," he said with an approving glance from pale blue eyes.

She smiled. "For that, I promise to mail all my garbage out of town."

"God bless you. How about agreeing to support my recycling concept instead?" he teased. "I can get federal funding and match services instead of cash."

"Really?" she asked, sidetracked. She whipped out her pad and pen. "Tell me about it."

He did, and by the time he was through, her cold hands had warmed and she was relaxed.

"You were tense when you came in," he observed. "Care to tell me why? Surely it wasn't because I inspire fear in young women?"

"I . . . uh, I just had a run-in with the

planning commissioner," she said. "Nothing important."

"Ummm," he said noncommittally. "I never approved of Moreland making that appointment," he said bluntly. "King was a real-estate agent before he took office, you know. A damned shady one, if you want my opinion. He gave it up when he went into office, but I'll bet my secretary that he still has all his old contacts. It just isn't good business. He has too much sway with the city commission, what with Moreland on such friendly terms with him."

"Are they friends?" she asked carelessly.

"They were in the service together," he replied. "I thought you knew all that."

"I'm new in town," she said, and let it go at that.

She walked back to her office in a silence fraught with concern. So many things were beginning to make sense: for instance, King's real-estate background. Was he somehow involved in that missing money? Was Bryan Moreland involved? Her eyes closed momentarily. Bryan! He'd probably never speak to her again after the confrontation she'd had with his friend. Perhaps it was for the best. She was getting involved with him — too involved. And she didn't dare.

She handed in her copy and went home, turning down Bill Peck's offer of a free meal. She didn't feel like company, and she didn't want to be pumped about her latest information. That was all Bill was after, she knew. She couldn't have borne talking about it.

The apartment seemed lonelier than ever as she dressed idly in a pair of worn jeans and a blue ribbed top that was slightly too small. She turned on the radio and as pleasant, soft music filled the apartment, she went into the small kitchen to whip up an omelet. She was going to have to force it down, at that. Food was the last thing on her mind.

The doorbell was an unwelcome interruption. The omelet was almost done, and she had to turn it off before time was up. Grumbling, she moved irritably to the door. It was probably some student selling magazine subscriptions. The apartment house was a prime target, despite the "no soliciting" signs, and she was in no mood for a sales pitch.

She swung open the door with unnecessary force and froze with her mouth open to speak. Bryan Moreland was standing there, idly leaning against the wall, his dark eyes pointedly studying the too-tight top she was wearing.

CHAPTER FIVE

He smiled at the expression on her face. "Who were you expecting?" he asked.

She swallowed. "Not you," she said without thinking. He was wearing slacks and an open-necked burgundy velour shirt that bared a sensuous amount of hair-roughened bronzed flesh.

"Why?"

"Well . . ."

"You might as well invite me in," he told her. "I've got a feeling it won't be a short explanation."

"Oh!" She opened the door wider and stepped aside to let him in beside her. He went straight to the armchair by the window and lowered his big body into it.

"Would you like some coffee?" she asked, stunned by his sudden appearance.

"If you can spare it," he replied with a wry smile. "I just put the lady mayor on a plane. I haven't even had lunch yet. That's why I came. I thought you might like to go out for a burger and fries."

It was almost laughable, the mayor taking a reporter out for a hamburger.

"Well, I . . ." she stammered.

"Aren't you hungry?" he asked. "Or are you still smarting from that round with Ed?"

She lowered her eyes. "I didn't mean to ruin your tour."

He laughed. "My God, is that why you ran away?"

"I thought you were angry with me," she admitted.

"I was furious. But that was this morning, and this is now," he explained quietly. "I don't hold grudges. You and Ed can damned well fight it out, but not on my time. Now do you want supper or not?"

She looked up, studying him. "I just cooked an omelet."

"Big enough for two?" he teased.

She nodded. "I can make some toast."

"How about cinnamon toast?" he asked, rising. "I'm pretty good at it."

"You can cook?" she asked, forgetting that she looked like something out of a ragbag, that she wasn't wearing makeup and her long hair was gathered back with a rubber band in a travesty of a ponytail.

"My mother thought it would be a good

idea if I learned," he recalled with an amused smile. "She gives me a refresher course every year at Christmas."

"What else can you cook?" she asked, leading the way into the small kitchen.

"The best pepper steak you've ever tasted."

"I don't believe you."

"Come to dinner Sunday," he said, "I'll prove it."

"At your apartment?" she asked as she handed him the bread and a cookie sheet spread with aluminum foil.

"At the farm. I'll pick you up early in the morning, and you can spend the day."

She thought for a minute, feeling herself sinking into deep water. She'd been too pleased at the sight of him tonight, too happy that he'd bothered to come and ask her out.

He came up behind her; and with a quicksilver thrill of excitement, she felt his big, warm hands pressing into her tiny waist. "I have a housekeeper, Mrs. Brodie. She's elderly and buxom, and she'll cut off my hands if I try to seduce you. Satisfied, Miss Purity?"

She felt her color coming and going as he drew her closer, his breath whispering warmly in her hair.

"I . . . I wasn't worried about that," she managed weakly.

Deep, soft laughter rumbled in the chest at her back. "Do you think I'm too old to feel desire?" he asked.

"Mr. Moreland!" she burst out.

"Make it Bryan," he said.

"Bryan," she repeated breathlessly.

"Why aren't there any men in your life?" he asked suddenly. "Why don't you date?"

Her eyes closed against the memory. "I date you," she corrected weakly.

"Before me there was someone. Who? When?" he asked harshly, his fingers biting into her soft flesh. "Tell me!"

"He was married," she said miserably.

There was a long, heavy silence behind her. "Did you know?"

She shook her head. "I was just nineteen, and horribly naïve. I met him while I was a freshman in college. He was one of the instructors. We went together for two months before I found out."

She felt him tense. "How far had it gone?"

She shifted restlessly. "Almost too far," she admitted, remembering the phone call that had saved her virtue. A phone call from his wife, and she'd answered the phone . . .

"And you gave up on life because of one bad experience?" he asked quietly.

"I learned not to trust men," she corrected, bending her head. "It was . . . safer . . . to stay at home, unless I was with girl friends."

"And now, Carla?" he persisted.

She chewed on her lower lip nervously. "I . . . don't know."

His hand slid down her hips, pulling her back closer to him. Involuntarily, her hands went to push against the intimacy of his, and he laughed.

"Turn on the broiler for me," he said, releasing her. "That omelet's going to be stone cold."

She obeyed him mindlessly, fighting down her confusion.

They ate in a companionable silence, and she felt his dark eyes watching her when she wasn't watching him. Something was happening between them. She could feel it, and it frightened her.

Afterward, she put the dishes in the sink to soak, refusing his offer of help to wash them, and led the way into the living room nervously.

"I can't stay," he said. "I've got to stop in at a cocktail party later tonight to try and twist the governor's arm for emergency funding for my revitalization."

"Dressed like that?" she asked without

thinking.

"It's informal," he teased. His dark, bold eyes traveled down the length of her slender body. "You look pretty informal yourself."

"I wasn't expecting company."

"Sorry I came?" he asked bluntly.

"No," she replied.

His jaw tightened, and she saw a strange darkness grow in his eyes as he looked at her. He held her gaze until she thought her heart was going to burst, until the only sound she could hear was the wild beating of her own heart.

"Good night, Carla," he said abruptly and, turning, went out the door without a backward glance.

She stood exactly where she was and caught her breath. He hadn't wanted to go out that door. She'd read it in his eyes. But he hadn't kissed her. He still hadn't kissed her.

"What's wrong with me?" she asked the room unsteadily, turning to look in the mirror. But all she saw was a disappointed face and a body in a too-tight blouse. The reflection told her nothing.

She had Daniel Brown, the informant, meet her for coffee the next afternoon in the small international coffee house where she had gone with Moreland that first time. Brown was a personable young man with an honest face, but she didn't quite like the way his blue eyes darted away while he spoke.

"Did you know that the mayor and James White were close friends?" he asked as they sat and drank coffee at a corner table.

She stared at him. "James White? Isn't he that rich realtor who was investigated for fraud last year?"

"The same. Do a little digging, and you may come up with some interesting little tidbits."

"Why are you furnishing all this information so generously?" she asked abruptly.

He looked uncomfortable. "I don't like corruption," he replied.

"Is that the truth?" she probed, "or are you just trying to get back at the people who helped you out of your job?"

He shrugged. "It's a dog-eat-dog world."

"Sometimes," she agreed. "Why do you think Moreland's involved?"

"He's got too much money showing to be a mayor," he replied vaguely.

"So he has. But I understood he was independently wealthy."

"Did you?" he asked. "You're seeing a lot of him lately."

"I'm working on a story," she said for the second time, to the second person, that week.

"He wasn't much of a husband," he said with a strange bitterness. "Don't get your hopes up in that direction, either."

She stood up. "My personal life is my own business."

"That's what you think." He sipped his coffee. "Check out White. You'll see."

She turned on her heel and left him there. Late that afternoon, she took her wealth of bits and pieces to Edwards and requested that he give it to the paper's attorneys and see if they could force the city attorney to release the airport land purchase records.

Bryan Moreland's farm was like a picture postcard. Well-kept grounds, white-fenced paddocks, silver silos, a red barn with white trim, and a farmhouse with a sprawling front porch and urns that must have been full of flowers in the spring and summer.

Mrs. Brodie grinned from ear to ear when Moreland brought Carla in and introduced her. The buxom old woman obviously approved, and the table she set for lunch was evidence of it. Carla ate until her stomach hurt, and Mrs. Brodie was still trying to press helpings of apple cobbler on her.

Moreland helped her escape into his study, where a fire was blazing in the hearth. It was a dreary day outside, drizzling rain and cold. But the den, with its Oriental rug and sedate dark furniture, was cozy. She stared at the portrait above the white mantel curiously. It was a period painting, and the man in it looked vaguely like Bryan Moreland.

"Is he a relative?" she asked.

He tossed two big, soft cushions down on the floor in front of the hearth and stretched out with his hands under his head. "In a manner of speaking," he replied lazily. "He was my grandmother's lover."

She blushed, and he laughed.

"And the picture hangs in here?" she asked, aghast.

"He's something of a family legend," he replied. "He'd be damned uncomfortable in the closet. Come here," he added with a sensuous look in his dark eyes as he gestured toward the pillow next to his.

She hesitated, drawn by the magnetism of his big body in the well-fitted brown trousers and pale yellow velour shirt, but wary of what he might expect of her.

His dark eyes took in the length of her body, lingering on the plunging V-neck of her white sweater, tracing her dark slacks down to her booted feet.

"If we make love," he said quietly, "I won't let it go too far. Is that what you're afraid of, Carla?"

She caught her breath. He seemed to read her mind. She only nodded, lost for words.

His eyes searched hers. "Then, come on."

She eased down beside him, curling her arms around her drawn-up knees with the pillow at her back. "Are we?" she asked huskily.

He traced the line of her spine with deft, confident fingers. "Are we what?" he asked deeply.

"Going to make love," she managed shakily.

"That depends on you, country mouse," he said matter-of-factly, and he removed his caressing hand.

She half-turned and looked down at him. His eyes were dark, smouldering, and there was no smile to ease the intensity of his piercing gaze.

"If you want it, come here," he said gruffly.

She didn't even think. She went down into his outstretched arms as if she were going home, as if she'd waited all her life for a big, husky, dark man to hold out his arms to her.

He crushed her against his broad chest

and lay just holding her as the fire crackled and popped cheerfully in the dimly lit room.

"It's been a long time for me, Carla," he said in a strange, gruff tone. "Kisses may not be enough."

She felt her body stiffen against him. "I can't . . ."

"Don't start freezing on me," he said at her ear. "I'm not going to throw you over my shoulder and beat a path to my bedroom with you."

"But you said . . ." she whispered.

"I may touch you," he murmured sensuously. His mouth brushed lazily, warmly, at her throat, while his big hands worked some magic on her back through the sweater. "Like this." He eased his hands underneath it, against the silken young flesh of her bare back. "And this," he added, sweeping his hands up to her shoulder blades, discovering for himself that she was wearing nothing under the sweater.

"No . . ." she whispered unsteadily, a protest that sounded more like a moan.

His thumbs edged out under her arms, brushing against flesh that had never known a man's hands, and she caught her breath at the sensations it fostered.

"I want to love you," he said softly. He eased her back on the rug, with her head and shoulders against the pillow, letting his hands move very gently on her rib cage in a silence burning with emotions.

"Bryan . . ." she whispered achingly.

He bent, and his mouth parted slightly as it touched hers in soft, slow movements. It was torture, the teasing, brushing touch of his mouth and hands, a delicious torment that made her heart beat violently against the walls of her chest. She had never wanted anything as desperately as she now wanted Bryan, and in a fever of wanting, she heard her own voice shatter as she cried out for his touch.

His mouth took hers violently, hungrily, pressing her head deep into the pillow while his hands taught her sensations so exquisite, she arched submissively toward them.

Once her eyes slid open to look up into his, and he smiled at the awe and emotion in them — a smile that was strangely tender and soft with triumph.

He drew her own hands to the buttons of his shirt and watched while she undid them, clumsily, because she was shaking from the lazy caresses of his deft hands.

"Here," he said quietly, drawing her mouth to his chest. "Like this. Hard, honey, hard!" he whispered huskily as her mouth brushed against the warm flesh that smelled of spice and soap.

She reached up to draw his mouth back down to hers and felt a shudder run through him as his body moved over hers in a way that was pleasure beyond bearing.

He hurt her mouth, bruised it, as all his hard control seemed to disappear at her yielding. He drew back suddenly, and his dark eyes were smouldering with hunger as they looked down into hers.

"I want you like hell," he said in a rough whisper. "Another minute of this and I'm going to take you. Is that what you want, Carla?"

Sanity came back in a blazing rush. She gasped at the emotions that lay raw and bruised at the harshness of his statement.

"No," she said shakily. "No, it isn't. Bryan, I'm sorry . . ."

He rolled away from her and got to his feet. He went straight to the bar and poured himself a large whiskey, downing it before he lit a cigarette — all without looking at her.

She pulled down her sweater and got to her feet, her tongue gingerly touching her bruised mouth. She felt vaguely ashamed at her abandon, and as she stared at his broad back, she couldn't help wondering if he thought she was like this with other men. In fact, she'd never let any man touch her like that. She was at a loss to explain why it had seemed so right when Bryan had done it. Her face flamed at the memory.

"I'll take you home," he said coldly. "Get your coat."

"Bryan . . ." she began apologetically.

He turned, and his eyes were blazing. "Get your damned coat," he said, in a voice that froze her.

Fighting tears, she gathered her possessions and followed him out to the car.

Chapter Six

She went around in a brown mood for the next week, alternately crying and cursing her own stupidity for getting herself emotionally involved with a man who only wanted one thing of her.

In between the tears, she waited vainly for the phone to ring, jumping every time it trilled, only to find some routine caller on the other end. The doorbell only rang once in all that time, and she dashed for it, her heart racing, only to find a neighbor inviting her to a rent party for another neighbor down on his luck.

How, she wondered, could she have thought Moreland was as involved as she was? Just because he took her out a few times didn't mean he wanted to marry her. She knew that, but had she really mistaken his objectives that much? All along, had he only been angling for a way to get her into his bed?

She could still blush, remembering the way it had been between them, that strange look in his eyes as they met hers while her body seemed to belong to someone else in her wild abandon. She wasn't easy, she wasn't! But, apparently, he thought so; and she still felt the whip of his anger even now, his smouldering silence as he'd driven her home and left her there, without even a word of apology. She hadn't been crying, but surely he could have seen that she was about to. Or perhaps he had. Perhaps it just hadn't mattered to him one way or the other.

That was the hardest thing to face; the fact that he just didn't care at all, except in a purely physical sense.

"No date with the mayor today?" Bill Peck chided as she sat down at her desk on Friday morning with an increasingly familiar listlessness.

She wanted to pick up something and throw it at him, but she kept cool. "I was writing a story," she reminded him. "It's finished."

"And it's been lying on Edwards's desk for the past week, where it will probably be lying this time next year," he reminded her. "The revitalization story's been done to death, and you know it. What's the matter,

362

honey, did your big romance go sour?"

She whirled, her green eyes flashing as they met his calculating ones. "You go to hell," she flashed in a tight, controlled voice. "What I do and how I do it are no concern of yours. I don't work for you; I work with you, and don't you ever forget it!"

A slow, mischievous smile appeared on his face, causing her anger to eclipse into puzzlement.

"That's my girl," he chuckled.

She slammed a pencil down on her spotless desk. "You beast!" she grumbled.

"It's my middle name. Now, are you finally back to normal? Business as usual?" He grabbed his coat. "Come on, we've got a press conference this morning. I've already cleared it with Eddy."

Eddy was his nickname for the city editor, and if Eddy said okay, she had no choice. But she got her purse and camera together with a sense of foreboding. "A press conference where?" she asked carefully.

"At city hall, where else?"

She froze, desperately searching her mind for an excuse, any excuse to get out of it. Another meeting. There had to be another meeting or an interview or a picture — oh, God, there had to be something!

"I said, let's go," Peck said, taking her

arm. "You haven't got an excuse. I need some pix, and I can't handle a camera with this finger," he added, holding up a bandaged right forefinger. "I cut it on a sheet of bond paper, can you imagine?" he sighed. "Worse than a knife cut."

"Can't you take Freddy?" she asked hopefully.

"What's the matter?" he asked with a sideways glance. "Afraid of him?"

She knew exactly what he meant, and she wanted to admit that she was terrified. She almost put it into words, but just at the last minute, she stopped herself.

"I'm not afraid of anybody," she said instead. "My father said it was better to go through life giving ulcers than letting other people give them to you."

"Wise man," he grinned. "On a trip to the Orient, did you say?"

It was just the question she needed to start her talking, and to take her mind off Moreland. They were in the elevator at city hall before she realized what Peck had been doing.

"You did that on purpose," she accused gently.

He glanced down at her, cocking his hat at an angle over his pale brow. "Who, me?"

"Yes, you, you lovely man."

He grinned at her. "Like to adopt me?"

"No. You're too tall."

He squatted down a little. "How about now?"

"Lose a hundred pounds, and we'll talk about it," she assured him.

The conference room was crowded, but she didn't spend one second looking around for Bryan Moreland. She took a seat beside Peck in the back section and lowered her eyes to her camera, keeping them down resolutely while she pretended to fiddle with light settings.

"You don't think you're going to get me a shot from here, do you?" Peck asked as he sat down beside her.

"I'll use the telescopic lens," she said under her breath. All around them, news people were milling around. A couple of them, radio reporters whom she recognized from other stories, called to her, and she managed a frozen smile and a tiny wave of her hand in response.

"What in hell is the matter with you?" Peck asked. "You look like you're trying to get smaller."

"Will you please shut up?" she begged. His voice was loud, and it carried. "Please sit down and pretend we aren't acquainted."

"But we work for the same paper," he

argued.

"Not for long, if you keep this up," she whispered back.

"You *are* scared of him!"

"Shut up," she said through her teeth, making a prayer of it as Bryan Moreland's big, husky form came into view. He swept the room with his dark, cutting gaze, and she felt the impact of it like a physical blow when his eyes stopped on her averted face. She stared straight ahead, ignoring him, while her heart felt as if it were going to jump out of her body.

She didn't look at him again until he was at the podium, with the City Council and the City Planning Commission gathered around the conference table with him. She recognized Edward King and Tom Green immediately.

"What's this all about?" she asked Peck in a muted whisper.

"The airport," he replied with a grin. "You made somebody take notice with that run-in with King, didn't you?"

She shifted restlessly and forced herself to listen to Moreland's deep curt voice describing plans for the new airport and the expansion of services it would mean by national airlines. For the first time, the city would have an international airport; a tribute to its rapid growth.

But when he finished, the land purchase still hadn't been discussed, and she noticed that the mayor didn't throw the floor open for questions, as he usually did at the end of a press conference.

She got her things together and started to dart out the side door, but Bill Peck left her, calling back that he had to talk to Tom Green, and Carla got trapped between the nest of chairs and a group of news people passing tidbits of information back and forth. The next thing she knew, she was looking up into Bryan Moreland's dark, quiet eyes.

Her heart dropped, and she could feel her knees trembling. She let her gaze fall to his burgundy tie.

"Good morning, your honor," she said with a pitiful attempt at lightness.

"Five days, two hours, twenty-six minutes," he said quietly.

She looked up, feeling all the dark clouds vanish, all the color come back into her colorless world as she realized the meaning behind the statement.

"And forty-five seconds," she whispered unsteadily.

He drew in a hard, deep breath, and she noticed for the first time how haggard he looked, how tired. "Oh, God, I've missed you," he said in a voice just loud enough to carry to her ears and no further. "I wanted a hundred times to call you and explain . . . I know what you must have thought, and you couldn't have been further off base. But I got busy . . . Oh, hell have supper with me. I'll try to put it into words."

The need to say yes was incredible. But she was cautious now, wary of him. He could hurt her now, because he could get close, and she wasn't sure she was willing to take the risk a second time.

He read that hesitation and nodded. "I know what you're afraid of. But trust me this once. Just listen to me."

She shifted and let a long breath seep out between her lips. "All right."

"I'll pick you up at six."

She nodded her assent and looked up, hypnotized by the strange expression in his eyes.

"Don't look at me like that," he whispered deeply. "There are too many cameras in here."

She knew what he meant without any explanation, and her face colored again.

"Reading my mind?" he asked with a wicked smile as his eyes dropped to the soft, high curve of her breasts. "Read it now."

She pulled her coat tight around her and tried to breathe normally. "I . . . I'll see you later, then," she managed weakly.

He chuckled softly as he moved to let her pass by him. His eyes didn't leave her until she was out of sight.

She was like a teenaged girl on her first date, waiting for him that night with her hair hanging loose over her shoulders, the single green velour evening gown she owned clinging to her slender curves like a second skin, bringing out the soft tan of her bare arms and shoulders.

She couldn't help feeling nervous. What was he going to expect from her now? The fact that he'd missed her hadn't really changed anything. And what about her? What was she willing to give? What did she truly feel?

In the midst of her mental interrogation, the doorbell screamed into the silence, and she jumped just before she ran to answer it.

He walked in by her even as she opened the door, his scowl fierce, his eyes dangerous.

"Hard day?" she asked softly.

"They're all hard," he said, turning to look down at her. The anger drained out of his hard face as he studied her soft curves with an expression that grew warmer, possessive, as the seconds throbbed past.

His massive chest rose and fell heavily under his dark evening clothes, his ruffled silk shirt. "Oh, honey," he said finally, deeply, "that is one hell of a dress."

"Do you really like it?" she murmured inanely, speaking for the sake of words, while her eyes told him something very different.

"I hope you haven't gone to any great pains with your makeup, little girl," he said finally, moving closer, "because I'm about to smear the hell out of it."

Her lips parted under a rush of breath while he pulled her against his big body, molding her slowly against him.

"It's been too long already," he said in a harsh whisper, bending his dark head until she felt the warm, uneven pulse of his breath against her trembling lips. "I can't get that evening out of my mind, Carla. . . ."

His mouth hurt. It was as if the hunger he felt made violence necessary, and his big arms bruised in their ardor while he took what he needed from her soft ardent mouth.

"Sleep with me," he whispered against her mouth. "I need you."

"Bryan . . ." she breathed, drawing back as far as the crush of his arms would allow.

"God, don't make me wait any longer," he growled unsteadily. "I'm so hungry for you I can hardly stay alive for wanting you. Carla, little Carla, why are you holding back? You won't regret it."

She swallowed and her eyes closed. "Bryan, there's never been a man," she said in a haunted voice.

She felt his arms stiffen around her, felt his breath catch.

"What did you say?" he asked.

She drew a steadying breath. "I said, I've never slept with a man."

"But, at the farm . . . My God, woman, you were on fire . . ."

Her eyelids pressed hard together as a wave of embarrassment swept over her, and her pale cheeks colored. "I know. But it's still true."

There was a long pause, and then his big, warm hands came up to force her face out of hiding, so that he could search it and her misty eyes.

"It was the first time for you . . . touching, being touched?" he asked finally, and there was a new tenderness in his voice.

All she could manage to do was nod. Her throat felt as if it had been glued shut.

The hard lines in his face relaxed, smoothed out. He looked at her as if he'd never seen a woman before. His dark eyes went down to her soft body, lingering on the high young curves that his fingers had touched so intimately.

"I remember looking down at you," he said absently, "and there was an expression on your face I couldn't understand. Now it all makes sense."

She chewed on her lower lip, vaguely embarrassed, because she remembered that moment, too — vividly.

He turned away, ramming his big hands into his pockets with a heavy sigh. "Well, that tears it," he said roughly.

She stared at his broad back, her eyes drawn to the thick, silver-threaded hair that gleamed like black diamonds in the overhead light.

"I'm sorry," she murmured inadequately.

"My God, for what?" he asked harshly, whirling to face her. His dark eyes blazed across the room.

The question stunned her. In the sudden silence, she could hear the ticking of the clock by the sofa, the sounds of traffic in the street as if they were magnified.

"Are you trying to apologize to me for not being the woman I thought in my arrogance that you were?" he asked, a new gentleness in his voice. "I don't want that."

She swallowed, dreading the question even as she asked it. "What *do* you want?"

A wisp of a smile turned up one corner of his sensuous mouth. "I could answer that in a monosyllable," he teased, watching the color come and go in her cheeks. "But, I won't." He shot back his white cuff and glanced at his watch. "We'd better get moving, honey. I ordered the table for seven-thirty, sharp. Ready?"

Confused by his sudden change of mood, she nodded absently and went to get her long black coat with its lush mink collar — an extravagance she'd once regretted.

He opened the door for her but caught her gently by the arm as she started out.

"I'm glad the first time was with me," he said in a strange, low tone.

Her face went beet red. She couldn't seem to meet his eyes as they walked together to the elevator.

He took her to a quiet restaurant downtown, with white linen tablecloths and white candles on the tables, and a live string quartet playing chamber music. It was cozy, and intimate, and the food was exquisite. But she hardly tasted it. Her mind was whirling with questions. He seemed to sense her confusion as they lingered over a second cup of rich coffee. He set his cup down in the saucer abruptly and leaned back in his chair, studying her with a single-minded intensity that began to wear on her nerves.

"You're very lovely," he said without preamble.

"Thank you," she replied, and lifted her empty cup to her lips to give her nervous hands something to do.

He drew an ashtray closer and started to reach for his cigarettes when the waiter came back, and he paused long enough to order another cup of coffee for them before he finished the action.

"Men my age get used to a routine of sorts with women, Carla," he said gently, blowing out a cloud of gray smoke from his cigarette. "You disrupted mine."

"I . . . hadn't thought you'd expect that from me," she said falteringly. "Not so soon, at least," she added with a wistful smile. "I thought I'd have time to . . ."

"Don't start that again," he said. "I should have known what an innocent you are. All the signs were there, like banners. I was just too blind to see them. Anyway," he added with a brief smile, "there was no harm done."

"Wasn't there?" she asked, gazing quietly at the hard lines of his leonine face. They never semed to soften very much, she thought, even in passion — especially in passion. She flushed. "You were so angry," she recalled.

He chuckled softly. "Yes, I was. Hurting like hell, like I hadn't hurt since years before I married. I could have choked you to death. Not knowing the whole story, I thought you were playing hard-to-get. And to tell the truth, I hadn't planned to see you again."

That hurt, more than she'd expected. Of course, most women her age were sophisticated and more permissive. But she'd been a late bloomer in all respects. Even now, when just looking at this dark, taciturn man could make her heart do flips, she couldn't consider an affair. She knew instinctively that it would tear her to pieces emotionally, especially when it ended. And it would end sometime. He was too sophisticated and far too worldly, to be satisfied with a novice for long.

"Why did you change your mind?" she asked gently.

He lifted his coffee cup with a well-manicured hand. "Because I missed you." A fleeting smile played around his chiseled lips. "It was unexpected. I've had women around since my wife died, but only briefly, and in one capacity. It occurred to me, belatedly, that I enjoyed having you around." He looked straight into her eyes. "In any capacity."

Her lips felt suddenly dry, and she moistened them with the tip of her tongue. "I couldn't handle an affair with you," she said hesitantly.

"I won't ask you to. But, if you don't mind, honey," he added with a wry smile, "I think we'll keep it low key. I can't handle frustration. It plays hell with my temper."

She smiled self-consciously, remembering. Her jade eyes looked into his. "I hope you know that I wasn't playing coy," she added seriously.

"I know it now." His dark eyes studied that portion of her above the table with a sensuous boldness that made her heart thump. "I'd say I wish I'd known it sooner, but I don't. I can still close my eyes and taste you."

She felt the heat in her face. "Low key, I believe you said?" she said breathlessly.

"Honey, for me this *is* low key." He chuckled. "Finish your coffee, and we'll take in a movie before we go home. Do you like science fiction?"

"I love it!" she said incredulously. "Don't tell me you're a sci-fi fan, too?"

"Don't let it get around but I sat through

two showings of *Star Wars*," he replied with a smile. "And if you aren't in a hurry for your beauty sleep, I'll sit you through two showings of this one."

"Who wants to sleep?" she asked, gulping down the rest of the rich coffee. "Why are you sitting there?" she asked, standing. "The box office opens again at nine!"

"Just give me a minute to ease my aching old bones out of the chair," he chuckled, leaning forward to stamp out his cigarette.

"Shall I get you a cane?" she asked with a mischievous smile. Her eyes traced his formidable bulk as he rose. "Or maybe a forklift?" she added, measuring him with her eyes.

"I'm not that big."

"You're not small," she returned. "I'll bet that's why you got elected."

He scowled. "What is?"

"Your size. The voters simply couldn't see your opponents when they were out campaigning against you."

His leonine head lifted, and he stared down his straight nose at her through narrowed, glittering eyes. "You," he said, "are incorrigible."

"Look who's calling who names," she replied saucily. "You wrote the book on it."

He smiled down at her, a slow, wicked

smile that was echoed by the look in his eyes. "Has anyone ever told you that this kind of teasing raises a man's blood pressure at least ten points?"

She turned and started toward the cashier's counter. "I won't do it any more," she promised. "At your age, that could be extremely dangerous."

"Why, you little . . ."

"You're the one who was complaining about your age, not me," she reminded him.

"You make me feel it," he said with exasperation in his voice.

She waited patiently while he paid the check, her eyes drawn to an impressionistic study of ballerinas on a huge canvas on the wall. The delicate pink and white contrasts were exquisitely implied.

"Do you like ballet?" he asked at her shoulder.

"Very much," she replied, turning to follow him out onto the sidewalk. "I studied ballet for two years, until they convinced me that I simply didn't have the discipline to be good at it."

"Discipline smooths the rough edges around any talent," he said with a sideways glance. "But I'd have said you have it, as far as reporting goes."

"Thank you," she said gravely. "I try to do

my best. Although sometimes, it's easier than others. I could have gone through the ground that day I got into it with Edward King on your ghetto tour."

He raised a heavy eyebrow at her. "That wasn't the end of it, either," he informed her. "I got an earful when I walked into my office."

She flushed. "He was pretty mad, I guess," she probed.

"Putting it mildly, he was frothing at the mouth," he replied.

She drew in a weary breath. "I'm bound to do my job," she said quietly. "I still feel that Mr. King is being unnecessarily evasive about that land purchase, and I intend to pursue it until I get the truth."

His jaw tautened. "I think you're making a mountain out of a lump, little girl," he said flatly. "Ed's like a mule. When someone tries to force him along, he balks. It's in his nature."

"And not being put off is in mine," she returned with spirit. She stopped under a streetlight and stared up at him. "Why can't I see the records of the land purchase?"

"I told you before, you'll have to knock that around with Ed. I'm not interfering," he said gruffly.

"Green says . . ." She caught herself just

in time. It wouldn't do to give away her hand, even though she was dying to know if Green's accusation about Moreland and King being such thick friends was true. And it was beginning to look bad; almost as if Moreland was involved, and had something to hide.

"Yes?" he said curtly, taking her up on the unfinished statement, his face like a thundercloud. "What does he say?"

She shrugged. "I'm sorry. Sometimes I forget to leave my job at the office."

He said nothing, leading her to the parked car in an ominous silence. "I'd better get you into the theater before we come to blows," he said, and she could hear the anger in his voice.

She felt a twinge of guilt, glancing at his set features as he climbed behind the wheel and started the black Jaguar.

"I'm sorry," she said gently.

Something in his posture relaxed. He pulled out into the traffic, all without looking at her. "Let's leave politics alone from now on. We both tend to overheat a little."

"All right," she agreed. She glanced at him again, her eyes searching his dark face for some softening. There was none.

"I don't hold it against you that you're the mayor," she reminded him.

A hint of a smile flared briefly on his lips. "I'll trade jobs any time you like."

"No, thanks." Her eyes were drawn to his dark, beautiful hands as he controlled the powerful car with ease and skill. The onyx ring on his little finger sparkled in the sporadic streetlights. "Why did you want to be mayor, anyway?"

"Are we conducting an interview?" he mused.

"No," she said, "but I'm curious."

"I saw some things that needed to be done. They weren't being done. I thought I could do them," he said.

"And, have you?" she asked, genuinely curious, because her brief time in the city wasn't enough for her to know.

"Some of them," he admitted. "I'm bound by the city charter and the council. My hands are tied a good bit of the time."

"It looks like you'll get your redevelopment program through, though."

His face clouded in the dim light. "Maybe. It depends on my support."

He pulled into a vacant parking spot right in front of the theater.

"That never happens for me," she sighed wistfully.

He half-turned in his seat. "What?" he asked with a curious smile.

"A vacant parking spot where I want to go." She shook her head. "You must be incredibly lucky."

"I was, until I met you," he replied, tongue-in-cheek.

She saw what he was talking about and felt the color run into her face just as he got out to open the door for her.

The movie was a dud, one of its main features being a brief flash of bare flesh and some passionate love scenes that Carla found frankly embarrassing to watch in mixed company.

"You little puritan," he accused gently when the film was finally over and they were leaving the crowded lobby. "I could see you blushing even in the dark."

"I'm a country girl," she muttered.

"Come out to my farm in the spring, and let's see if you blush any less," he challenged dryly.

"Will you hush?" she burst out.

He laughed at her, a pleasant, deep sound. "I'd rather tease you than eat. Ready to go home, little one?"

No, she thought, watching him out of the corner of her eye as they walked down the sidewalk toward the car. I never want to leave you. The thought was incredible and she could barely believe what her stirred senses were telling her. She got a tight rein on her emotions, and slid gracefully into the car when he held the door open for her.

"I am a little tired," she admitted, forcing down her disappointment.

"I'll drop you by your apartment before I go home for my warm milk and crackers," he said dryly, sparing her an amused glance as he started the car and pulled out into the street.

"If you're drinking warm milk," she observed, "it's probably spiked."

He chuckled softly. "Probably."

They managed a companionable silence the rest of the way back to her apartment. It wasn't until they went up in the elevator that he broke it.

"Do you like to bowl?" he asked.

She laughed. "I like to try," she admitted. "Most of the time the ball goes down the alley."

"I'll teach you," he told her. "All it takes is the right technique and a little practice."

"I'd like that," she said, smiling up at him.

He searched her soft green eyes and scowled as they left the elevator and walked down the carpeted hall to her door.

"Is something wrong?" she asked, when they reached her apartment.

He rammed his hands in his pockets and

sighed heavily. "Time," he said, sketching her face with restless eyes.

"Time?" she prompted.

"You need to be spending yours with a younger man," he said.

"I thought I was," she replied, darting a mischievous glance up at him.

He shook his head. "It's only a matter of time before someone mistakes me for your father."

"Only if I wear roller skates and braid my hair," she assured him.

He reached out a big hand and touched her cheek lightly. "Are you sure?" he asked.

Her face went solemn. "Am I too young for you?" she asked gently. "I know so little . . ."

"That makes you a novelty in my life," he replied. He pulled at a lock of her long, dark hair. "I know very little of innocence. My wife was far from being a novice when I married her. And I wouldn't have married her if Candy hadn't been on the way."

"What a lovely name," she murmured.

"She was a lovely little girl," he replied quietly. His dark eyes clouded.

Her fingers went up to touch his chiseled mouth. "You've never talked about it, have you? Not once. Not to anyone."

"You read me very well, little one," he told

her, catching her soft fingers to press them against the hard lines of his cheek. "No, I haven't talked about it. But I think I could, with you."

"I'm flattered."

"It's not flattery." He drew her palm to his mouth, and she felt the warm excitement of his lips against its softness, running through her like electricity.

She could smell the clean, tangy scent of his skin as the action brought his dark head closer. She felt her heart storming against the walls of her chest. He affected her as no man ever had. Everything about him attracted her; the bigness of him, the dark masculinity, even the scent of his cologne. She wanted with all her might to reach up and bring that hard mouth down against her lips.

He looked up and saw the expression in her face, and something seemed to explode in his dark eyes.

"Don't tempt me, honey," he said in a soft, deep tone. "If I start kissing you right now, there won't be any stopping me."

She flushed. "I wasn't . . ." she protested weakly.

His dark eyes sparkled wickedly. "Weren't you?" he teased.

She lowered her eyes to the heavy rise and

fall of his massive chest, hating her inherent shyness.

"Don't be embarrassed," he said gently, and she felt his fingers lightly touching her hair. "Delicious things happen when I touch you. You'll never know what it cost me to walk away from you that day at the farm."

She smiled at the carpet. "I felt terrible," she murmured. "I didn't sleep for two nights, and I was sure you hated me."

"You do inspire violent emotions, little one," he said wryly, "but hatred isn't one of them. Not for me." He sighed, leaning his forearms over her slender shoulders. "I knew you weren't sophisticated, but that innocence — I thought it was more a pose than anything else, and I indulged you. But the way you responded to me . . ."

She lowered her eyes to the steady rise and fall of his massive chest. "I've got a mental block about sleeping with men," she admitted quietly. "I believe in forever afters."

"And probably, unicorns," he teased lightly. "I'll be honest, Carla, I've tried marriage and I find little to recommend it. I enjoy my freedom."

"And the women that go with it," she said with a wry glance.

He looked vaguely uncomfortable. "Do

you want to know something irritating, little girl? I haven't had a woman since the night of that cocktail party."

She flushed at the frank statement. "Lack of opportunity?" she asked breathlessly.

"Lack of interest," he replied. His heavy brows drew together in a scowl. "I want you. No one else."

"Bryan, I'm sorry . . ."

He laughed mirthlessly. "God deliver me from innocence," he said in a gruff undertone. "It may be gold floss to fiction writers, but it's hell on a man's appetite."

She felt her temper catching fire and abruptly she jerked away from him, opening her door. She stood just inside it, her pale green eyes flaring up as they met his puzzled glance.

"Let's just say good-night, and goodbye, and it's been fun," she said tightly. "I'm dreadfully sorry I leave a bad taste in your mouth, but I want more out of life than one night in a man's bed! Good night!"

She slammed the door and locked it, leaning her hot forehead against it tearfully, feeling its coolness drain some of the heat away. There was no sound outside in the hall for several seconds. Then there was a harsh, muffled curse and the sound of heavy footsteps dying away. Tears welled up and overflowed in her eyes, dribbling down her cheeks and into the corner of her mouth.

I hate him, she thought raggedly. Her eyes closed tightly. I hate him so much . . .

An ache made her chest feel hollow as the sobs racked her slender body. A picture of his dark, handsome face floated around in her mind as she went to change clothes. It haunted her like an attractive, persistent ghost.

She did hate him — she did! Her even white teeth chewed on her lower lip as she stripped off the dress and exchanged it for a flowing gold and green patterned caftan. He didn't care a jot for her pale dreams of a home and children and a man to share with. He simply wanted her body — probably because it was the first that had been refused him.

The tears started again. She wiped them away with a vicious hand and went back into the living room. She didn't normally drink, but there was about two inches of wine in an old bottle in the cupboard, and she sloshed it into a juice glass and threw it down her throat. It stung pleasantly, giving her heartburn.

"Story of my life," she muttered, "cure's worse than the ailment."

She poured a glass of milk and washed

the wine down with that, idly contemplating ways she could get even with Bryan Moreland. All of them seemed to end with her in his arms.

Her face went hot at the memory of the last time she'd been there, of a pleasure so intense it hurt. The touch of his hands, his mouth, the sight of his dark, quiet face above her with a strange glow in the orange firelight.

"Oh, God, I love you," she whispered shakily, her eyes closed as she saw him again and again in her mind. "I love you so."

The sound of her own voice sobered her, especially when she realized with a start what she'd been muttering. It shocked her so that she didn't hear the telephone until its third insistent ring.

Her heart jumped impatiently as she picked it up, hoping to hear Moreland's deep, slow voice on the other end. But it wasn't him. It was her informer.

"I just wanted to see what you'd come up with," Daniel Brown said lightly. "I hadn't heard anything from you lately."

"I'm still working on it," she said, aware in her heart that she hadn't really been working on it very hard. Part of her was terrified that Bryan Moreland just might be mixed up in the land deal.

"I know someone who can get you a copy of those financial records, if that's the impasse," he said. "By tomorrow morning, if you like. I could meet you in that little coffee shop on the mall."

"It wouldn't involve a break-in, would it, Dan?" she asked quickly. "Our lawyers would frown . . ."

"I've got a girl friend at city hall," he interrupted. "She'll do it for me. Well?"

She swallowed. "I'd appreciate any help you could get me," she said finally. She was hurting so much from the confrontation with Moreland that very little of the conversation was registering in her mind.

"I hope you're not getting too involved with His Honor," he added suddenly. "He's in it up to his thick neck, and I can get proof of that, too."

Her face went white. "What kind of proof?" she asked in a voice far calmer than she felt inside.

"How about a check for one hundred thousand dollars, made out to him, signed by James White?" he asked smugly.

She felt her heart stop, and for one long, insane instant she wondered if it would ever start again. "For what?" she managed.

"His share of the kickback, of course," Brown replied. "Moreland, White and King are all in it together. It was White's land. He had his agent, King, propose it to Moreland for the airport at a two-hundred percent profit, and Moreland buffaloed it over the City Council. It was worth about one-third of what the city paid for it, and one third is what the city got. The rest of it was split among the three men. White got the city's actual cost, plus a few thousand. The rest of it was split between Moreland and King. I'll bring you a photostat of the check, too."

She twisted the telephone cord round and round her finger. Her voice faltered when she found it. "I'll meet you at the coffee shop at ten-thirty."

"I'll be there."

CHAPTER SEVEN

She still didn't want to believe it. It didn't sound like Bryan Moreland. He had money — at least, she'd heard that he did, and the farm was big enough to be proof of some kind of independent wealth. And he had integrity. She'd have staked her life on his honesty, his forthrightness. Loving him had nothing to do with that opinion, either. She'd have felt that way if they'd been bitter enemies. She smiled to herself wistfully. After tonight, that might be the truth.

The doorbell sounded in the stillness, and she sighed wearily as she went to answer it. It was probably one of the neighbors. . . .

She opened the door and looked up into a dark, quiet face with lines she hadn't seen before. He looked absolutely worn out.

"Got a cup of coffee?" he asked calmly.

She nodded, feeling her heart shaking her with its sudden, insistent pounding.

She stood back to let him in, pausing long

enough to close the door before she led him into the kitchen and poured him a mug of fresh, hot coffee.

He leaned back against the counter to sip it, his dark eyes sliding up and down the caftan appraisingly. "You look very exotic in that," he remarked casually.

She shrugged. "It's kind of like walking around in a tent," she replied.

He smiled fleetingly, but the smile didn't reach his solemn eyes. Abruptly he set the cup down and reached for her, slamming her body against his, wrapping her up in his big, warm arms, holding her as though he was afraid she might vanish any second. His lips were against the side of her neck, pressing gently, softly.

She melted into him with a muffled sob, feeling the warmth and strength of his big body with a sense of wonder. Her arms stole inside his jacket and around him, her fingers tracing the hard, rippling muscles of his broad back.

"Damn you," he whispered in a searing undertone. "I haven't had a minute's peace since I met you."

"Neither have I," she said miserably. "Oh, go away, Bryan . . . !"

"I can't," he said, drawing back to look down at her with brooding, strange eyes.

"You've cast a spell on me."

A little of her old audacity came back. "That's funny, you don't look like a toad."

"Don't be funny," he said, and his face was as hard, as formidable as ever. "I don't feel like laughing right now."

"What do you feel like?" she asked without thinking.

His eyes narrowed, glittering at her out of his leonine face. "Like picking you up and throwing you down on the nearest bed," he said harshly. "Not for one lousy night, but every night for the rest of my life."

She stared at him as if she wasn't sure she'd heard him. "What do you mean?" she asked softly, afraid of the answer even as she asked the question.

"Don't you know?" he laughed mockingly.

She dropped her gaze to his white shirt. "Bryan . . ."

He tipped her face up to his descending mouth, and it bit into hers before she could even begin to form a coherent thought. He was rough with her, as if he'd been holding back as long as he could, and his control was wearing thin.

"Open your mouth," he whispered unsteadily, roughly, his hand tangling in her long, loosened hair, as he pulled her head roughly back onto his shoulder. "Wide,

Carla . . ." he said huskily, his arm crushing her, his kiss deepening intimately, blotting out thought, regret, sanity.

A moan broke from her throat, and he pulled away just enough to search her drowsy, confused eyes. "You see?" he asked in a voice that was deep and slow and not quite steady. "I could make you submit. I don't even have to work at it. I touch you, and your body flares up against mine like a torch." He brushed his open mouth against her forehead. "You can talk about morality from now until hell freezes over, but if I pressed you, you'd let me have you, Carla. Not because of an uncontrollable desire, but beause you're in love with me."

She felt the shock run through her body as if she'd touched a live wire. He knew! But how could he, when she'd only just discovered it herself?

He felt the sudden stiffening of her body in his arms and drew back to study her. "Don't panic."

She swallowed hard. It was unnerving to meet that level, intense gaze. "I . . . I didn't realize . . . it showed," she said weakly.

"You have a very expressive face, little one. It was flashing like a neon sign tonight, even through that burst of temper." He locked his hands behind her back and swung her lazily back and forth. "I walked around the block twice, muttering to myself, until it suddenly occurred to me that the only reason you were so angry was because you wanted me as much as I wanted you." He smiled wryly. "Then it stood to reason that you cared too much for a casual fling, and all the puzzle pieces just fell into place. I came back to see if I was right."

The embarrassment was like a living thing. She felt weighed down by it. "I . . . it's still an impasse," she said quietly. "I know you could force me, but I'd hate you."

He shook his head. "You'd love me," he corrected. His eyes looked deep into hers. "It would be everything either of us could want, for the rest of our lives."

"But, desire isn't enough. . . ." she protested weakly.

A corner of his chiseled mouth went up. "Did I neglect to mention that I'm in love with you?"

Tears burned in her eyes, hot and overflowing down onto her flushed cheeks in a tiny flood. He blurred above her.

"Don't," he whispered. His fingers lightly brushed away the tears.

"It's like coming to life all over again," she murmured shakily, "after being dead inside. Sunlight . . ."

"I know." His lips brushed her wet eyes. "You taste of wine," he whispered at her mouth. "Trying to drink me out of your system?"

"Umhum," she murmured. She smiled wistfully. "It didn't work."

"Liquor won't do it," he whispered, kissing her softly, possessively. "But a few weeks behind closed doors might. We'll go on the way we have for a little while longer," he added seriously. "Until you're very sure. But I don't have a doubt in my mind how it's going to end."

"Neither do I," she murmured. Her eyes studied the strong, hard lines of his face.

"What are you looking at?" he asked.

"You never seem to really relax, to let go," she said gently. "I was wondering if you ever do, even with a woman."

He smiled gently at the expression on her face. "Oh, I let go, all right," he laughed softly. "Would you like me to show you?"

She lowered her eyes shyly. "I think you'd better go home."

"I think so, too." He studied the caftan. "I can't feel anything except skin under that flowing thing, and I'm getting ideas right and left."

"I wasn't expecting company."

"But you were hoping, weren't you?" he

asked perceptively.

"Yes," she admitted, her heart in her eyes. "Oh, yes, I was."

He stopped the words with his hard mouth, kissing her roughly, briefly. "Sleep well. Meet me at the office around twelve, and I'll take you to lunch."

She blanched, remembering her meeting with Brown, the accusations . . . but she put them all out of her mind for the time being. She smiled. "I'll be there."

She didn't sleep for a long time, thinking about the night that had ended so unexpectedly. It was hard to believe that a man like Bryan Moreland could actually be in love with her. She had so little; he had so much. But between them, they seemed to have everything.

Her mouth was still bruised from the pressure of his, her ribs still ached from the embrace that had seemed to crush her. A man couldn't pretend that kind of emotion, she thought dazedly. And to realize that a man she loved could feel that way in return amazed her.

Brown's words came back to haunt her, tearing the delicate fabric of her dreams. Tomorrow, she'd go to meet him, and maybe all his accusations would vanish like nightmares in the daylight. She wouldn't —

she couldn't — believe what he'd told her. Bryan Moreland wasn't a crook; she was sure of that. She fell asleep finally, with a picture of Moreland's leonine face in her soft eyes.

Daniel Brown was waiting for her in the small coffee shop where she'd arranged to meet him, his long pale fingers nervously clutching the fragile stem of the half-empty wineglass that held what remained of a cup of coffee and a smear of whippped cream. He looked up as she entered, and a relieved expression crossed his face.

She forced a smile she didn't feel and sat down in the chair he pulled out for her.

"Nippy out today, isn't it?" she asked, slipping out of her heavy black coat.

"A little." He took a quick sip of his coffee. "Can I order something for you?"

"Espresso," she said.

He gave the waitress her order and sat back down with a heavy sigh.

"Have you got it?" she asked suddenly. Better to have the truth all at once, if it was the truth, than to dig it out a sentence at a time.

But even as she hoped he might not be able to produce that damning evidence, he reached in his pocket and pushed a folded sheaf of photostat copies across the spotless white linen tablecloth at her.

With a hard swallow, she opened the papers with trembling fingers and looked at the first of the copies. Her heart felt suddenly like an anchor in her chest. Her green eyes closed momentarily. It was a check for one hundred thousand dollars, made out to Bryan Moreland, signed by James White. Her gaze flashed to Daniel Brown's curious, wary face.

"I know what you're thinking," he said unexpectedly. "Look at the second photostat before you say it."

Puzzled, she turned to the second sheet, and saw what he meant. This photostat was the endorsed back of the check, with Moreland's unmistakable signature.

Dully, she thumbed through the rest of the material. There was a photostat of a page of financial records with the disbursement of five hundred thousand dollars to James White Realty for a tract of land marked airport land purchase. Another sheet was from the tax assessors office, showing the fair market value of the property at one hundred thousand dollars. It was enough, more than enough, to give to the paper's legal staff. In fact, the very obvious overpayment might be enough to make an accusation and prosecute.

"This will destroy Bryan Moreland politically," she murmured.

"Probably," came the cool reply. "But the evidence speaks for itself. They were trying to cover up an overpayment of four hundred thousand dollars — of which your aging boyfriend received one-fourth. Explain that, if you can."

She stared at him, pausing while the waitress put the cup of espresso in front of her. "Now tell me the real reason why you're doing this," she asked quietly.

He looked taken aback. "I told you already, I . . ."

Her eyes narrowed. "I know what you *told* me. I want the truth."

He shrugged, averting his gaze. "All right, maybe I felt like a little revenge. We were in love, you know."

"You and who?" she persisted.

"Mrs. Moreland, of course," he said bitterly. "She was much younger than he was, and he treated her like dirt. She was nuts about me."

Those words haunted her all the way back to the office. Something wasn't quite right, although revenge might be a good motive for helping to nab a crook. But if it wasn't revenge . . .

When she handed over the photostats to Edwards, he and the legal staff were convinced that they had a blockbuster of a story.

"You've done a damned good job, Carla," Edwards told her with a rare smile. "I knew you'd pull it off."

"Brown won't testify, you know," she said. "And I can't reveal my source by telling where and how I came by those photostats."

"We'll work that out," he assured her.

"What if . . ." she cleared her throat. "What if it's a frame?"

He studied her closely. "You know better than to get involved with a news source."

She nodded, and smiled bitterly. "You can't imagine how well I've learned that lesson."

"Go eat something," he said with a paternal pat on her shoulder. "It will all come right."

Bill Peck stopped her just as she started out the newsroom door. "Want to have lunch with me and talk about it?" he asked with uncharacteristic kindness.

She shook her head. "Thanks. But there's something I've got to do first."

His eyes narrowed. "Don't go. He'll rip you into small pieces."

Her thin shoulders lifted fatalistically. "There's very little left to be ripped up," she said in an anguished tone. "See you."

She walked into the waiting room of Moreland's office with a heart that felt as if it had been pounded with a sledge hammer. Her face was pale, without its usual animation, and her body felt as taut as rawhide.

"Go right in, Miss Maxwell," his secretary said with a smile.

"Thank you," Carla said gently. She opened the door to his office with just a slight hesitation.

He was sitting behind the big desk, his dark eyes riveted to her trim figure dressed in a gray suit and black boots. A smile relaxed the hard lines in his face and made him seem younger, less intense.

"Sexy as hell," he remarked with gentle amusement.

She swallowed, and not to save her life could she return his smile. "Hello, Bryan," she said in a loud whisper.

The smile faded. "What's wrong?" he asked gently. "Did you stop by to tell me you couldn't make it for lunch?"

Her shoulders lifted slightly, as she gathered her courage. "I don't think you're going to want to take me out when you hear what I've come to say."

His heavy black brows collided. "Sit

down."

She shook her head. "If it's all the same to you, I think I'll stand," she said miserably. She fumbled in her purse for the photostats she'd made of Brown's material. "I think this will explain it all," she said, handing them to him. She waited while he studied the documents, his eyes narrowing, his face becoming as hard, as formidable as she remembered it from their first conflict.

His dark eyes flashed up to her face, blazing. "Well?" he growled. "What about it?"

She curbed an impulse to turn and run. "Do I really have to tell you that?" she asked in as calm a voice as she could manage. "We're going to publish this information. We can't afford not to."

His jaw tautened. "You think this check is a kickback?" he asked in a strange, deep tone.

"We know it is," she agreed tightly. "It's painfully obvious that you don't pay five times fair market value for a piece of land unless somebody benefits. We've already checked with the man who owns the land. All he got out of the deal was two hundred fifty thousand dollars. That leaves the other half unaccounted for, except for your cut. Either White alone or with another conspirator pocketed the rest, and we can prove it.

I'm sorry, but . . ."

"You believe I'd take a kickback?" he asked with barely controlled rage. "You really believe I'm capable of that kind of vice?"

"You accepted a check from James White for one hundred thousand dollars," she said in a voice that trembled, "just two days after the check for the airport land left city hall. What else am I supposed to think?"

"Get out."

He said it so softly, so calmly, that she did a double take. He didn't raise his voice, but then, he didn't have to. There was an arctic smoothness in his words.

She turned to go. "I'm sorry," she said inadequately, her voice a bare whisper. Inside, she felt as if she were frozen forever.

"Not half as sorry as you're going to be, I promise you," he said. "One more thing, Carla."

"What?"

"Was it really necessary to get that involved with me to get the story?" he asked coolly. "Did you have to pretend an emotional interest, or was that just a whim?"

Her face reddened. "But, it wasn't . . ."

He laughed shortly, leaning back in his chair to study her with eyes that shone with hatred. "I should have been suspicious at the beginning," he said mockingly. "A woman your age wouldn't have been so interested in a middle-aged man. I suppose I was too flattered to ask questions."

"But, Bryan, you don't understand . . . !" she cried.

He ignored her. His eyes were those of a stranger. "Go print your story," he said. "You might add a postscript. I got my funding for downtown revitalization this morning. I may leave this office, but I'll take the city slums with me."

Tears blinded her. She turned and ran out of the office leaving a puzzled secretary staring after her.

The story hit the stands the next afternoon, with a blazing banner headline that read, "Kickback Suspected in Airport Land Purchase." The story carried Carla's byline, even though Edwards had had a hand in writing it. She hadn't slept the night before at all. She could imagine the anguish Moreland was going through. She'd destroyed him. And he thought that she'd been pretending when she said she loved him. That hurt most of all, that he could believe she'd be that cruel for the sake of a story. But, after all, didn't she believe that he'd been crooked enough to take a kickback? How could she blame him?

Over and over she heard his deep voice growling at her accusingly. It began to haunt her. And Daniel Brown's voice haunted her as well, admitting that he'd been in love with Mrs. Moreland, that she was "nuts about him." From what she'd heard about Angelica Moreland, she was hardly a lovable woman. And she would have had to be a good deal older than Brown, who was still in his middle twenties. None of it made sense. If only she could get her mind together enough to think logically!

She walked into the newsroom the next day with a feeling of unreality. Her mind was still on yesterday, but Peck snapped her out of it with his greeting.

"We're into it now," he greeted her grimly. "Moreland's filed suit for defamation and character assassination."

"Did you expect him to admit he was guilty?" she asked with a bitter smile.

He grinned back. "Hell, no." His pale brows drew together. "Something bothering you besides the obvious? Making accusations sometimes goes with the job, honey. Reporters don't win popularity contests, you know."

"I know." She slumped in her chair. "What do you know about the late Mrs. Moreland?"

"Angelica?" He shrugged. "She liked men and money, and she hated her husband and motherhood. That about wraps it up."

"What kind of men did she like? Young ones?"

"Angelica!" he exclaimed. "My God, she liked them older than her husband. I think it must have been a father fixation. She was never seen with a man under fifty except Moreland."

Her lips made a thin line. "Do you know anybody who could help me get some information on Daniel Brown's private life?"

One eyebrow went up and he grinned. "Think Moreland's innocent?"

Her chin lifted. "Yes." Her eyes dared him to make a comment.

He only smiled. "So do I." He laughed at her expression. "Don't look so surprised, honey. I've known His Honor for a lot of years, and he's got more integrity than any other public official I know. Sure, I'll help you dig out some info on Brown. I think he had an angle, too."

She returned the smile, feeling a weight lift off her shoulders. "Then, let's go. I want to see a man I know at the city police department about some personnel records."

"I'll check with a contact of mine," he said, following her out the door. "My God, don't we remind you of the news staff on that hit television show?"

She laughed. "Which one? The one where we solve crime and make America safe for consumers, or the one where we fight for truth, justice and the . . ."

"Never mind. Let's sneak out before Eddy can ask where we're going."

"I don't think he cares if we even work today," she replied. "He looked sick when I poked my head in to ask about assignments, and he didn't even offer me one."

"He's brooding over the lawsuit," he told her. "The attorneys warned him that he mightn't have enough concrete evidence to avoid one, but he took the chance. Without asking old man Johnson," he added, grimacing.

"He didn't ask the publisher?" she exclaimed.

He shrugged. "He couldn't reach him by phone, and the deadline was coming up fast. He took a gamble on the hottest story in years. Now Johnson's all over him like ants over honey."

She felt herself shrinking inside as she remembered whose byline the story carried. "How much trouble am I in?" she asked softly.

"I don't know," he replied, glancing at her

sympathetically. "I wish I could tell you your job's secure, regardless. But I can't. That's the first thing Moreland's going to want by way of recompense if the evidence against him is false."

"Which I think it is," she murmured weakly. She stuck her hands in the pockets of her coat as they walked outside in the chill air. "It's going to be winter soon," she remarked, shivering.

He drew in a breath of cold air, unaware of the pollution judging by his expression. "What's that poem, 'keep spring within your heart, if winter comes, to warm the cold of disillusion . . .' "

"I didn't know you like poetry," she said, feeling the words with a sense of aching grief.

"An occasional line," he chuckled. "Even though it goes against the grain. Come on, we'll catch a bus downtown."

"Lead on."

Carla, who was used to a two-man police department, couldn't help but be awed by the mammoth precinct with crowds of lawbreakers and blue uniforms and plain-clothes detectives. She felt uncomfortable among all the unfamiliar faces.

"Don't worry," Peck assured her, "none

of them bite."

"Care to lay odds?" she whispered.

"Shhh!" he said sharply. "Not here!"

She flushed at his teasing tone. "I wasn't trying to gamble with you," she protested.

"Discussing a capital crime, right in front of the city's finest!" he clucked. "Shame, shame."

"Will you stop," she muttered. "I'm a good girl, I am."

"So was Ma Barker."

"Why did we come here?"

"To see Leroy."

Her eyebrows went up, but he moved forward to haul a patrolman off to one side. There was a lot of whispering, and gesturing, and the tall, dark-haired, middle-aged policeman was giving Carla a look that made her feel vaguely undressed.

They joined her at the door, and Peck took her arm, propelling her out onto the street with Leroy right behind.

"We'll grab a cup of coffee and talk," Peck said, leading them toward a nearby cafe. "Carla Maxwell, Leroy Sample."

They exchanged mumbled pleasantries and walked along in a companionable silence. Once inside the old cafe, which featured worn, bare wood floors and vinyl-covered booths repaired with black electrical tape, they talked over strong coffee.

"What do you want to know about Daniel?" Leroy asked with a grin. "I don't know much, but I'll do my best."

"Is he local?" Peck asked, all reporter now, not the jovial companion of minutes ago.

"No," Leroy replied. "He came here from Florida about six months ago, and was he a ball of fire! He was going to clean up all the corruption in the city and close down drugs and gambling for good."

"And then . . ." Peck prodded.

"You want the truth?" Leroy asked, lowering his voice. "He was offered a little temptation to turn his head, and he turned it. Some of the rest of us have been made the same offer, but we nixed it. He liked the dough."

"You think somebody's paying him still, even though he's been fired?" Peck asked.

"We all know he was feeding you that bull on Moreland," the patrolman said angrily. "With all due respect, I hope he sues the hell out of you. If Moreland took money, he had a legitimate reason. He's not on the take. I'd know."

Carla felt her heart lift, and she prayed silently that this fierce policeman was right. "Who's paying Brown?" Peck asked point blank.

Leroy looked uncomfortable. "I do my job the best way I can, and I try hard not to stick my nose out too far. Those guys play rough, Peck. I've got a little girl three months old."

The reporter sighed. "You make me feel like a heel for asking. I know how dangerous it is. I've had my share of threats, too. Okay, if you can't tell me, send me to somebody who can."

Leroy sipped his coffee. "Now you make *me* feel like a heel."

"It isn't deliberate," Peck said with a smile.

The policeman took a deep breath and looked around at the sparsely peopled cafe. His eyes came back to Peck. "I'll deny it if you finger me as your informant."

Peck looked vaguely insulted. "Have you forgotten that I stood a thirty-day jail term two years ago when Judge Carter tried to get me to tell who gave me information in the Jones murder?" he asked.

Leroy laughed. "Yeah, I had. Sorry." He leaned forward on his forearms. "You go ask James White who helped him ramrod that land deal through the city council, and you'll get your man."

CHAPTER EIGHT

Carla and Bill Peck wore ruts in the city park as they walked. A rally protesting the low wages paid garbage collectors was going on around them, part of the sanitation strike plaguing the city, but they ignored the peaceful marchers.

"He's right," Peck said finally, turning to Carla under a leafless oak amid the crunch of dead leaves underfoot. "The best defense in the world is a good offense. We may still be able to pull our acorns out of the fire."

She blinked at him. "I don't understand."

"We'll go to see James White. We'll carry along a file folder of documents incriminating him. We'll allow him to give his side of the story before we print the whole disgusting mess."

"But we don't have any incriminating documents!" she burst out.

"We will have," he grinned. "Come on. Time's a-wasting. We may save your job yet, and Eddy's, too."

"Let's go to it, then," she agreed, smiling as she hadn't felt like smiling for days. Maybe she could clear Moreland's name. That would make up for so much, even if he never forgave her for what she'd already done. If only she'd listened to her heart. If only she'd been suspicious of Daniel Brown's eager help. If only she hadn't been so determined to get a scoop, to make Bill Peck proud of her. She sighed as they walked briskly back toward the newspaper office. Oh, if only . . .

The paper had already gone to bed for the day when she and Peck left again, armed with an impressive folder of information. They still had not mentioned a word to Edwards whose face was almost as long as his legs.

Carla had already called to make an appointment with James White on the pretext of purchasing some land. She knew the foxy little man wouldn't be eager to meet with the press, especially after his honorable mention in the story on Moreland.

They were ushered into his private office by a young, buxom blond secretary whose smile was as empty as her pale eyes.

White rose, gray haired and thin, with astonishment plain in his pale face when he suddenly recognized Bill Peck.

"Reporters!" he burst out. He glared at them. "Don't sit down," he warned, reaching for the telephone. "You won't be here long enough!"

Carla felt suddenly nervous and unsure of herself, but Bill Peck was not taken aback at all.

"Dial," he warned the older man, "and you'll be on the front page tomorrow afternoon."

White gazed at him warily, but he hesitated, his finger still on the dial.

"We came armed this time," Peck added, holding up the file folder. He smiled confidently. "I think you're going to want to cooperate, Mr. White. That way, you just may escape a long jail term."

White put down the receiver and laughed self-consciously. He whipped out a spotless handkerchief and wiped his perspiring brow. "Jail?" he said. "Surely you're joking, Mr. Peck. I've done nothing illegal. In fact, the only crime I'm guilty of is getting my client better than fair market value for a piece of land."

"And crucifying a blameless public official in the process," Carla broke in, feeling her advantage. She moved forward, and Bill Peck sat down, letting her carry the ball.

She took the file from Peck and lifted it in front of James White's nervous face. "It's all here, Mr. White. Everything. How you arranged a five-hundred percent profit out of that worthless land. How you set up Bryan Moreland, you and your co-conspirator, to take the blame for it by sending him a check for his revitalization project just in time to make it look like a kickback from the land deal. We know all about it. We even know," she added narrowly, "about Daniel Brown's role."

White sat down, suddenly looking his age. He leaned back in his chair and wiped his mouth with the handkerchief. His spare frame seemed to slump wearily.

"I engineered it," he admitted quietly. "There's no sense in denying it any further."

Peck pulled out a pocket tape recorder and turned it on. "I'm recording, Mr. White," he advised the man, "and I think it would be in your best interests to give the truth."

"Why not?" White sighed. "I'm ruined now, anyway, you'll see to that. Yes, I engineered the airport land deal. I got Ed King to present it to the City Council and convince his friend Moreland that it was the best site available." He nodded at Carla's shocked face. "Moreland had so much on his mind with the sanitation strike and that downtown redevelopment scheme that he wasn't able to check into the site too closely, so he left it all up to Ed, whom he trusted." He laughed shortly. "Bryan and I have been friends for a long time, he had no reason to distrust me or Ed. We had it made. We sold the land to the city for five times its true value. Then I had Daniel Brown start making noises about Moreland accepting a kickback, right after I sent my good friend a donation for his downtown redevelopment. It was flawless. Absolutely flawless. Until you people came along and started poking around," he added bitterly.

"Who actually owned the land, Mr. White?" Carla asked.

"The deed says, Will Jackson," he replied.

"But isn't it actually owned by Daniel Brown?" she persisted, smiling at White's shocked expression. "Yes, I made some phone calls to Florida. Brown used Will Jackson as an alias when he purchased that land, at your instructions."

"At Ed King's," White corrected gruffly. "Why the hell did I ever get mixed up with that little snip? If I'd handled it by myself . . ."

"If," Carla sighed, closing her eyes momentarily as a wave of unbearable grief and tiredness washed over her. She turned away as Bill Peck moved to call the police. It was too much, too soon. All her suspicions, all her digging, and it hadn't been enough to save Bryan Moreland from a public crucifixion. She'd finally gotten at the truth, and all it had cost her was the one man she could ever truly love. A single tear rolled down her cold cheek, trickling salty and warm into the corner of her mouth.

"It's great," Edwards laughed as Carla and Bill Peck played the tape for him and summarized White's arrest. "Just great! We'll scoop every paper in town with this, even the broadcast boys! We'll save face!"

Carla stared down at her black boots. "You'll print everything, including how Moreland was set up?"

Edwards looked at her with a compassionate smile. "Yes. And it might be enough to convince him to drop the lawsuit. We'll run another banner headline. 'Moreland Innocent of Kickback.' How's that?"

"Will it please you-know-who?" Peck asked, tongue-in-cheek, gesturing toward the ceiling.

Edwards frowned. "God?" he asked.

"The publisher!" Peck burst out.

"Oh, him." Edwards shrugged. "Nothing

ever has before. I'm not sure it will. But it may save my job, and Carla's."

Peck grinned. "I'll settle for that."

But, it appeared, Bryan Moreland wouldn't. Edwards called Carla into his office two hours after the paper was on the streets, looking uncomfortable and vaguely ill.

"Sit down," he said gruffly.

She perched herself on the edge of her chair and sat up straight, her hands clenched in the lap of her burgundy plaid skirt. She could feel the ominous vibrations, like the growing chill of the weather.

"Get it over with," she murmured. "I hate suspense."

He jammed his hands in his pockets and studied his feet. "Moreland called me."

Her heart jerked, but she didn't let the emotions dancing inside her find expression in her face. "Oh?"

"He's willing to drop the lawsuit, especially in view of our efforts — your efforts — to clear his name. But I couldn't get across to him that it was your investigation that cleared him," he added apologetically. "When I mentioned your name, he blew up." He sighed. "What it boils down to is this. He'll drop the lawsuit if I fire you. That's my only option." He shuffled angrily.

"Johnson says if I don't fire you, we'll both get the boot."

She felt every drop of color draining out of her face, but she forced a smile to her lips. "I expected it, you know," she said gently. "I was looking for a job when I found this one."

"Yeah," he said curtly. His eyes studied the expression on her pale face. "I'm sorry as hell."

She shrugged. "It's been an experience. How long have I got to clean out my desk?"

He sighed bitterly. "Until quitting time. I'm giving you two weeks' pay, maybe that'll get you through to another job."

She tried to mask her apprehension with a smile. "I'll be okay. If things get too tight, I can always go home to Georgia," she reminded him. "The editor of Dad's old paper would give me a job on the spot. All I have to do is ask."

That, at least, was true. But how was she going to leave this city, and Bryan Moreland behind, when the picture of them would haunt her until she died? If only she could see him once more, touch him . . .

"I said, you might have a shot at the radio station," he repeated, interrupting her melancholy thoughts. "I hear they're looking for a leg person."

She smiled and rose, offering him her slender hand. "Thanks, Eddy. I've enjoyed working here."

"You're one hell of a reporter," he said with grudging praise. "I hate to lose you. If it weren't for that damned lawsuit — the truth is, our budget won't stand it, and he's got every law in the books on his side."

"It was my fault . . ."

"And mine," he said firmly. "Nobody held a gun on me and made me print it. The evidence was there. I didn't know it was engineered any more than you did. By the way," he added, "there's every indication that Ed King is going to be recalled even before his case comes up," he grinned. "That ought to make you feel a little better."

She returned the smile. "It does. See you around, Eddy."

Bill Peck sat, perched on the edge of his chair, watching Carla clean out her desk, an enigmatic expression on his face. He ignored the phone that was screaming insistently beside him.

"Where will you go?" he asked gruffly.

She shrugged. "Back to my apartment to wallow in self-pity."

He chuckled in spite of himself. "Hell,

does anything get you down?"

"Crocodiles," she murmured as she put the last of her notepads into a brown bag with her other possessions. "I never go near swamps for that reason." She closed the bag and turned, her eyes soft as they met his. "Thanks for everything, my friend."

His face tightened. "Thanks for nothing," he grunted. "I helped cost you your job. If I'd interfered at the beginning . . ."

"I believe in fate," she interrupted. "Don't you?"

"Suppose I called Moreland, and told him the truth?" he asked quietly.

"No," she replied, turning to face him. "What happened between Bryan and me . . . it's nothing to do with anyone else," she finished weakly. "If he wants to think that it was all my fault, let him. I'll be gone soon, anyway."

"Gone where?" he asked.

She smiled. "Home. I've missed it."

"Not a whole hell of a lot," he replied doggedly, "Or you wouldn't have stayed this long."

"I've learned things here that I could never have learned in a small town," she reminded him. "And you've shown me the ropes. I'll never forget you."

"Don't get mushy," he growled, moving

forward to perch himself on her desk. "When are you leaving?"

"I've got two weeks before I have to make a definite decision," she told him, grateful for her own foresight in keeping up her savings deposits. It would give her a little more leeway.

"Then you may stay in the city?" he probed.

She looked down at the brown bag, testing its weight and rough texture. "I don't know. I don't want to think about it right now. It's been a rough week."

"Yeah."

"Thank you for helping me do it," she said fervently.

"I like the guy," he said, and his pale eyes smiled at her. "Keep in touch, okay?"

"Okay. If you hear of any openings around town, let me know."

"I'll keep both ears open." The smile went out of his eyes. "I've gotten used to you. I won't want to look at this damned desk for a week."

"Have Betty sit on it," she suggested with an impish grin.

"Two-ton Betty?" he groaned. "Who'll pay to replace it?"

"Definitely not me," she told him. She took one last look around the busy office, its rushing reporters and ringing telephones and editors calling over the din. "How quiet it is here," she sighed.

"Good thing you're leaving," he replied. "Working here has deafened you."

"Don't take any wooden tips," she cautioned.

"You, too."

She turned and walked out the door into the lobby. The temptation to cast a farewell glance over her shoulder was strong, but she didn't yield to it. With her head high, she walked out onto the busy sidewalk and merged in with the crowd.

Not going to work was new to Carla. Since her eighteenth birthday, she'd had a job of some kind, even if it was only a summer one working for her father. But to see four walls day after day, no new faces, no people, was like slow torture. She kept the television on, but the soap operas were more than she could bear, and the radio got on her nerves after the second day.

There was too much time: time to regret her behavior, time to think about Bryan Moreland and his ultimatum that the paper fire her. How he must hate her. Not only had she betrayed him falsely, but he even thought her declaration of love was part of that betrayal, that she'd pretended affection for him solely to get a story.

She almost laughed at the thought. And he'd said that no normal woman would be interested in a middle-aged man. Didn't he realize how very attractive he was? How strong and charming and exciting he was to be with? Didn't he realize that she'd have loved him if he'd been totally gray and walked with a cane? Age didn't matter. Time didn't matter. She'd have given anything for just a few years with him — to love him, to bear his children, to grow old with him.

Tears blurred her eyes. The firing was a message, as surely as if he'd given it in person. He was telling her, in the most deliberate way possible, that he wanted her out of his city. And she had a feeling that if she approached any other news media for a job, the doors would all be closed.

It must have come as a tremendous shock to him, realizing that two of his most trusted friends had set him up as the scapegoat for their land deal. And to top it all off, to think that a girl reporter would lead him on and flatter his vanity just to get the goods on him . . .

"But it isn't true," she whispered tearfully. "Oh, Bryan, it isn't true!"

She dropped down onto the soft cushions of the sofa and cried like a lost child. It was the first time she'd yielded to tears since her firing, but it seemed to ease the hurt a little.

By the end of the week, she was regaining some of her former spirit. She'd already decided that her only course of action was going home, but she wanted to wait until her father returned. That would be just another three or four days, and she couldn't spend them sitting in the apartment staring at the walls. She became a sightseer, taking buses all around the sprawling city to visit the park, the museums, the historic landmarks. It was all new to her suddenly, as if she'd gone around blind as a reporter and was just now seeing the city without her blinders.

The days went by quickly, and on the very last one she found herself retracing her steps through the ghetto she'd visited with Bryan Moreland. The slums were already being bulldozed down now, and signs were going up heralding the construction of new, modern apartments for low-income groups. She couldn't help feeling a surge of pride for the man who'd fought so hard to bring this dream to fruition. If only she could tell him how very proud she was.

Her slender figure looked even thinner than usual in the gray suit she was wearing. A pale green scarf around her throat emphasized her green eyes, and the braided coil of dark hair seemed even darker against it. The black coat and boots she wore seemed to fit in with the darkness of her mood as she walked aimlessly back toward the downtown business district, her sad eyes on the dirty, cracked sidewalk. She felt so miserable, so lost and alone. Her chest lifted in an aching sigh and she didn't notice where she was going until she ran head-on into another pedestrian. Strong hands came up to grip her arms, and she looked up with an apology on her lips. Then her heart leapt inside her chest.

Bryan Moreland's dark, angry eyes were looking straight down into hers, and she couldn't even manage a weak greeting, the shock of seeing him was so great.

CHAPTER NINE

She stood there looking up at him like a slender statue, without life or breath or strength.

His face was hard, haggard, and she searched its leonine contours with a drowning hunger, lingering on the curve of his mouth, the darkness of his narrow eyes.

"Excuse me," she said finally, breathlessly, moving back as if the touch of his hands scorched her.

He let her go abruptly and pushed his big fists into the pockets of his beige overcoat. "I thought you were on your way out of town, Miss Maxwell," he said roughly.

She nodded. "I . . . I leave tomorrow," she managed. "The . . . uh, the slums . . . it's going to be quite a feat."

"My going away present to the voters," he remarked curtly. "I won't run for reelection."

She dropped her eyes, feeling cut to the

quick. "It was all my fault," she mumbled. "Saying I'm sorry won't even scratch the surface, but I am, oh, God, I am," she whispered fervently.

He laughed shortly, without a trace of humor. "Chalk it up to experience, honey," he said sharply. "Maybe next time you'll be a little more cautious about your methods."

She glanced up at his set face through her long, dark lashes. He looked as formidable as ever, only harder. Her heart almost burst at the sight of him.

"There won't be a next time," she said absently. "I . . . I'm not going back into journalism." She smiled wanly. "I hate the very idea of it, now."

He scowled. "Guilty conscience, Miss Maxwell?" he asked mockingly. "A little late, isn't it?"

Tears blurred him in her eyes. "Yes," she said in a whisper.

He drew in a deep, harsh breath. "Just for the record, you'd never have gotten me as far as the altar. I wanted you pretty damned bad, but one night would have worked you out of my system." His smile was cruel and mocking. "Too bad things worked out the way they did. Another date or two, and I'd have had you."

A strange sound broke from her lips. It

was like the end of a dream. She'd cradled the thought that at least he'd cared for her once. But now, she didn't even have that. Not even that! He'd only . . . wanted her!

Without thinking, she turned and ran away from him, the crowd blurring in her tear-filled eyes as she tore through it, deaf to the sound of her name being called roughly behind her.

She elbowed through a crowd waiting for a city bus at the corner and darted out across the busy street, too overwrought to notice that the pedestrian light was red. She never saw the taxi that turned the corner and sped straight toward her. She was dimly aware of a horrible hoarse cry from the curb and a sickening thud that seemed to paralyze her all over. Then there was a strange cold darkness that she fell into, swallowing her up in its veiled cocoon.

The first conscious breath she drew was incredibly painful. She felt a strange tightness in her chest and her hand encountered bandages under the thin nightgown she was wearing.

She couldn't remember what had happened. She was only aware of crisp sheets, medicinal smells and metallic noises all around her.

Her eyes slid open lazily, thick from drugs. They widened as Bill Peck came into view at her bedside.

"God, you gave us a fright," he said heavily, rising with a weary smile to stand beside the bed and hold her hand.

"Have I . . . been here long?" she whispered.

"Two days," he replied. "Give or take a few hours."

"How bad am I?" she asked, wondering how she could even talk, she hurt so much. It felt as if every bone in her body was broken.

"You've got several fractures, three broken ribs, a concussion, and you're damned lucky the cab driver had lightning reflexes or you'd be dead," came a rough angry voice from the doorway.

She turned her head, groaning with the effort, and found Bryan Moreland standing there, dark and forbidding, and looking as if he hadn't slept in a week. His sports shirt was open at the neck, his hair was ruffled, and he was plainly irritated.

"Sorry to disappoint you," she whispered miserably.

Some unreadable expression flashed across his face. "Who the hell said you have?" he demanded.

Bill Peck let go of her hand with a grin. "If you don't mind, honey, I'm going to get out of the line of fire. Get well, huh? And if you need anything, just call."

"Thanks," she said weakly.

He winked at Moreland and closed the door gently behind him.

Carla turned her eyes back to the wall, moaning softly with the pain. "What do you want now?" she asked wearily. "A leg?"

"I want you to get well."

She bit her lower lip to keep the tears at bay. "I want to go home," she said tearfully. "My father . . ."

"Is still on his cruise," he finished for her. "He sent a cable the first day you were in here. Peck and I went to your apartment to get some gowns for you, and it was waiting under the door."

"Oh." She felt the tears wind down her cheek. She was hurt and she wanted her father.

"You're coming with me," he said without preamble.

She turned on the bed, her eyes staring at him as he stood looking down at her, his dark face daring her to argue.

"I can't," she told him.

"Maybe not, but you're sure as hell coming," he said doggedly, his jaw going taut as he studied her young, bruised face. "Mrs. Brodie's going to live in for the duration, until I get you back on your feet."

Her lips trembled. "You don't owe me anything."

His face seemed to darken, harden. "You got hit because I upset you. I might as well have thrown you under the wheels myself."

She closed her eyes. Would she ever be free of guilt? She wondered miserably. First hers, now his. She didn't want to be on his conscience. And most of all, she didn't want to go home with him, to have to see him every day, knowing that he hated her, blamed her, that he was only salving his conscience by having her around.

"I don't want to go," she whispered.

He gave a harsh sigh. "I don't want you around any more than you want to come," he growled at her, "but there isn't much choice. You can't go home with no one to look after you, and I'm damned well not going to let you stay with Peck!"

"Why not?" she asked sharply. "He'd take care of me."

"So will I," he said, his dark eyes unfathomable as they studied her thin form under the sheets.

Her eyes closed, and tears washed out from under her tight eyelids. "Please don't make me go," she pleaded unsteadily. "Haven't you punished me enough?"

There was a long silence, and when she looked at him, his back was turned. He was staring out the window blankly, his hands rammed into his pockets. "It's only for a few days," he said tightly. "Until you're back on your feet. We'll both grit our teeth and bear it. Then you can damned well go home and get out of my life."

She turned her face back to the wall, hating him, hating what she felt every time she looked at him. It was going to be pure hell, and if there had been any way she could have talked her way out of it, she would have. But all the doors were locked behind her.

She studied the white fences and bare trees and chilly-looking Herefords as Bryan Moreland's sleek Jaguar wound up the farm road.

All her arguments hadn't prevailed against the brooding, irritable mayor. He simply silenced her with a hard look and went right ahead. Even Bill Peck wouldn't take her side against Moreland. It was as if every friend she had had deserted her. No one was willing to stand against Moreland.

Mrs. Brodie was waiting for them at the

front door, smiling and sympathetic. She reminded Carla of a loving, kind aunt, standing there in her white starched apron.

"There, there, you poor little girl, we'll soon have you back on your feet," she cooed, following along behind Moreland as he carried Carla down the hall into a spacious bedroom with a blue and white French provincial color scheme.

"I could have walked," she protested as he laid her down gently on the canopied bed.

He stared down into her eyes without rising, and she was aware that Mrs. Brodie had disappeared, calling something back about fetching Carla some hot chicken soup.

"And broken Mrs. Brodie's romantic heart?" he chided. His dark eyes searched her wan, bruised face. Reluctantly his hand moved up to tuck a strand of dark hair behind her ear. "You do look terrible, little girl," he said gently.

The kindness in his voice brought tears surging up behind her eyelids. "Don't," she whispered brokenly.

His face shuttered. Abruptly he rose from the bed and moved away. "Mrs. Brodie will bring you some soup, and I'll get your suitcases. You'll probably feel more comfortable in a gown."

She stared at him with her heart in her

eyes. The tears spilled over onto her flushed cheeks just in time to catch Mrs. Brodie's attention as she came in with soup and coffee on a tray.

"Oh, poor dear," she murmured, setting the tray down on the bedside tale. "Does it hurt very much?"

Carla took the handkerchief she offered, and dabbed at her red eyes. "Terribly," she whispered, but she wasn't talking about physical pain.

"I'll get you some aspirin directly. Right now, you eat this soup." She placed the tray on the bed across Carla's slender hips. "Bless your heart, I'm so glad Mr. Moreland brought you to me. I wondered what was wrong, of course, but it isn't my place to pry. He's just been so bitter lately, and the way he rides that big black stallion of his, it's a wonder he hasn't killed himself." She sighed, watching with maternal concern as Carla started sipping the delicious broth. "That dreadful King person. How could he do something so terrible to a man like Mr. Moreland?" She sighed, her ample bosom rising indignantly. "Pretending to be his friend, and all — can you imagine? Thank goodness someone took the time and trouble to get the truth."

"Amen," she breathed softly.

"It was your paper that did it, wasn't it?" Mrs. Brodie asked shrewdly.

She dropped her eyes to the spotless blue coverlet. "It was my paper that started it," she said miserably.

Mrs. Brodie patted her shoulder gently. "It all came right, dear. Don't worry."

Nothing had come right, but she only smiled. "The soup is very good," she murmured.

And Mrs. Brodie beamed.

Moreland made a conspicuous effort to stay completely out of her way in the evenings. Naturally, his job kept him away in the daytime. But even when he came home, he found things to keep him busy. Farm business, paperwork, phone calls, anything, it seemed, to keep him away from Carla's bedside. Even Mrs. Brodie noticed it.

"Why, Miss Maxwell will get the impression that you don't want her here, Mr. Moreland," Mrs. Brodie teased gently one evening when he made a rare visit to Carla's room.

Carla, who was sitting wrapped up in her fleecy white robe in an armchair by the window, only glanced his way. One look at the formidable, dark face, was enough to tell her how little he wanted to be in the

438

same room with her.

"Mr. Moreland is busy, I'm sure," Carla said with a gentle smile. "It was . . . very kind of him to let me come here to recuperate. I already feel I'm imposing, without his having to entertain me."

Moreland's eyes were flashing fire. "Don't let her stay up too late," he told Mrs. Brodie. He turned and went out the door, his face like stone.

"I just don't understand," Mrs. Brodie sighed.

Carla did, but she couldn't begin to explain it and she wasn't going to try.

A few days later, she dressed in her jeans and a pale green T-shirt that matched her eyes. It was an effort just to stand, but once she'd dragged a brush through her long, waving black hair and washed her face she felt a little more alive. The bruises on her flawless skin were beginning to fade a little, to a purplish yellow, but she didn't bother with makeup. What would be the use? She couldn't attract Bryan Moreland again if she were the world's most beautiful woman. He hated her too much for that.

She made her way down the hall on unsteady legs, glad that Mrs. Brodie had driven into town to do the shopping. Being here on her own had given her some incentive to rush her recuperation. The sooner she was able to go home, the better. If only her father's arrival hadn't been delayed.

"What the hell do you think you're doing?" came a startled, deeply angry voice from the direction of the study.

She froze in her tracks, half turning as Moreland exploded out of his study into the hall. He was dressed casually, too, in worn jeans and a deep burgundy velour shirt that she recognized with a blush as the one he'd worn during her last brief visit here.

"I . . . I was just going to the kitchen," she said weakly.

He moved closer, towering over her. "You crazy child," he said in a soft, deep tone.

Her wounded eyes lifted to his, and he drew in a sharp breath.

"You shouldn't be on your feet this soon," he said, his hard mouth compressing into a thin line as he studied her thin figure in the tight jeans and top.

"The sooner, the better," she said quietly. "I have to go home."

"When you're able," he agreed. His eyes narrowed, glittered, on her face. "My God, little one, you look so thin. As if a breeze would blow you all the way home."

He clouded in her vision, and she averted

her face from the concern she read briefly in his gaze. "Don't feel sorry for me," she said tightly.

"Is that how it sounded?" he asked. His lean fingers came out to close over her shoulders. "I've got a pot of coffee in the study, and a roaring fire. Come keep me company until Mrs. Brodie gets back. I don't want you staggering around alone."

"I'm not drunk, you know," she whispered, unnerved by his closeness, the electrifying touch of his warm, caressing hands on the delicate bones of her upper arms.

He drew her imperceptibly closer, and she could feel his smoky, warm breath against her forehead, the bridge of her nose. "Would you like to be?" he asked in a bitter, brooding tone. "Maybe it's what we both need. To get staggering drunk and hold a wake over the past."

She pulled away from him before he could read the submission in her eyes. "I . . . I would like some coffee," she agreed.

He hesitated for just an instant before he took her arm and guided her into the study.

She hadn't realized it was the same room; she'd been too wrapped up in Moreland. But as she recognized the fireplace and the rug, her face went white, and she stood like an ice sculpture in the doorway, just staring at it. The pain of memory was in her eyes, her face, her whole posture. A muffled sob escaped from her tight throat as she remembered with vivid clarity the sight of the two of them lying in each other's arms on the soft rug, the feel of his big arms warming her, loving her.

"I can't," she said on a broken gasp, turning away. "Please I'd like to lie back down."

He caught her flushed face in his big hands and turned her shimmering eyes up to his. "Lie with me, then," he said in a soft, haunted tone. "Go back with me."

Tears ran down her cheeks as her hands pressed warmly against his chest. "We can't," she whispered achingly. Her eyes touched every line of his face. "I ruined everything," she murmured bitterly. "I killed it."

"Did you?" He bent, his mouth touching her own lightly, teasingly, tasting the tears that had trickled down from her eyes.

"The story . . ." she whispered. Her eyes closed, as she savored the feel of him against her, the tangy scent of him — cologne mixed with soap. . . . "Bryan," she breathed as his lips touched and lifted against hers.

"We made love on that rug," he whispered deeply. "Do you remember?"

A sob broke from her throbbing throat.

"Every second," she said without pretense. "The story . . . had nothing to do with it. I loved you. . . ."

His open mouth caught hers, pressing her lips apart as he bent and lifted her completely off the floor, cradling her trembling body against him as if she were some gentle, fragile treasure.

"Don't talk," he whispered against her soft, yielding mouth as he carried her toward the fireplace. "Make love with me. We'll heal each other."

A sob was muffled under his hard, devouring mouth. Her warm arms clutched at him, holding him as he laid her gently on the rug and came down beside her.

"I love you," she whispered softly.

"I'm years too old for you," he murmured against her cheek, his lips maddeningly slow and enticing.

"I'll push your wheelchair," she gasped as his mouth burned against her throat. "I'll polish your crutches. Bryan . . . I want children with you. . . ."

She moaned under the hard, uncontrolled passion of his mouth as it forced hers open and searched it with an unfamiliar intimacy that made her blood run hot. This kind of ardor was something she'd never experienced before; she stiffened in instinctive fear at first. But his arms tightened, and his ardor became suddenly gentler, coaxing, and with a sigh, she gave herself over to him completely. She wouldn't fight anymore. Whatever he wanted. Anything. Everything. Her cool fingers moved under the hem of his soft burgundy shirt and ran over his firm, hair-covered chest with a sense of awe. It was so good to touch him, to savor the powerful masculinity that drew her like a magnet. She loved him so. If all he wanted was a mistress, even that didn't matter. She moaned, her fingers digging into his muscular flesh as the kiss deepened sensuously.

Abruptly he drew back and rolled away from her to lie breathing heavily, his hands under his head, one knee drawn up.

She turned her head on the rug, staring at him not comprehending. "Did I do something wrong?" she asked softly.

"Pour me a cup of coffee," he said roughly. "It's behind you, on the table."

She sat up, feeling vaguely rejected, and turned around to the coffee table. She poured coffee into the two china cups and added cream in his, remembering how he liked it. She lifted his and set it on the rug beside him, then turned back to get her own, grimacing with the movement.

"Now do you know why I stopped?" he

asked, raising an eyebrow at her as he sat up and lifted his cup.

She stared at him, lost in the warm darkness of his eyes.

He chuckled softly. All the hard lines were gone from his face. He looked years younger, carefree — loving.

"Your ribs, darling," he said gently, as he sipped his hot coffee. "You aren't up to violent lovemaking yet."

The "yet" made her pulses go wild. She stared down into her black coffee. "You don't . . . hate me?" she asked.

"Look at me, country mouse," he breathed.

She lifted her shimmering, soft eyes to his and caught her breath at the emotion she read in them.

"I love you to the furtherest corner of my soul," he said quietly. "I've never loved this deeply, this completely. But you were a baby, and I was afraid of you. I didn't think you were capable of feeling deeply at your age."

She felt the warm glow wash over her body like scented water, and she smiled at him. "And now?"

He chuckled deeply. "If you could have seen the look on your face when you walked in here . . . it told me everything. That you cared. That you'd been hurting the way I had. That you loved me. It was like waking out of a nightmare."

"I'm so sorry," she began.

He pressed a long forefinger against her lips. "It's over — forgotten." His finger traced her soft, pink mouth. "Kiss me."

She leaned forward and drew her lips against his slowly, teasingly. "Like that?" she whispered saucily.

He caught the back of her head and ground her mouth into his for a long moment, making her ache with the barely contained passion in his kiss. "More like that," he replied with a mocking smile when she drew back, blushing.

She dropped her eyes to her coffee. "Did you really want me here?"

"Are you out of your mind?" he asked conversationally. "It was all I could think about. I reasoned that if I could get you here, keep you here long enough, you might be able to forgive me."

Her eyes misted once again as she looked at him. "For what?" she asked incredulously.

"For almost costing you your life," he said, and his face went rigid with remembrance. "Oh, God, when I saw that taxi heading for you . . ." He stopped and caught his breath deeply. "I prayed every step of the way until

446

I got to you, and I swore that if you lived I'd make it all up to you somehow."

"But it was I who'd caused you so much pain," she countered.

"We hurt each other," he said, summing it up. "But that's over. I want you to live with me."

"Yes," she said quietly.

"Aren't you going to ask me about the terms?" he asked with a slow grin.

She shook her head.

"Unconditional surrender?" he probed.

She nodded with a smile.

He caught her hand and took it to his lips. "Marry me, then."

"You don't have to."

He gave her a measuring glance. "I thought you just said you wanted children with me?"

She blushed wildly. "Well . . ."

"Yes or no?"

She met his teasing eyes levelly. "Yes. A boy, and maybe another girl," she added gently, sensing his pain.

He nodded. "The farm will be a good place for them to grow up."

She clutched his hand as if all the past few minutes were a delicious dream she was afraid of losing. "Oh, I only wish my father was home so that I could tell him."

"He is, and I already have," he said.

She gaped at him, tugging her hand loose. "He is?" she burst out.

He nodded. "I called him. He was here for those first few critical hours until we were sure you were going to be all right. Then I persuaded him to pretend he was still on vacation so I could take you home with me."

"However did you get him to agree?" she asked, aghast.

He touched her cheek gently. "I told him I was in love with you, country mouse, and that I was reasonably certain you were in love with me."

Her eyes closed briefly. "Is it real, or am I just dreaming again?" she said, more poignantly than she knew.

He stood up, drawing her with him. His face was strained. "We'd better go call your father before I give in to the temptation to show you how real it is. Think how shocked Mrs. Brodie would be," he added wickedly.

She reached up and touched his cheek. "Are you sure?" she asked quietly. "I'm not worldly, and . . ."

"Hush." He brushed her mouth with his. "You're my priceless treasure, and I'll treat you like paper-thin glass. All right?"

She flushed and turned away from his

mischievous smile. "I thought we were going to call Dad."

He drew her into his arms. "In just a minute," he agreed, bending his head. "I think it can wait that long, don't you?"

She went on tiptoe to meet him halfway, her warm smile disappearing under the slow, expert pressure of his mouth. Yes, the phone call could wait. Everything could wait. She closed her eyes and gave herself up to the one man in all the world whom she could love forever. In the back of her mind were the lines of a poem . . . "Keep spring within your heart, if winter comes, to warm the cold of disillusion." The winter approaching would find spring flowering in her soft eyes.

ABOUT THE AUTHOR

The prolific author of over 100 books, **Diana Palmer** got her start as a newspaper reporter. A multi-*New York Times* bestselling author and one of the top ten romance writers in America, she has a gift for telling the most sensual tales with charm and humor. Diana lives with her family in Cornelia, Georgia.